Horse Power

A Kyle Shannon Mystery

Linda Mickey

Happy reading!

Linda Mickey

Finish Off Press

Libertyville

Horse Power

A Kyle Shannon Mystery

Finish Off Press Ltd.
872 S Milwaukee Avenue #134
Libertyville IL 60048
www.finishoffpress.com

ISBN: 978-0-9833778-0-1

Printed in the United States

For Seth

God forbid that I should go to any heaven in which there are no horses. - *Robert Browning*

Acknowledgements

I would like to individually acknowledge all the people who have helped me with this book however that is not possible. So family, friends, and colleagues – please know that I am deeply grateful to all of you for your support and encouragement.

For specific expertise provided for this novel, I thank Mike Sliozis, Illinois State Police Lieutenant, retired, Ken Pfoser, Biology and DNA scientist, Northeastern Illinois Regional Crime Lab, Sherri Gallagher, president, German Shepherd Search and Rescue Dog Association-Illinois Chapter, Terry Lemming, Illinois State Police, Jim Wipper, former Coroner, Lake County, Illinois, Agita Grants, owner of Amberland Artisans, the Libertyville Police Department, the Vernon Hills Police Department, Doug M. Cummings, Bonny Koffler, Sandra Burkett, and Tess Schmieg. Finally, thank you to David Burke for bringing Bright Hope Equestrian Center to life (see map on the following page).

Finally, I am particularly indebted to public libraries. Without them, I would not have discovered mysteries nor would I be writing them myself.

Bright Hope Equestrian Center

Frank and Dixie Villano, Proprietors
Isabella (Izzy) Villano, Trainer

Eduardo Duran – Land owner

Farmhands:
Henry Slavin
Chuck Floriak
Jorge Estaban
Ramon Gutierrez

Owner's and Their Horses
Brisa Duran - Jamaica Jerked Chicken
Nolan Grinnell - Ephraim's Lifting Fog
Lori Boc - Pivot Divot
Sal Fabrini - Sunny Disposition
Izzy Villano - Maida
Dixie Villano - Raider

Other Animals:
Oscar the Goat
Cats: Carson, Pirie, Scott, Neiman, Marcus, Lemon
Dog: Ronig – Lori Boc's German shepherd

BRIGHT HOPE EQUESTRIAN CENTER

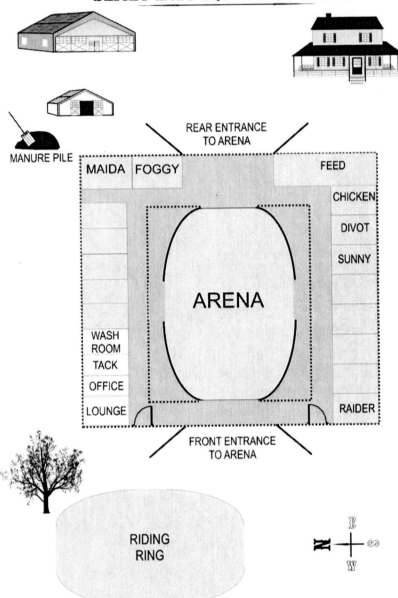

CHAPTER 1

*B*am-whack.

Sunny's hindquarters seemed spring-loaded his hooves hit the wall so fast. Driven by twelve hundred pounds of raging equine, the kick connected with such force the vibration traveled through the cement and tingled in my legs. The gelding tossed his head, his nostrils flaring with each exhale of hot breath.

Thump-thwack.

I stood frozen.

His hooves battered the stall wall again. Ears pinned, his eyes rolled back until the whites showed. When the volley ended, Sunny's chest heaved like he'd won the Preakness.

"What's going on? What the hell did you do to him?"

Isabella Villano, second in command at Bright Hope Equestrian Center, charged around the corner and came to an abrupt halt in front of me, her hand on the hilt of a knife attached to her belt. She wasn't tall enough to look me in the eye but her anger propelled her to nearly my height. I backed up a step.

"I didn't do anything. I swear."

"Look at him! He's freakin' goin' nuts. Did you go in the stall? What's that you're holding?" She grabbed the rectangle of paper from me, nearly cutting my palm as the edge pulled across my hand. "You waved it at him, didn't you?"

She glanced at the black text surrounded by a border of purple and gray. It read Sunny Disposition, Owner: Sal Fabrini.

"Very nice. Very la-de-da." Izzy glared as she crunched the paper and dropped it to her feet. "Now explain what got Sunny all upset."

"I was about to slide that into the frame on his stall door. When I got to here, he started kicking."

Izzy rubbed her cheek while she looked at Sunny. "That makes no sense. He doesn't go goofy just because a person is nearby. For all he knows, you're bringin' him sugar."

Sunny circled away and stopped in the back corner of the stall, lather glistening on his chest. Speaking in a low monotone, Izzy stepped gradually into the stall, her right hand extended. She kept up the soothing babble as she approached and touched Sunny's neck. He dropped his head and let her rub his muzzle. As suddenly as it began, his raging ceased; here and gone in minutes like the passing of a midday summer storm.

"Kyle, leave slowly and calmly. Bring me a rub rag and the bottle of witch hazel, please."

I had no idea where they kept rub rags but when I looked into the tack room, I spotted a pail stuffed with cloths sitting on a bench. I grabbed several, then went to shelves full of fly spray, hoof polish and other equine care products and read labels until I found the liniment. Running back to Izzy, I slowed to a walk as I approached the stall door.

Cross ties were hooked to his halter, holding Sunny in position so he couldn't turn around while Izzy inspected him for injury. She kept one of her hands on him, patting him gently as she moved from his head to his hindquarters. Then she squatted at his side.

"Did he hurt himself?" I asked.

Izzy unwound Sunny's protective leg wrap bandages and then carefully cupped her hands around the horse's legs, sliding slowly knee to hoof. She repeated the maneuver on each limb.

"I don't find heat or swelling," she said. "That's a good sign but I'll check him again in an hour or two and I'll give him a good rubdown now, just in case."

She poured witch hazel into her palm and then rubbed his legs briskly, her hands making a slap, slop noise as a minty, menthol astringent odor filled the stall. When Izzy had massaged each leg, she rubbed Sunny with a rag, starting on his neck just behind his ears and working back to his hind quarters. When she reached his hip, he flinched. She stopped immediately. Then slowly, barely touching him, she placed her hand on his rump. Again Sunny shrank from her touch.

Izzy brought her eyes level with Sunny's hindquarters. After a moment, she stepped away from him and moved slowly around the stall, her boots pushing shavings out of the way. She was near the stall door when she gasped and bent down. Uttering one expletive after another in quiet, even tones, she stood again. Then, after unclipping the cross ties, Izzy patted Sunny's shoulder, gave his neck a hug, and came out of the stall, pushing the door latch into place.

A bruise blossomed on my arm the minute she clamped her fingers around it and dragged me down the aisle.

CHAPTER 2

Being manhandled by a boss was not in my job description but then there was nothing about this job that was typical.

I'm a temp. Usually I work in office buildings, managing projects or departments in corporate settings, clearing backlogs or covering open positions. I am stabled in a cubicle with a desk and computer until my assignment ends and Office Right Staffing Service sends me somewhere else.

Eduardo Duran, owner of Duran Building and Grading, was my boss. In a manner of speaking. I worked for the Villanos but Duran Building and Grading paid for me. Duran decided the stable needed office help so he called a temp agency. And that is the short version of how I, an office temporary worker, happened to be at Bright Hope Equestrian Center.

"Come with me." Izzy, maintaining her lock on my arm, moved me down the aisle to the feed room and slid back the door latch. "Oh, for Pete's sake. Who locked you in here, Oscar?"

She released me and nudged the goat with her knee, maneuvering him away from an overturned aluminum trash can. Oats speckled the floor like snowflakes.

Cocking his head and locking his legs in place, he looked up at me, his pale blue eyes blinking rapidly. A caricature of his species, Oscar had a distended belly, knobby knees, and two lumps where horns had been before the vet sawed them off. A misshapen white beard curled under his narrow chin like tangled fishing line.

"You're gonna eat yourself sick," said Izzy. She wrapped her arms around his middle and dragged him toward the door. "Go on. Scoot."

Barely five foot five, stocky but muscular, Izzy could move a fifty pound hay bale as if it were luggage with wheels. I couldn't even pick one up. I'd tried once when no one was looking. My shoulders were sore for days. Oscar's stiff-legged resistance was no match for a determined Izzy. As soon as she had him out of the feed room, his stubby tail twitched twice and he scampered away.

"Stupid goat," she muttered, pulling a broom from the corner and sweeping marble-sized goat droppings into the aisle.

When she finished, she motioned me to a hay bale. I sat down, rubbing my arm. Izzy placed the filthy rub rags on the bale next to me and peeled back the folds. Inside was a thick, well-worn leather strap contraption that reminded me of a blackjack but without the hard, bulbous end.

"You saw how Sunny flinched when I rubbed his hindquarters?" Her eyes flashed like someone had thrown a match into a pool of lighter fluid. "I found this in the shavings. There are welts on his rump. He's been beat."

"Why…what?" Imagining the bulky strap biting into Sunny's skin made me shudder. "Who would do something like that?"

"I sure as hell plan to find out. Someone's gonna pay for this." She exhaled. It was almost a growl. "Sorry I yelled at you before. Sunny was making such a racket I knew he was mad about something."

"I read that his former owners abused him but there's nothing in Sunny's file about him being dangerous."

"He's not. I just don't know what he'd do if a stranger barged into his stall when he's like that. See, Sunny's a Saddlebred, Arab mix. That breeding makes him high spirited. His former owner didn't think about that and bought him because he's pretty and then tried to beat him into being a different kind of horse. After we got Sunny from the humane society, he was aggressive but it was all defense because he was afraid. We pulled his shoes, let him get shaggy, fed him good and, well, just let him be a horse. He spent the whole winter loose, either in the riding ring or the arena. Whenever I could, I got near him, sittin' quiet, talkin' to him. Touching him real gentle."

"Like horse whispering?"

"Not that mystic. We just love 'em, don't give them a reason to be afraid of us and wait for them to heal. It's been almost a year since we got him and he's doing so good even you could ground drive him."

I was sure that ground driving him was a lot harder than it looked. Sunny wore a harness but was not hitched to anything. Izzy followed behind on foot at the end of long reins, walking or running where the cart would be if there was one. If the horse got upset, the handler was already on the ground so there was little risk of injury to animal or trainer.

"Last week, I tried him out in the training sulky," Izzy went on. "He was as good as gold. Depending on how that goes, I'll reintroduce him to the saddle."

She had shelved her anger and, when she spoke again, there was no indication of how riled up she'd been.

"So what's with the signs?" she asked.

"Everyone around here uses the horses' names instead of the owners' names. When you talk about people, you say Foggy's dad or Divot's momma. It's pretty confusing so I thought stall signs would help me. Besides, all these empty holders ought to be put to use."

"That one for Sunny. Sal doesn't own Sunny. Not yet anyway. Sal won't buy him unless he can be ridden."

"Sorry. Chuck told me to make up a sign for him."

Chuck Floriak was one of the farm hands. He helped feed the horses, clean out the stalls and handled most of the barn maintenance. A burly young man with a crooked smile, ruddy skin and eyes that matched his faded jeans, Chuck was much too bulky to be a jockey so he dreamed of training racehorses instead. As often as anyone would listen, he shared his plans for his own racing stable that someday would be filled with Triple Crown winners.

"Why would Chuck be telling you what to do?"

"When he came into the office this morning, he saw the signs and said I was missing one for Sunny."

"Chuck was jumping the gun a bit. Sal will buy him eventually, but Sunny's not ready for a rider yet. And it looks like some SOB is making sure he won't be."

Izzy folded the rags back over the strap, stood up and placed the package on a shelf behind a can of equine vitamins. "He pitched a fit a couple of weeks ago. I wonder if gettin' beat set him off then too." She turned to me, an eyebrow arched. "You've been around horses before, haven't you?"

"When I was ten, I was horse crazy so my folks gave me eight weeks of riding lessons as a birthday present. I'd ride my bike out to a barn owned by this marvelous old woman. She was something. Compact like you and fiercely independent. Drove herself to the hospital when a horse kicked her and broke her arm." The memory made me smile. "I had to do it all, muck out the stall, clean feet, feed and water. When the chores were done, I would saddle the horse and have my lesson. I thought I'd forgotten everything but being here...well, I'm amazed at what I remember."

"You didn't stick with it?"

"We couldn't afford more lessons. After I got out on my own, I was too busy working. Bright Hope brings back some wonderful memories."

Izzy's features softened and the bright young woman I was accustomed to seeing emerged.

"I can take a few minutes before I work Foggy," she said. "Go get your signs and I'll introduce you to everyone."

I hurried to the tack room. The signs and my list of boarders were on the bench next to the pail where I'd dropped them. Cutting through the arena, I met Izzy at the last stall in the south wing.

"Guess I should stay out of the arena," I said, steadying myself against the wall while I dumped sand out of my sneakers.

"No sand problems if you got boots on and you should be wearin' boots. A half ton on top of your foot will break bones for sure if you're not protected."

Raider, Dixie's buckskin Quarter horse, stuck his nose to the bars along the top of his stall. His ears moved forward and back to the beat of a swishing black tail. In sharp contrast to his sandy colored coat, a black dorsal stripe ran the length of his spine and his short black mane stood upright on his neck like brush bristles.

Izzy broke a carrot into quarters and pushed a piece through the bars. Raider slurped it up with his lips, manipulated it to his teeth and crunched down. He pawed at the ground.

"He's begging," I said.

"He's a pig. See that bump in his cheek? He hasn't finished chewing the first piece but he wants more. Mom spoils him rotten." She patted the bulge. "Chew it, you rascal."

We moved on, stopping at each stall while Izzy helped me match owner to horse by describing the human clients so I could picture who I'd met and who I hadn't.

Pivot Divot, a rangy palomino with a long neck, had the stall east of Sunny. Divot was fifteen-two hands, or sixty-two inches, taller than Raider by four inches. Horses are measured from the ground to the top of their shoulders and each four-inch segment is called a "hand." If Raider was any shorter, he'd be considered a pony.

Lori Boc, Divot's owner, was an equine pharmaceutical sales rep and a member of a search and rescue team. Divot was in training to be a trail horse so Lori could use him for rescue work.

"Divot's like molasses," said Izzy. "He's thick, slow and sweet. Look at him. All that commotion right next door and he's barely awake." Then she pointed to Divot's neighbor. "And this is Brisa Duran's horse, Jamaican Jerked Chicken. We call him Chicken."

"He looks like a Dalmatian."

"That black saddle with the sterling silver conchos in the tack room? That's his western saddle. He goes English, too."

"Must be nice to be the daughter of one of the richest men in the county. You get a saddle that matches your horse."

Izzy touched her forefinger to Chicken's nose. He stuck out his tongue and let it hang six inches below his lips.

"Did Brisa teach him that?" I asked.

"I have no idea," said Izzy, laughing as Chicken's head bobbed and his tongue came out again, this time without the prompt. "I expect Chicken will be for sale soon. Brisa's ready for an A-circuit show horse."

"Bright Hope works with difficult and problem horses," I said. "Was Chicken once abused like Sunny?"

"When he came to us, he was a little head shy, but we cleared that up easy. Chicken's here because, instead of training fees for Chicken, we get Chuck for free and that's why Brisa can't move to a show barn. Uncle Ed refuses to pay someone else for training because he's already paying us with Chuck. It's hard on Brisa. She wants to compete at the better horse shows and we're not a show barn. Mom and I smuggle her to McHenry now and then for special work with a Saddlebred trainer over there."

"I guess I see his point. Since he owns the place..."

"He doesn't own Bright Hope. Just the farm."

"Aren't they the same thing?"

"Bright Hope is a business that leases space. Ed Duran owns the two hundred acres this barn sits on. We lease the barn from him."

"The same way a card store leases space at a mall?"

"Yeah, only the deal's more complicated here because Uncle Ed pays the help, all except one guy. Jorge's our employee but

Chuck, Henry and all the others are on the farm's payroll."

What Izzy had just described sounded like an Ed Duran kind of arrangement. I recognized it because I was in one myself. Were all his business deals so complex?

We walked past the feed room and the rear barn doors to the next stall where a dapple gray with a black mane and tail put his ears forward. He snuffed, blowing air out with enough force to stir the dust along the rim of the stall where the vertical iron bars met the wood planks. Dark pools watched me from a sculpted head set on an arched neck.

Izzy slid back the stall door. "Come closer. This fella's worth meeting in person."

The stallion nickered and shoved his massive head toward me, bumping me gently.

"Pet his muzzle."

Softest velvet. I moved my hand along his jaw and rubbed the short smooth hair of his summer coat. "He's the most beautiful horse I've ever seen."

"When Nolan found him, he was skin and bones, standing in a heap of muck. I honestly don't know how much longer he would have lived."

"That's horrible. I hope his owner went to jail."

"Actually, Foggy's owner was dead. Sudden massive heart attack. Nolan was on vacation and overheard the resort owner telling the cops about a horse they needed to rescue. Nolan tracked down the executor of the estate and the guy sold Foggy for a hundred bucks just to wash his hands of him."

Nolan Grinnell was a big man with broad shoulders, legs like telephone poles, and baseball mitt hands. I met him the previous weekend and we chatted over coffee while Chuck harnessed Foggy for Nolan's weekly driving lesson. Nolan told me he fell in love with horses as a child in the Chicago housing projects. A mounted policeman visited Nolan's grade school. The children had been encouraged to touch the horse.

"I was good and hooked," Nolan told me. "Never got over wanting one of my own. When my auntie moved us to Waukegan, I saw lots of horses. Made me want one even more."

Izzy gave Foggy a final pat and stepped out of the stall. "I'm teaching Nolan to drive. We think he's got a real winner here so we're pushing him to move into a show barn, too. Of course, showing takes serious money and Nolan can't even pay his board bill right now."

Next door, separated from Foggy by a solid wooden wall, a seal brown bay mare stood dozing, her tail occasionally flicking at the flies. Flies were ever-present. I'd become so accustomed to their constant buzzing that I didn't pay much attention to them. Like the horses, fly flicking was now as automatic for me as breathing.

After opening the stall door, Izzy took a peppermint candy from her pocket, unwrapped it, and held it in her open palm. The mare picked it up with her lips and then chomped merrily, her eyes shining.

"Candy? I thought horses got sugar cubes."

"Maida prefers peppermints. When she was just a filly, I was eating a candy cane and she pestered me like crazy. It took awhile before I figured out what she wanted. I've been giving her peppermints ever since."

"She already has a sign." I touched the polished brass nameplate. "Horse show prize?"

"Won that my senior year of high school."

"She can't see Foggy. You keep them apart because he's a stallion?"

"He and Maida are so accustomed to one another that she doesn't get excited around him anymore. That wouldn't be true for another mare." Izzy gave Maida a final pat. "Much as people romanticize them, the only reason to have a stallion is to make baby horses."

"Geldings are better pets, aren't they?"

"Even better than mares 'cause they don't have any raging hormones. Foggy's the first stallion we've had in a long time and we got lucky with him. He's a perfect gentleman."

When I pushed the last stall sign into place, Izzy said, "If you see Mom, ask her to track me down. I want to talk to her about what happened to Sunny. And thank you for the signs. They look great."

Izzy turned around and headed toward Foggy's stall. I looked down at my feet. My white sneakers were smudged with dirt and manure. Could I write boots off as a business expense?

Back in the barn office, I sorted through the mail that arrived while I was meeting the horses. Several checks were there but none from Nolan Grinnell. He was two months in arrears. What happened to a horse if its owner got too far behind in the rent? Was it evicted like human tenants were?

I took Nolan's folder from the file cabinet. The seizure clause was on the second page. After ninety days of unpaid board and/or training bills, a warning would be sent to the owner. If the bill was not paid within ten days after receipt of the certified warning letter, the horse would become the property of Bright Hope Equestrian Center and could be sold to settle the debt including associated collection expenses.

It was nearly time for the certified letter and, as office manager, it was my job to send it out. Maybe Nolan didn't realize Bright Hope hadn't been paid. Checks really do get lost in the mail.

When Dixie Villano came into the office at noon, she carried a familiar brown paper sack stamped Penzler's Corner Market. The independent convenience and deli store was located near Vernon Hills and I managed to stop in several times a week for coffee or take-out lunch. Mary Penzler made the best coleslaw in the world and her husband, Pete, put together sandwiches so thick that polite princess bites were impossible.

"Come on, Miss Office Manager. We're going to have a lunch meeting." Dixie pushed the stool next to the desk, sat down and placed a sandwich in front of me. "Mary says hi and she sent along some coleslaw. I tried to buy you potato salad but she insisted the coleslaw is your favorite."

"It absolutely is." I unwrapped my lunch. "What are we meeting about?"

"Lots of things."

Dixie Villano and Izzy were nearly the same height and both had long hair, but Dixie looked nothing like her daughter. She was slight and wiry. Her hair was sandy brown and thin while Izzy's thick black ponytail reflected her Italian heritage. Dixie was closing in on fifty and, though there were few gray hairs on her head, she'd spent a lot of time in the sun; something guaranteed to put age on a person. Other than the wrinkles in her face and her leathery skin, nothing else about her was old. Her brain was as sharp as Emeril Lagasse's best chef's knife and she knew that Black Eyed Peas was a rap group not a vegetable. I'd never seen her in anything but riding breeches and boots with spurs, which she always removed before coming into the office. Like a man removing his hat, she told me. Polite folk do not wear spurs anywhere but in the barn.

"What kind of things?" I asked after I stabbed the last of the coleslaw with my fork.

"You are aware my husband, Frank, has been missing for several months."

I nodded slowly and put down my sandwich.

"People say Frank ran off," Dixie went on. "They think he didn't like the life, or me, and wanted out. That's not true. This stable is our dream. We talked about creating a horse haven from the day we met twenty-five years ago." She paused, then said quietly, "Frank's dead."

"What!"

"He'd never leave me. Something dreadful has happened to

him."

Her lips were stretched thin and her chin quivered. As she laid her sandwich on its waxed paper wrapper, the strain of her situation crossed her face like a cloud's shadow drifting past the moon.

"I just put a picture of Frank on the mantle in the lounge. I want you to make sure there's a fresh yellow flower in the vase next to it at all times. Yellow's for remembrance."

I nodded.

"Until I know for sure, until they find my Frank, I don't want anyone to forget him or to think he left me. I know he'd be here with me if he could be."

She finished her lunch in silence. Then, as suddenly as she had opened the subject, she closed it.

"OK. On to other topics. You've been here almost two weeks and you spent most of your time cleaning out this place. I gotta tell you, even when Frank was running the business, the office never looked this good. Now that the new computer has arrived, you're probably ready to get into some serious recordkeeping?"

Unable to answer with my mouth full of sandwich, I merely nodded. The computer was barely out of the box because it had been a struggle to figure out where to put it. The room we called the office was only ten feet square. The old executive desk took up too much space and was the first thing to go out to the trash. Its faux Danish modern replacement included a printer stand that slid underneath the writing surface. With the removal of countless outdated magazines and papers, I had achieved enough floor space to add a short stool for guest seating and a four-drawer file cabinet.

"You must have questions that I've been too busy to answer," Dixie said.

I brought up Nolan Grinnell and his unpaid bills.

Dixie sighed. "Nolan's business dropped off substantially when the recession hit and he's struggling to make ends meet. His wife is into Jack Russell terriers and, from the gossip I hear around the barn, she and Nolan are arguing about whose animals should be sold. She claims Foggy costs as much as her dogs, which is probably true. Nolan insists Foggy is not for sale, no matter what. She says her job pays for her dogs and if he wants to keep Foggy, he'd better get to work."

"What does he do?"

"Sells commercial insurance. Some of his best clients went under and he's having trouble writing new business."

"So you've talked to him about this?"

"He came to me at the end of last month. He said he'd get me a check by the fifteenth. That hasn't happened, has it?"

I shook my head.

"From what you're telling me, he has less than two weeks to make good or Foggy belongs to me?" She sighed again. "Frank insisted on that clause so no one could stiff us but I never imaged it would be enforced. Do I have to?"

"I'm no lawyer but it sounds pretty straightforward to me. No pay, no horse. Do you want me to check with your attorney?"

"Heavens no."

She rubbed her forehead as though I'd just given her a pounding headache. Which I probably had.

"Let me think about it for a couple of days. I'll talk to Nolan the next time he's here and see how things look."

"OK. What else?"

A mischievous grin appeared on Dixie's face. "You're leaving early today to go shopping." She pointed at my shoes. "You are not allowed into the barn again in sneakers. Finish up the mail and the bank deposit, then get yourself over to the store and buy yourself a decent pair of boots." She rose. "You can get them at Sundowner's. Their stuff will be fine for your purposes. And bring back a flower for Frank."

She turned and left before I could thank her for lunch or ask her more questions so I did as instructed and drove to Sundowner's after stopping at the bank.

The western wear store was crowded with racks and rounders the way popular restaurants squeeze too many tables onto the floor. The service counter in the center divided the western tack and clothing from the English. Alan Jackson's voice, drifting down from overhead speakers, lured me to the western side where the boot display was on the back wall; women's on the left, men's on the right. Round toes, pointy toes. Regular heels, sloped heels. Boots that looked like cowboy boots and boots that looked like hiking boots. Black, brown, green, blue. Manly boots of snakeskin and girly boots vivid with bouquets of inlaid leather flowers.

"Y'all need boots? Lama or Justin?"

A short, buxom saleswoman in jeans and a white shirt approached me, the fringe on her red leather vest swaying to "She's Got the Rhythm, I've Got the Blues."

I didn't answer her. From the look on her face, those names were supposed to mean something to me but they didn't. Nose wrinkled, she glanced at my sneaker-clad feet.

"It's like Reebok or Nike. People wear one brand or the other. Which are you?"

"Reebok."

"Then you'll need Lamas. Color?"

I shrugged.

"Brown. Size?"

"Eight?"

She went to the rack, ran her finger down the boxes until she found a size seven and a half and pulled it out. After handing me a pair of cotton socks, she sprinkled baby powder inside the right boot and handed it to me. I sat down and stuck in my foot. It didn't get very far.

"Push."

I pushed. And pushed some more. This was harder than zipping my pants after Mom's Thanksgiving dinner.

"Use these here boot hooks."

She picked up two metal J-shaped hooks with red plastic handles and put the curved end through leather hoops on either side of the boot top. I grasped the handles and stood up for leverage.

"Grunt, honey. Boots don't go on unless you make some noise."

I absolutely was not going to grunt but a harrumph escaped as I pushed for what I vowed would be the last time. My foot slid into place.

"Works like a charm." The saleswoman leaned forward, pressed on the toe and then grabbed the sides. "Walk."

She watched as I took several steps away and back.

"Your heel slips? That's good."

I struggled into the other boot, forked over my credit card and drove back to Bright Hope trying to figure out how I was going to get the boots off now that they were on.

CHAPTER 3

I forgot to close the shutters before I left and the full brunt of summer had made the lounge as hot as a wood-fired pizza oven. Instead of generating a cooling flow, the ceiling fan merely sliced through Polar Tec thick air. Sweat formed wet circles under my armpits and pooled at my waistband. Frank's yellow rose wouldn't last five minutes in this heat. I put the vase on the cement hearth against the back wall of the fireplace. Cool air sinks, right?

The message light on the office telephone was flashing. Duran planned to spend the weekend at the farm and needed time with Dixie to talk about Chuck and Henry's work projects for the fall. He didn't want his visit to interrupt the farm's normal routine so he asked that she not mention he was coming.

Henry Slavin was the farm foreman, overseeing the other five or six workers, keeping track of expenses and spending most of his time on a tractor working in the fields. There when I arrived in the morning and still riding the rows when I left in the afternoon, he was usually so far away that I had no clear view of him but he waved if he saw me. He wore plain jeans, a denim work shirt and a baseball cap over his salt and pepper hair that was mostly salt.

The first time Henry and I met, he pulled off his work gloves revealing rings on almost every finger of his hands, most of tooled silver. The ring on his right pinkie was set with a small oval of amber the color of wild honey.

"His daughter designs jewelry," Izzy told me. "She and the rest of his family are still in Poland. Anyway, she sends him a new ring for his birthday and he wears them all instead of replacing one with another."

"One per year? Is he marking time? Is that why he wears them all?"

Izzy thought about it for moment. "Yeah, I guess so. Eight fingers, eight rings, eight years."

"One finger is empty."

"His birthday is coming up soon. He must be getting ready for the new one. Been here too long and now he has to make room for the new ring. Guess he can't wear them all anymore."

Sal Fabrini's message was short; he confirmed his appointment to discuss Sunny's progress.

How would they handle that? How much would they tell him?

Clad in my new boots, I went to the arena to deliver the messages. My feet, accustomed to the soft support of athletic shoes, were constricted by the tight leather. Toes immobile, ankles unable to bend, I stiff-legged my way through the sand like I was on stilts, throwing one leg forward and then the other.

So this is why cowboys walk like they have a stick up their butt.

Dixie stood in the center of the arena watching Izzy ride a chestnut mare that seemed a lot more interested in the big, bad light patch on the ground than on what Izzy wanted her to do.

"It won't eat you, I promise," said Izzy, clearly exasperated. "Mom, this is ridiculous. She's going to do it again. I can feel her butt tense."

As soon as her hooves touched it, the mare vaulted over the light patch, her ears flat back and her tail jerking rapidly from one flank to the other. She side-stepped several strides before she pivoted to stare at the dangerous bright sand, her sides heaving.

I didn't understand her fear. Trigger never balked when Roy Rogers was on his back. Black Beauty endured the worst possible treatment without shying from adversity. Hidalgo raced across the sands of the Sahara without giving up. But Lady Go Lucky could not walk calmly through sunbeams.

"Go up to it slowly. One step at a time," said Dixie. "Give her a chance to see it won't attack her."

Izzy turned Lady in a complete circle, and then prodded the mare forward with gentle taps of her riding crop and steady pressure from her legs and heels. Although the horse was quivering with fright, she obeyed. Then Izzy stopped her two feet from the light patch.

"Relax the reins so she can just stand there a minute or two. Let her get a good look at it." Dixie turned to me. "Hi, Kyle. Back so soon?"

I pointed to my boots.

"How do they feel?"

"Weird. Very tight."

"They'll stretch to fit your foot. In a week, they'll feel like a second skin. Be sure to wear cotton socks so the moisture is absorbed. In this heat, your feet will sweat." She glanced at her daughter. "Slowly, Izzy. Don't rush her." She watched as the mare moved a step closer to the light. "What else?"

I handed Dixie the messages. She read them both and groaned.

"I guess I should have expected this. Ed hasn't been over for a visit since he decided to hire you. I suppose he wants to see how things are going." She rubbed her forehead. "Well, thanks to you, the office is presentable. Ed doesn't own the business but it helps if he thinks I know how to run it. He's been concerned since Frank disappeared. Probably worried about getting his rent money. But let's look on the bright side. At least I know I'll be here through the fall if he wants to talk about Chuck and Henry. Hope he doesn't pull Chuck away for farm work. I can't afford to hire a replacement. I'll call Ed back after chores tonight."

Apparently the barter arrangement between Dixie and Ed

Duran was worrisome. Maybe I'd do a little research. There are temp agencies for everything. Perhaps there was one that supplied stable hands. If Duran could remove fifty percent of her labor force at any time, she needed a back-up.

The rattle of a diesel engine reached our ears. It revved and chugged, the sound diminishing as the tractor moved away from the barn. Dixie spun around and her eyes landed on the back door of the barn.

"Oh hell, I missed Henry again."

She marched toward the door and, shielding her eyes, looked across the yard toward the out buildings and the horse trailers parked nearby. I followed and stood next to her, listening intently to an engine surge.

"No Henry," I said.

A mammoth yellow cat loped toward the low wooden outbuilding everyone called the garage.

"Just Lemon," said Dixie, "He'll sack out on the cool concrete and won't come outside again until after sundown."

"One of your mousers?

"Almost the last one left. He's so ornery the coyotes are afraid to eat him."

"Is that why there are so few cats around? The coyotes get them?"

Dixie looked at me, a great sadness in her eyes. "Lemon and the few you see here in the barn are all that's left. Lemon will survive. He doesn't like the horses but when the coyotes moved in, he stopped roaming the hayfields. I can't say the same for the others. If they continue to stray outside, their days are numbered."

"But without cats...."

"We'll be overrun with mice." Dixie pointed into the rafters. "That's Neiman and that's Marcus."

I followed her finger and saw matching tortoise shell puffs of fur with yellow eyes watching us from above. "And the tabbies that spend all of their time sacked out on the hay bales in the feed room?"

"Carson and Pirie. Scott disappeared a couple of days ago. That's it. Lemon and those four. I worry about them. Sure would hate to lose them." She sighed. "We had twenty a year ago."

The engine clatter grew louder again and we looked to the east. Henry, perched in the cab of a shiny green John Deere, waved as the tractor rolled into the field beyond the farmhouse.

For the first time, I really looked at the house. Bleached gray clapboards were visible through thinning whitewash. Grey wicker furniture lay scattered on the covered porch, blown or knocked over and never righted again. One window was boarded up; the house looked like it had a black eye. In front, dead vines covered an arbor arching over a broken birdbath. If the exterior was in such poor shape, how did it look on the inside?

"He's turning under the last of the alfalfa," said Dixie, still watching Henry. "We're not supposed to get any rain so it's a good time to do it. Guess I'll have to catch him tomorrow morning. He'll be plowing until well past dark."

"Alfalfa hay? Is that what the horses eat?"

"All of Ed's hay is sold to some dairy farmers in McHenry County. I get mine from a Wisconsin farmer who charges a lot less. Ed grows premium and he's very fussy about it, measuring this and calculating that. It has something to do with fiber and sugar content."

"When he spends the weekend, does he stay with Henry and Chuck in the farm house?"

Dixie laughed. "The owner of Duran Building and Grading? I don't think that's quite up to Ed's standards. When you leave tonight, drive up the road about a mile and you'll pass the main house. It's quite a shack."

If there was a sizeable project in Lake County, Duran Building and Grading was involved in some way. A recent article in the local newspaper had said Ed Duran was about to bid some contracts in Chicago. That meant he was bigger than big. Dixie was absolutely right. Men like Ed Duran do not stay in places like the farmhouse beyond the barn.

Just then, Chuck Floriak maneuvered past us. He had a peculiar habit of raising and lowering his shoulders when he walked, three steps, shrug, three steps, shrug, as though he were trying to adjust the way his tee shirt stretched across his broad shoulders. We watched as he jockeyed a wheelbarrow full of manure out the back door and over to the mountain of dung where he up-ended it and added the contents to the enormous heap.

"Chuck," Dixie called, her voice loud and clear. "That manure pile looks like Mt. Everest and it hasn't been touched since April."

"No," Chuck called back.

"Why not?"

One shoulder went up. "Too busy. Repaired all of fence."

"I know but you and Henry are supposed to spread at least one load a week."

Another half-hearted shrug and Chuck's head was down, his face hidden below the bill of his cap. Apparently he knew he'd dropped the ball.

"The pile is smoking. It's getting too close to the barn. It could cause a fire."

I stared at her. "Could it?"

She lowered her voice. "I doubt it but why take chances? If they were spreading like they should, the pile would be half that size. It wouldn't be close enough to the buildings to be a problem."

"You told Chuck that he and Henry are supposed to spread. What does that mean?"

"We muck out stalls twice a day. Twenty horses produce a lot of shit – if you'll pardon the expression. At least once a week, someone is supposed to spread manure in the hay fields because if they don't…well, you see the result. I saw a brand new loader arrive not too long ago so there's no excuse for not doing it."

"Manure is good for the hay?"

"Best fertilizer there is – manure that's cooked for awhile." She called out again. "Ed's coming out here. He'd better not see that pile looking like that or you and Henry are going to be in big trouble."

Chuck's head snapped up, he dropped the wheelbarrow with a clang and ran towards the fields calling Henry's name.

*   *   *   *

"I need you to photocopy this paperwork before Ed gets here tomorrow."

Dixie blew into the barn office the next morning at roughly the speed of sound, waving a sheaf of papers at me.

"Where's Izzy? Sunny's in the arena ready to go."

"She's in the barn somewhere," I said.

"Please go find her. As John Wayne said, 'we're burnin' daylight'."

I set the papers on my desk and went out to find Izzy. It wasn't hard to track her down. I followed high-pitched cursing to the back of the building where I found her, shoulder against the door, trying to slide it open. The muscles in her arms twitched and her eyes bulged with effort. I hurried over to add my weight to the endeavor, setting my boot heels against the concrete floor. Straining, unable to get any real traction, I pushed. After several tries, the door shuddered and then rolled into place.

Izzy straightened, wiping sweat from her forehead with the back of her hand. "Damn door. Every summer it swells and we can't get it open. You need me?"

"Your mother does. She's in the office."

"OK."

Turning toward the barnyard, now fully visible through the

open doorway, Izzy shaded her eyes and called out, "Chuck, I'll take care of the horses today. Mom wants you to keep working there. The smoke is making the customers nervous. Hey, you're using a pitchfork and a shovel? Where's the loader?"

"Don't know," said Chuck. "Maybe out in fields someplace?"

"Henry should be helping you. And first thing tomorrow morning, please oil this door. We can hardly move it." She turned toward me. "The men busted butt whenever Dad needed something done. I don't think they like taking orders from a woman. Especially me. I'm a woman and the kid."

"It looks like they got some of the pile moved yesterday. This tip is gone."

"Yeah, but that stuff is so packed down at the bottom a pick axe can hardly break it up. If they get half that pile cleared out by Sunday quitting time, it'll be a miracle."

I looked toward the hayfields to the east of the farmhouse but I didn't see Henry. Nor could I hear the tractor. Chuck stopped long enough to wipe the sweat from his neck with his shirt tail and turn his cap backwards. From the undisturbed end of the manure pile, white smoke drifted lazily skyward.

Izzy followed my gaze. "Chuck's going to be melted by noon. Being out in the sun is bad enough. It's got to be hotter 'n hell on ole Mt. Manure."

"Just one giant compost heap."

"Been like that since spring."

"Do they ever get rid of it all?"

"Nope. The horses take care of that." She watched Chuck struggle with the loaded pitchfork. "If he hurts himself, he won't need to file for worker's comp. Uncle Ed'll just kill him." She rubbed her elbow, then snorted. "That wasn't very nice, was it? Ed's got some great guys. I just don't get why they haven't worked the pile lately. Last fall it got done once a week." Izzy's eyes clouded. "Last fall, Dad was here."

She pointed down the aisle. "Let's go back through the barn. Sunny's in the arena. After yesterday's fiasco, I don't want anything upsetting him."

"How's he doing?"

"Mom checked him out. She agrees someone beat on him." A scowl creased Izzy's face. Her voice faltered. "I don't know whether someone hates horses in general or Sunny in particular."

"Maybe someone is mad at Sal?"

"But why pick on the horse? Sal doesn't own him yet and if Sunny doesn't settle down, Sal might not want him. We've got a lot invested in that animal." Izzy stopped near the restroom. Just above a whisper, she said, "I don't think there's any way to really secure this place but, if you have a chance, call around to some of the other stables in the area. See if they've had any problems and what they do about security. Keep it cool though. Nobody can know about this."

I followed her into the lounge where we found Ed Duran sitting on the floor, back against the wall, his cell phone pressed to his ear. He waved at us and wrapped up his conversation.

Eduardo Duran was a compact man with bronzed skin, black hair and probing dark eyes that looked out from under the Caterpillar baseball cap he always wore. There was a scar on his left bicep that, according to Izzy, had been a gang tattoo. I didn't know much about gangs but his demeanor told me that he brooked no nonsense. You played straight with Ed Duran or you didn't play.

"Uncle Ed!" said Izzy. "What are you doing here? We didn't expect you until tomorrow."

He rose from the floor, brushing dust from his jeans. "Came out last night. Thought I'd surprise everybody."

"Well, it's a good surprise." Izzy hugged him, then stepped back, her hands on her hips. "What were you doing on the floor? Why don't you sit on the couch?"

"You sit on the couch," he said, a definite edge to his voice. He shoved an iced coffee at her. "Here. You look like you could use a break."

After she took a deep drink, Izzy sank onto the tattered sofa only to come upright abruptly, rubbing her backside. A broken spring pierced the brown corduroy fabric and Izzy had just stabbed herself on it. She moved to the end cushion and sat down again.

"Now I know why you're on the floor," she said.

"That couch is a health hazard. You're lucky someone doesn't have tetanus." Duran passed an envelope to Izzy. "Brisa told me Nolan's in trouble on his board so I pulled his file. Everything's signed, sealed and now delivered. If you don't have the money from Nolan by the end of the month, Brisa owns his horse."

Izzy pulled several sheets of paper from the envelope and looked them over. "I don't think Mom will go for this, Uncle Ed. You know how she is. I'll tell her you're here but I'm not going to say anything about this."

She tossed the remainder of her coffee into the wastebasket, passed me the envelope and went out the door. It seemed to me that her departure had been rather abrupt. Duran either didn't care or didn't notice.

"See you later, kiddo." He looked at me. "You're going shopping today. This place needs decent furniture."

The customer lounge was sparsely furnished with the old sofa, two folding lawn chairs and a fake fichus tree covered with enough dust to bend its leaves. Above the sofa was a framed print of mustangs galloping across the prairie. It too was covered by a film of dirt. Cobwebs hugged the corners of the ceiling. Black and dingy white vinyl tiles covered the floor.

I opened the envelope and looked over its contents. Duran had signed a boarding contract, the health care forms and had included a check plus copies of an insurance policy and registration transfer papers. Everything was dated the first of the following month.

"I can't afford new furniture any more than I can afford Kyle," said Dixie, entering the room. "Ed, you're driving me crazy."

Duran grunted. "I'm paying for the furniture, too. And by the way, Kyle should schedule Missy Maids or Monday Maids or some maids outfit to come clean this place. You don't want to put new stuff into this dust bin."

Dixie glared at him. "This is a barn. It's full of horses – not to mention the goat, the cats, and the clients' dogs. There's an indoor riding arena full of sand and there's an outdoor riding ring full of dirt. Do you expect everyone to take their boots off when they come into the lounge or the office?"

"Hell no, but you can look more like a business. How about a place to sit and work with your clients? The office is too small for any type of meeting. I'm gonna talk to Henry in an hour. Where do you propose we do that?"

"The picnic table?" Looking at me, Dixie shrugged. "OK, Kyle. If he gets this out of his system, maybe he'll leave us alone." She glanced at the drooping rose. "And please see to Frank while you're out. Flowers don't last long in this heat."

Duran looked at me, a question in his eyes but he let it pass. "I'll be back later. We gotta talk about Brisa's horse."

"And I'll be in the arena," said Dixie. "Let me know when Sal gets here and then go buy that furniture. I'll see you later."

I was on the telephone with a cleaning service when Sal Fabrini came into the office. He was about thirty-five, slightly taller than I am and a lot broader. His deeply tanned olive skin contrasted handsomely with a blue linen shirt that was open at the neck. I expected a gold chain but there wasn't one. His Rolex made up for it, however. The watch was the size of the moon. Very white teeth shone through a beard and mustache so neatly trimmed I was reminded of a manicured lawn. He entered the office with a confident air, giving me a half bow.

"Good morning," he said in a strong bass voice.

I offered him coffee.

"No thanks. Coffee'd out. Where's Dixie?"

"In the arena. I'll get her."

He held up his palm. "Wait a sec. That monument to Frank on the mantel. Any word?"

"No."

"Then what's she doin'? It's creepy."

Sal turned toward the lounge and the Frank Villano memorial. When he looked back at me, there was something in his eyes. As soon as I tried to define it, it was gone.

"If Frank was dead," Sal continued, "someone woulda found him by now and, from what I hear, there's no trace of him. His truck is gone and so is he. I don't think we're talkin' Jimmy Hoffa here. Frank's not wearing concrete shoes; he just flew the coop. Some hottie, like Lori or Brisa, got in his blood and he took off."

Hottie?

I felt my hackles go up. While I agreed that Lori and Brisa were both attractive women, I didn't equate them with that particular term.

"Why are you telling me this?" I asked. "It doesn't match anything I've ever heard about Frank Villano."

"That picture on the mantel got me thinkin'." Sal rubbed his mustache. "Brisa may be a doll-baby, but she's Ed's only kid and he'd kill anyone who bothered her."

Like you perhaps?

"He used to be in a gang, you know, before Brisa's mother put the ball and chain on him." He went quiet. After a moment, he said, "Four months. I think Frank's been gone four months."

"Dixie filed a missing persons report, didn't she?"

"Who knows? She gets nuts whenever anyone asks about Frank so don't ask her."

Dixie came into the office at that moment and, thankfully, gave no indication that she was aware of our conversation. I made myself busy getting out of the way.

"Perfect timing," I said as I vacated my desk. "Take my chair."

I left Dixie and Sal to go over Sunny's progress and went into the arena to watch Izzy work. Sunny was hitched to the two-wheeled training sulky and when I stepped into the arena, they were making the turn at the north end. The gelding moved out at the trot, his hooves rising and falling in the sand, making occasional hollow-sounding clop-clops as his rear hooves clipped his front. Izzy commanded him to walk. Shifting gears smoothly, Sunny slowed. Then she turned him into the center of the arena and pulled back on the reins. Sunny stopped and stood quietly, ears flicking forward and back. After waiting a minute, Izzy left the sulky and looped the long reins over her arm. Walking to Sunny's head, she threw her arms around his neck, hugging him tightly. Her delight seemed to be infectious. She led away a very different animal than the aggressively fearful one I'd seen charging about in his stall the day before.

I went on through the arena to the back door to watch Chuck work the manure pile. He wasn't there; the pitchfork lay on the ground. It didn't look to me like he'd made any progress at all. Beyond that I saw one of the workers trimming the dead vines from the arbor by the farmhouse. Sunlight glinted off a piece of yellow equipment at the distant end of one of the fields. It was too far away for me to see more detail.

Ed Duran appeared at my shoulder, looking out on the same scene I surveyed.

"So?" he asked, turning toward me. "How do you like it so far?"

"I like it fine. Dixie's great."

"Good. The office all organized, is it?"

"It's coming along. There's a lot of paper to sort through."

"I told you there'd be filing."

Boxes and boxes of it. Staple jabs, paper cuts. My favorite kind of work.

"That's an understatement," I said. "Dixie's focused on the

horses, not on pushing paper. I don't think she'd opened mail for a couple of weeks."

"The very reason you now have a job. You wash the office floor?"

This temp does not do floors.

"Chuck washed the floor."

"Ah. Henry said something about Chuck bein' helpful but I didn't get what he was talking about." He pointed at the manure pile. "Chuck was out there last night, too. Who's doin' his chores?"

"Izzy told him she'd take care of the horses today. Dixie was hoping that would be done before you got here tomorrow." I looked at him, watching his eyebrows knot. "Only you're here today...and last night, too?"

Duran returned my gaze but there was nothing decipherable in his eyes. "Funny thing about that manure pile. In the time it takes to pile the manure up to that height, they could have spread it. No wonder my nitrogen levels are off. Glad I got here last night. Got a good look at how things are."

CHAPTER 4

His comment made me gulp. When bosses get a good look, they tend to make decisions that alter the status quo. I had the feeling that Ed Duran was about to do that.

He turned to me. "I know the horse trade isn't your background but Mary Penzler said there's no one better for fixing up a mess and Dixie Villano's business was getting pretty messy."

Now my being at Bright Hope made sense. I assumed a referral had started the process but I'd never had the chance to ask who gave him my name so he could request me specifically from Office Right.

"You're concerned about her."

"She's a great gal and you got to admire her determination but ..." He trailed off, reaching for his wallet. "Here. Come back with furniture for that customer lounge. Something that won't put holes in my ass."

I took the five one-hundred dollar bills. It was a lot of money to spend on someone who just rented business space from you. Izzy had called him "uncle." What was the relationship between Ed Duran and Dixie?

"How did the meeting with Sal go?" I asked Dixie when I returned to the office.

She was sitting at the desk, writing on a legal pad. "Not well. Sal made some noises about not buying Sunny. He's bidding some important rehab project in Chicago and he's worried sick over it because Ed is bidding the same project."

"Duran Building doesn't do rehab work, does it? And why move into Chicago? Lake County doesn't have enough work to keep him busy?"

"I suppose Ed has visions of dining with The Mayor."

"Still, all that red tape and there must be hundreds of competitors. Is a dinner with Daley worth it?

"To Ed it is. It's validation. Means he's made it to the big time." She stopped writing and looked up. "Sal has good reason to worry. Ed's a bona fide minority. That automatically gives him an edge in the bidding."

"But only for government work."

"True, but that's where Sal was making most of his money. He has some kind of connection and he gets a lot of the smaller city jobs, like rehabbing this housing project. He told me he's been forced to bid private sector jobs out here now, the stuff no one wants. Like condo association stuff."

Hey, I live in an association. What am I – liver and onions?

I let her comment pass. "Sal told you all this in the meeting?"

"He tried to be nice. Gave me some excuse that he fired his bookkeeper so doing that plus everything else takes up all his spare time. He let slip that he's hauling equipment himself from jobs in the city to jobs out here to save money. The hauling is what eats up his time, not the loss of a bookkeeper."

"So he doesn't have time for a horse?"

"That's what he says but I think money's tight, too"

"Don't all contractors have to move their equipment from job to job?"

"Not the big ones. Duran Grading has so much equipment that Ed doesn't have to hold up one job while equipment is being used on another."

"I've heard rumors that Ed bought his first bulldozer with drug money. Is that how he got started?"

Dixie shrugged. "Who knows? Ed's wife died shortly after Brisa was born and he poured himself into his work to deal with the grief. Brisa's twenty-three. Twenty plus years is ample time to get a good business going and his timing was absolutely perfect. He got into construction just as Lake County decided to have a building boom." She pushed herself up and passed me the pad. "File this for me, please. I've got horses to work."

I left Bright Hope with five hundred dollars in my pocket. After driving south for ten miles and mulling over options, I still had no solid idea of what I wanted to accomplish. In the first few stores, the furniture was too expensive and too nice for a barn. The discount department stores had plenty of tables but no sofas or chairs. I gave up. It was well past noon and my lunch bag sat in Dixie's refrigerator. I turned the car toward Penzler's.

Penzler's Corner Market is a one-story prefab building with white aluminum siding and light gray asphalt shingles on the roof. A six-foot window overlooks a cement patio cordoned off from the gravel parking lot by two white plastic planters filled with orange day lilies.

Inside, the front half of the store is stocked with grocery and sundry products. The Penzlers have arrangements with a local dry cleaner so, in addition to paying for purchases, customers can drop off their laundry at the checkout counter. The deli cases are at the rear and it is here that Pete Penzler holds court, preparing thick sandwiches from whole grain breads and a wide variety of meats, cheeses, and fillings. Mary, his wife, is in charge of the sides: coleslaw, potato salad, bean salad, fruit salad, all made with low fat and low sugar dressings and all second-helping delicious. She bakes many of the breads, pastry and dessert items herself. Her cinnamon rolls are a local favorite; people drive for miles to get them. She once told me her secret ingredient is the water left over from boiling the potatoes for her potato salad. Whatever it is, her rolls are not the bland, tasteless dough that passes for cinnamon rolls elsewhere. Mary Penzler's are dense and the flavor is in the dough, not the icing. In fact, she uses very little icing, just a drizzle stripe or two to add some sweet to the spicy cinnamon filing.

After I got my tuna salad sandwich and coleslaw, I went outside to one of the picnic tables on the patio slab in front of the store. I adjusted the umbrella, shielding my eyes from the August sun. The dog days of summer had arrived but, unusual for this time of year, a stiff breeze discouraged the yellow jackets. They buzzed around the garbage, crawling in and out of the empty soft drink cans but left me alone to snarf down my sandwich in peace.

I was just about finished with my lunch when Mary slid onto the bench opposite me and pushed a snickerdoodle at me. During the summer months, her apron covered short-sleeved cotton dresses dotted with tiny pink or yellow flowers. In the winter, Mary favored wool sweaters and long skirts. Her pale skin showed no age spots but a couple of freckles were scattered across her nose. She wore no make-up or jewelry except for the thin gold band on her left hand.

"What brings you out in the middle of the day, dear?"

I explained my mission. "Five malls, seven stores. I certainly ought to be able to find reasonably priced and durable furniture at one of them. The big stuff has to be delivered. That may eliminate a couple of my options."

"Now that you've had some lunch and relaxed a bit, it will come to you. You'll find what you want now, I'm sure." Mary pointed to my boots. "I'll bet Office Right Staffing Service doesn't get much call for cowgirls."

I fiddled with my fork. "I don't work for Office Right now. At least not for this job."

"But I told Ed to call Office Right. And you are with Dixie?"

"It's a weird arrangement, Mary. Office Right refused to send me to a horse barn. Margaret said the chance for injury was too high."

Margaret, my Office Right supervisor, had told me all about the Bright Hope assignment; it was long-term, possibly six months or more. Then, after she had me hooked, she told me Office Right couldn't offer me the assignment because it was against their policy. Their insurance wouldn't cover me.

"Margaret, I promise I won't get hurt. Besides, according to you, I'm not working for the stable anyway. I'll be employed by Duran Building."

"There's no way Office Right will approve you working in that environment. It's got worker's comp claim written all over it."

"But I need a job!" I sounded like an Irish banshee foretelling a death...the death of my checkbook. "What am I going to do?"

Margaret was silent for several moments. I was just about to give up when she said, "I have an idea." She lowered her voice until I had to strain to hear her. "I shouldn't suggest this but you could take the job as an independent contractor."

"How do I do that?"

"Well, first you get yourself to your accountant so you thoroughly understand the tax implications. Then you become self-employed."

That didn't sound like what I wanted to do. I'd never worked on my own before. "I don't want to be self-employed. I want to work for Office Right."

"And we appreciate your loyalty. But when you signed on with us, didn't we suggest that you register with more than one service so you would have a greater opportunity for work?"

"Yes."

"Did you do it?"

"No. I didn't think I'd need to."

"Times are tough for all of us. There just aren't that many jobs and certainly not at your level. You need to hedge your bets and register with other services. Or take on contract work when it comes your way."

"I guess I have some thinking to do. Can you recommend a good accountant?"

"You don't use one?"

"When all you have to your name is a small savings account and a big mortgage, you don't need an accountant. You just need some tax software."

"I suppose that's true. Hold on."

An FM radio station kept me occupied until Margaret came back on the line. She read me a telephone number.

"Got it? His name is Greg Lacey. He seems to have a specialty in new business and independents. Everyone I've sent to him has been very pleased. Call him. In the meantime, if something else comes in, I'll let you know right away."

I hung up feeling confused and concerned. Mom always said that a door doesn't close without a window opening. Great adage if the window is on the ground floor. I felt as though this particular window was a lot higher, say on the fortieth floor. Did I want to jump out? I looked at the telephone number. It wouldn't cost anything to check it out.

Greg Lacey had a deep, almost melodic voice and I couldn't help wondering what he looked like. Sometimes he huffed a bit and I pictured him with a bushy mustache that tickled his upper lip. Lacey asked me a lot of questions about my former employment, my desire to be more independent, my tenure with Office Right and my personal finances.

"To the IRS, it's all a matter of control and who has it," he said. "Your client will hire you to do specific work. They have control over what needs to be done. How that work is performed should be under your control. Let's get specific. Based on your conversation with the stable owner, you know what she wants you to do but has she indicated how you are to do it?"

"I haven't talked to her directly yet. Margaret said the office needs to be organized and cleaned up so a part time clerk can eventually be hired. I got the impression Dixie Villano is focused on training horses, not on paying bills or filing."

"Then it's doubtful she will care how you accomplish the tasks. In this scenario, she needs work performed but how you perform it is entirely up to you. Ergo, you qualify as an independent contractor."

"But what if she determines what days I work. That gives control back to her."

"That's not necessarily a determining factor. It's not unusual for a business to want workers, whether employees or independent contractors, to be present during working hours. You won't receive any benefits, nor do you expect any, and neither party anticipates that the work will go on indefinitely. I'd say this qualifies as independent contractor stuff. Now, assuming you decide to go forward with this, there are several things you need to consider."

"Such as?"

"Recordkeeping, providing for your retirement, health insurance, self-employment insurance."

Being an independent contractor sounded like I would no longer be independent. I'd be bound by the requirements of running a business, keeping track of details like expenses and estimated tax payments and mileage. Did I want to do that? Did I have a choice?

I hadn't worked steadily since leaving my corporate job. So far the lulls between assignments hadn't been too long but I couldn't go forever without a paycheck and each period of unemployment had me wondering about my sanity in choosing this method of earning a living. I didn't want to go back to the corporate stress pool and I had made some significant financial concessions to avoid doing it. So here I was, sitting at Penzler's Corner Market, telling Mary about how her referral had made me an independent contractor. This was all her fault.

Apparently I hadn't been out of focus for long because Mary

was still talking.

"So Ed told me he wants to partner with Dixie. What do you think?"

"About?"

Mary smiled. "I thought you were somewhere else, dear. One of the reasons Ed wants Bright Hope in tip-top shape is that he hopes to go into business with Dixie doing horse vacations. He called it a vocation vacation. Imagine a week at a horse training facility. The visitors attend workshops with Dixie and Izzy and do the chores. He will put the folks up in a bed and breakfast right on the property." She winked at me. "Equestrian Escapades Ltd. has a nice ring, don't you think?"

"I think he'd better talk to Dixie before he goes very far with it. Imagine what the insurance costs for something like that would be."

"Doesn't matter if Ed passes the costs on to the people," said Pete, scooting onto the bench next to Mary. "Ed plans to charge a bundle for it."

"Have you seen Izzy or Dixie work the horses?" asked Mary. "Would people pay to watch?"

"Yes, I think they would," I said, "Vocation vacations are hot right now. Several of the local papers have done stories about getaways at vineyards, cattle ranches, different places."

"Would people pay to shovel shit?"

"Pete!" said Mary. "Mind your mouth." She looked thoughtful. "You know, dear, now that I think about it, Dixie won't like Ed's idea much. It goes against her beliefs."

I scrunched my garbage and tossed it into the bin. "I agree with you. Equestrian Escapades doesn't match Dixie's devotion to animals in trouble or that framed mission statement above the mantle."

That statement was so important Frank Villano's memorial was next to it. The declaration had something to do with helping troubled horses overcome adversity and reach their full potential through a gentle, loving approach.

"With Frank missing," said Mary, "I worry about Ed trying to run things. He's a strong man with strong opinions. I hope he doesn't try to bowl over Dixie like he does Brisa." Mary reached out and patted my hand. "I'm glad you're working out there, dear. Dixie is a fine person and I knew you two would hit it off."

I looked at my watch. "I'd better get going. I've got furniture to buy."

They waved me out of the parking lot. I felt completely rejuvenated, thanks to the Penzlers – and that snickerdoodle. Even Milwaukee Avenue's five lanes of honking horns and lane jumpers didn't bother me as I drove back to the mall.

This time around, I found exactly the right items. After ordering a couple of inexpensive leather chairs, I stopped at a discount store for a small dinette, chairs, occasional tables and lamps. Most of it required assembly but I was sure the customers would get a kick out of helping me with it. The trunk and backseat of my car were completely filled but I had everything I wanted.

On the drive back, I thought about furniture placement, which led me to think about the fireplace and the last item on my list. It didn't take long to swing by Jewel's floral department. Dixie had specific requirements. A yellow rose. If that wasn't available, yellow anything but carnations or glads.

"No funeral flowers," she had told me. "I'll do funeral flowers when we find him."

"Yellow for remembrance." I thought as I got back into the car. "Dixie sure is a sentimentalist."

Duran's black dual-wheeled pick-up truck was still parked in the shade by the riding ring when I returned. It was a lot of truck with a masculine, hard-hitting look; its spotless mirror finish reflecting everything around it. Stencils on the door panels read Duran Building and Grading in bold red script. I looked over at

Dixie's muddy white Ford F10 and my own used Altima. As I went inside, I thought about what our vehicles said about us. Dixie had no time, I had no money and Ed Duran had plenty of both.

Duran was talking to Henry when I stepped into the lounge. The two men looked up.

"Dixie's in the arena," said Duran, smiling. "Mission accomplished?"

"Yes."

"Good. You know Henry, my foreman?"

"Nice to see you up close again," I said. "Usually we wave at each other across the fields."

Henry removed his cap. "You help a lot. Thank you."

We shook hands, my fingers wrapped in his enormous palm. I felt his rings bite into my skin and pulled back. Henry looked distressed.

"I hurt you," he said, looking at his fingers as though they didn't belong on his hand. "I didn't think. I am sorry."

"Jesus, Henry," said Duran. "Do you have to wear those things all the time? I've warned you it's not safe."

"No harm done." I held up my palm.

Henry nodded, staring at his hands. I excused myself, going into the office to set down some of my parcels before dealing with the flower.

The stable office was small; the desk taking up much of the floor space. I had arranged it so the desk backed up to the north wall and was pushed tightly against the west wall so there was room for a file cabinet. Shelving over the file cabinet created more storage. Above the desk was an opening to the lounge where two ivy plants sat on the ledge. The tiny arch provided light and air movement but did not serve any other purpose that I had been able to discover. At five feet, it was too high to be a functioning pass-through.

The men were still at it when I went back out to the lounge to put the rose in the bud vase. Duran and Henry watched, both of them frowning. Sal thought the memorial was obscene. By the looks on their faces, so did they.

"Sorry, Ed," said Dixie, stopping just inside the door. "I didn't realize you were still in here."

"No problem. Henry and I were discussing the fall chores list. I left a copy on your desk."

"Thank you. Anything special this year?"

"You might say that. It took a year of arm-twisting but I finally bought the place across the road."

"You did? When?"

"Last week. I was afraid that old geezer's family was going to sell to some developer and another strip mall would go in. Now it'll protect this place."

"Are you going to farm it?"

"Yeah, but I haven't decided what crops yet. I'm thinking truck farm with a nice vegetable stand."

"Retail? Tours for children? That kind of thing?"

"No kids. The liability insurance I got is already too much. I'm thinking small. And all organic. Henry, here's a list of farms out in McHenry County that are like what I want to do. You and Chuck check them out next week."

"Sounds like quite an undertaking," said Dixie. "I suppose Henry will be tied up with that all winter?"

"Henry's staying here to run this place." Duran clapped a dour Henry on the back. "I think Chuck will do great over there. Henry trained him well. He should be proud." Duran looked at me. "You got a trunk full? You want Jorge to bring stuff in?"

"Please."

"Jorge is in tack room." Henry stepped forward. "I will get him."

The two men carried boxes into the lounge and stacked them in the corner. Dixie hovered, looking at the illustrations on the cartons and offering comments. Just as we finished unloading my car, we heard frantic shouts of alarm. Someone was making a real commotion.

It was the pitch that caught my attention, elevated and intense. I'd heard Chuck bellow before but this was frenzied, like the call a person uses if a house is on fire. But Chuck wasn't shouting about fire. He was yelling about bones.

Duran left the lounge at a run, the screen door banging behind him. Henry dropped the end of the box he carried. He mumbled something in Polish, switched to Spanish to speak to Jorge, and then he too hurried out. Dixie grabbed my arm and the two of us followed the others cutting through the arena.

When we arrived at the barn's back door, Duran and Henry were standing near Chuck. He prodded at something in the manure with his shovel.

"What's going on?" asked Izzy, leaning over her mother's shoulder. "What'd you find, Chuck?"

"Look," he said, poking again. "It's a bone."

"Stop that!" Duran put his hand on Chuck's arm. "I told you to stop messing with it." He pulled his cell phone from his belt and made a call. "The police are coming. Put that shovel against the barn and go inside. You, too, Henry."

The men looked at each other and then Henry came in immediately, turning sideways to get past Dixie and me. Chuck complied more slowly, as if he was reluctant to leave his find. Duran followed them, gently pushing Dixie and Izzy back into the barn.

When we were near the lounge, Duran steered me outside. "You go on home. You don't need to be here for this."

"Don't you think I should stay? As an employee and as a witness, the police will have questions for me even if I don't have any answers."

"Why spend the night while the cops go through their routine?

Like you said, you don't have any answers for them anyway. You weren't there when Chuck found the bones so you don't know enough to be any good to them. They'll waste time on you and that keeps us all here that much later. I'm sending Jorge home for the same reason."

"What about Dixie? She looked upset. I can help her."

"Izzy's here. Besides, no use everyone getting all stressed about this. They're deer bones," Duran walked me to my car, his hand on my elbow. "Poachers have been here before. They carved up the animal and buried the guts in the manure knowing it wouldn't get discovered for a long while, if ever."

"But -."

"Trust me. It'll blow over tonight and if it doesn't, the cops can harass you in the morning. There's nothing you can tell them that can't wait."

Duran watched me pull out of the parking lot, waving when I turned onto the road. As I drove away, I saw him run toward the south end of the barn. Why wasn't he going back inside with the others? When I stopped at the Wadsworth Road traffic signal, two Lake County Sheriff's squad cars flew past me.

*　　*　　*　　*

I was up early the next morning and before I did anything else, I turned on the news. The morning shows featured the bizarre burial at Bright Hope Equestrian Center. Sometime during the night, the bones were confirmed to be human remains but authorities didn't have an identity for the victim and had not divulged whether the skeleton was male or female. The media filled air time by describing the Lake County Major Crimes Task Force's evidence collection process. Television made the most of its stable footage with long shots of the mass of manure surrounded by florescent yellow crime scene tape and evidence techs working the scene like ants on a dollop of jam.

With all the police activity, I didn't think Bright Hope would be open but if it was, I wanted to be there. Besides being helpful, I wanted to find out what was really going on. As soon as I was dressed, I called the barn office. A message on the voice mail explained there had been a death and that the barn would not open until noon at the earliest. Callers were instructed to check back at that time.

How were the horses reacting to the unusual activity around them? Horses are prey animals – food for the predators of the prairies. Being watchful and nervous is part of their genetic makeup. I hadn't been around the horses long but I was sure Chicken would be pacing his stall, tossing his head, sweat foaming on his chest. And I worried about Sunny. How would he handle the bedlam?

Flashing lights and numerous strangers making lots of noise would bother more than the horses; however, unlike the animals, only the humans would comprehend the implications. Dixie and Izzy had to be deeply troubled by these events. The clients were another matter. I didn't know them well and had never met some. Would Nolan be angry? Would Brisa be frightened? What about Sal and Lori?

I pulled on a pair of jeans and then struggled with my boots, stomping and tugging without success until I remembered the talcum powder. Once dressed, I ran errands that didn't need to be run, checking my watch every ten minutes and wondering if I should call Bright Hope before noon. By the time my stomach gurgled, I was closer to Penzler's than to my townhouse so I decided to get a sandwich there before heading out to the barn, if the barn was going to be open. As soon as I pulled the Altima into a spot in Penzler's lot, I called Bright Hope again. Dixie's hesitant hello greeted me.

CHAPTER 5

"It's Kyle. How are things?"

"A nightmare. I had to move Chicken. His stall is too close to the back door and all the activity. Worked himself into quite a sweat. Brisa's frantic and won't leave him so now Ed is all upset. He's trying to get her to go home but she's refusing. They had quite an argument."

"Shall I come out?"

"Please. I was just getting ready to call you. I have no idea when the police will go away. They tell me they're almost done in the barn so I can use the office in about an hour."

"Then I'll see you in an hour."

As I made my way to the rear of Penzler's, I saw Mary replenishing the potato salad in the refrigerated case. She always wore her gray braids wound around her head and no matter how many times I saw her, I thought of halos. I'd never known anyone else who had such a deep-seated faith in humanity. Pete manned the broom, pulling morning rush crumbs into a little pile by his feet. He looked up and then set the broom aside to envelope me in his thick arms. Someday his traditional greeting would crack a rib. Mary shooed him aside.

"How are you, dear?" she asked, putting her arm around my shoulders and squeezing lightly. "We heard the awful news."

"Tell us what in the blue blazes is going on out at Dixie's place," said Pete, going behind the meat case. "I turned the damned radio off. They weren't saying anything; just droning on about a death investigation at Bright Hope. We want details, not some speculative drivel. It was driving us nuts."

"It was driving you nuts, dear," said Mary. She reached across the case and rubbed his hand. Then she turned to me. "Do you have any information you can share?"

"Not a crumb. Dixie got after the hired hands to spread the manure out in the fields. I have to admit that smoking heap did make me nervous."

"Fires happen," Pete said, glancing at Mary. "You can't always prevent them."

I waited for her reaction. The subject of fire was a little close to home. A memory flowed through Mary's eyes. She straightened slightly and the moment passed.

"Dixie was right to react," said Mary. "You know how awful it was for us. How would she feel if a fire started because she ignored what that smoke represented? Guilt would tear her apart."

"Izzy said customers were nervous about the smoke," I said. "I wasn't the only one bothered by it."

"You can't have uneasy customers," said Pete. "Pretty soon, they stop being customers."

"Dixie said the workers let that chore go much longer than usual."

"That's because Frank's not around."

"Izzy thinks they don't want to take orders from a woman."

"That's ridiculous," said Mary.

"I saw it myself. The minute they were told Ed Duran was coming to the barn, their whole attitude changed."

"Poor Dixie," said Mary. "First Frank and now this."

"It probably is Frank," said Pete.

"In a way, I hope you're right, dear," said Mary, looking thoughtful. "Poor Dixie just hasn't been herself since Frank disappeared. How can she run the business when her whole life is filled with uncertainty?" She dismissed the topic with a quick blink.

"I wanted to ask you yesterday but those customers came. How is Jake?"

Jake Prince is the information systems manager for a Lake County company where I worked as a temp. After my assignment ended, we started seeing each other, although getting together a couple of times a month was all our busy schedules would allow. Sometimes I wished for more time with him and sometimes I was glad it was so sporadic.

"He's out of town. Again."

"Business or pleasure?"

"Both. A convention in San Francisco and he tacked on a couple of days to see Napa Valley."

Mary's head was cocked and her eyes held more questions. Guess she noticed my tone.

"You wanted to go with him."

"I wanted to be invited to go with him."

Mary's gentle smile reminded me of my mother, who gets the same look on her face when I'm being illogical.

"You would have turned him down," Mary said.

"I have to work."

"He knew that, dear."

"It would have been nice to have been asked."

"He calls you, doesn't he?"

"Email, Mary. Lots of email."

I didn't stay longer with the Penzlers. After Pete made my tuna salad sandwich and Mary packed up a big bag of cookies, I hurried out to the barn. On the roadway near the entrance, I saw people leaning against the shady sides of television satellite trucks or sitting in cars with the air conditioning running. As I turned my car into the driveway, a man scrambled out of the CLTV truck and ran to a camera mounted on a tripod. If Chicagoland TV thought I was news, apparently nothing of significance was happening at Bright Hope.

A white squad car partially blocked the gravel drive and a buxom officer, perspiration dripping down her cheek, stepped forward as I approached. She held a clipboard in the crook of her left arm. I put my window down.

"Name, please. And some ID."

I gave her my name and pulled my driver's license out of my wallet.

"You the secretary?" She looked at my license and then at my face. "The owner said you'd be coming. Park in front by that white pick-up. You can go anywhere inside the barn but not outside, 'specially not behind the barn. You see yellow tape, you stay out. Any questions?"

I shook my head, thanked her and eased forward until my Altima was next to Dixie's truck. A silver SUV was parked near the riding ring in the shade of an old maple. Ronig, Lori's German shepherd, watched me warily from his cage in the rear.

Ronig was the size of a small pony. I'd seen him outside his cage only once but the black-and-tan German shepherd, despite all his tail wagging, was one of the most striking and intimidating animals I'd ever encountered. Bred in Germany to German standards, he was at least twenty-five percent larger than any shepherd I'd come upon before. Lori introduced us and when he jumped up, he nearly knocked me off my feet. I'd learned the hard way that if I got near the vehicle, he went crazy so I stayed well away from it. That dog's bark could be the crashing cymbals of the Chicago Symphony and I didn't want to set him off.

Inside, I paused at the customer lounge screen door and watched as Lori paced in front of the fireplace, muttering. Her walnut hair was pulled back in a ponytail, held in place with a purple scrunchie. Wayward wisps framed her face. Boot cut jeans hugged her tall, muscular frame. She stopped once to look at Frank Villano's photo and then resumed a halting march from one end of the room to the other.

"Thank god you're here," she said as I came through the door. She held a wad of tissues and her eyes were red. "What can you tell me? The cop at the front gate wouldn't tell me anything and she was worse than airport security. Checking my name against a list. Wanting to see inside my truck. Doesn't she need a warrant for that? Ronig changed her mind in a hurry. She didn't like him at all. I think she was going to keep me out but Dixie heard him barking and told her to let me in. What's going on? What happened? Sal called and said they found bones. The news said they're human. Is that true? Is Divot OK? Will you check on him?"

"Whoa." I held up my hands. "I'm sure your horse is fine."

He's probably sound asleep.

"I just got here myself," I said, "so the only things I know are what you've already seen for yourself on the news: Chuck uncovered some bones in the manure yesterday and the bones turned out to be human."

"But you worked yesterday, didn't you?" Her voice caught. She sounded close to tears. "Weren't you here when it happened? Sal said you were here."

"I ran to the back of the barn along with everyone else when we heard Chuck shouting. That's the extent of my involvement."

"The cops'll shut Dixie down, won't they? I called Brisa to warn her as soon as I heard the news. I'm sure we'll have to move our horses."

"They don't have a reason to shut Bright Hope down."

"Henry said the police will close the place and he and Chuck will lose their jobs and he won't be able to bring his family over."

"Lori, I don't know how long Henry has been in this country but it sounds like he doesn't understand our process. Trust me; they can investigate with the business running."

I looked at the coffee maker, saw it was empty and started a pot. It was ninety degrees outside and a balmy eight-five in the office. Perfect coffee weather. Someone was sure to want some if it was made and I needed caffeine to go with the Mary Penzler cookie I craved.

I had consumed my sandwich during the drive to the stable but I am a stress eater. Raise my adrenaline level and I want something sweet. How convenient that I had a whole bag of gooey chocolate chip cookies fresh from Mary's oven. One or six of those would do just fine.

"Keep an eye on the coffee," I commanded Lori. "I'll go see what's what."

Grabbing a cookie, I hurried into the aisle. There was no crime scene tape visible at any of the arena doorways so I cut through to the back aisle of the barn. Yellow plastic stretched across the rear door between Foggy's stall and the feed room. As I approached, the stallion's head appeared at his stall door.

"What have you seen, boy?" I rubbed his muzzle. "Did you take notes?"

He nickered softly.

While I certainly didn't expect him to magically solve our mystery, his big brown eyes held the wisdom of the ages. Horses have been on the planet a long time. To mankind, they represent wealth, freedom, and power. Perhaps that explains the nearly genetic affinity we have for them.

As far back as I can remember, a love for horses has been part of me. I treasure my father's boyhood copy of The Black Stallion, watch equestrian sports on television and write checks to equine-affiliated charities. I often wonder what it would be like to own a horse like Ephraim's Lifting Fog. Nolan was a fortunate man indeed to have this magnificent creature in his life. For the briefest second, I wondered if I could afford Foggy if Nolan had to give him up. I hated the idea that Brisa might take him away.

Realism squashed my fantasy in a hurry. There was no way I could compete with Ed Duran's limitless supply of money. I inhaled deeply, patted Foggy again and went to the back door to look out at the activity around Mt. Manure. As I watched the evidence techs use large wood-framed strainers to sift through the manure, I scanned faces looking for Ian Page, my detective friend from the Vernon Hills police force. Page was a member of the Lake County Major Crimes Task Force so I knew he was working the case.

When homicides or other major crimes happen, the task force handles the investigation. Individual communities within the county are too small to devote the forty or fifty officers necessary to work a big case so they pool their resources, contributing funds, equipment, or one or two officers from their police departments. The officers receive specialized training and have acquired the expertise needed to solve complex cases. Page was on the task force when I met him. Now he commanded the detectives assigned to it.

I didn't see him nor did I really expect to. The techs work the evidence; the detectives work the witnesses. Page was questioning someone somewhere but he wasn't behind the barn.

The brring of the telephone brought me up sharply and I hurried to answer the extension near Foggy's stall.

"Bright Hope Equestrian Center," I said, trying for a lightness I didn't feel. "This is Kyle. How may I help you?"

"Brisa around?"

It was Ed Duran.

"I haven't seen her but I'll try to find her for you."

"Wait!"

I waited.

"She's been talking about Sal Fabrini a lot lately. You know him, right? I don't like him sniffing around her. He's connected. Know what I mean?"

You don't really expect me to answer that.

"Well? Do you?" Duran's volume raised a decibel. "Do you?"

"He knows someone in Chicago government so the city awards him contracts."

I didn't mention that the process works the same way in Lake County. Somehow I suspected Ed Duran already knew that.

"Better connections than that. His father lives in Little Italy."

Duran's implication that Sal was somehow associated with the Italian mafia surprised me. Although, it had been years since I'd been in that neighborhood, Little Italy reminded me of pasta and meatballs on tables covered by vinyl red and white checkered tablecloths, not organized crime families. More importantly, why was Ed Duran talking to me about this?

Duran drew a deep breath. "He made my Brisa crazy this morning. He called somebody about the dead guy and that somebody called her. How'd he know about it so fast?"

"Television?"

"Or maybe he did a favor for some old friends from the 'hood?" He paused. "Anyway, Brisa gets this call, gets all hysterical and rushes over to the barn. Now somebody else is tellin' her that the police are going to close the place. That's stupid. I own the place and nobody shuts me down unless I shut me down. But Brisa's not hearin' me."

"Sal called Lori Boc," I said. "You know her; she owns the big dog." Duran grunted so I went on. "Lori called Brisa, probably so she would hear the news from someone she knows, not the television. I guess Henry was the one who thought the police would shut down Bright Hope. Lori or Henry relayed that to Brisa."

Duran was silent for several seconds. Finally, he said, "Keep an eye on Brisa for me. I want to know right away if she starts liking Fabrini. I've been down that road with her once. We're not going there again."

"Mr. Duran, I can't —."

"Yeah, you can. An extra hundred a week."

I didn't have a chance to decline because he had already hung up. I stared at the receiver still in my hand. My cheeks were hot and my stomach flipped like I was on the Space Mountain roller coaster at Disneyland.

My boss had just issued orders that I wasn't sure I could or should follow. I had faced similar dilemmas during my corporate days and it was one of the reasons I so enjoyed being a temp worker. No political entanglement.

But that was the least of the things about the conversation that troubled me. Several words leapt to mind. Snitch. Mole. Spy. I knew what happened to those people. They ended up face down in dark alleys – or under tons of horse manure.

This temp does not do espionage!

Vowing I would set Ed Duran straight as soon as I had a chance, I returned to the office by taking a swing past Divot's stall as I had promised Lori I would. The palomino was dozing, leaning against the stall wall, one hind foot cocked slightly, a soft, guttural horsy snore rumbling in his chest. Swishing softly to some unknown rhythm, Divot's tail moved from right flank to left but he didn't even flick an ear as I went by.

When I got back to the lounge, Lori was gone. Guess she wasn't all that worried about Divot after all. The door to the office was closed. I thought Dixie might be inside and almost went in until I heard men speaking. I should have moved away but when I recognized the voices, my curiosity held me in place.

"Please." It was Chuck, his accent thickened by frustration and anger. "I got work to do. Time to feed horses. And I still gotta move shit pile."

"Your boss isn't going to be mad," said Ian Page. "We have to talk to you about what happened yesterday and he knows that. And you're not going anywhere near that shit pile until we say you can."

"This is fifth time you ask me questions. How many times you gonna ask me same thing?"

"As many times as it takes." There was a pause and then, "Tell me about Frank Villano. What did you think when he disappeared?"

"You think that's Frank? Holy Pope John!"

So at least Page had thought of it. Pete's pronouncement was right on target.

"It could be a lot of people," said Page in a conversational tone. "In a minute, we're going to talk about Ramon Gutierrez. But for right now, let's talk about Frank Villano."

"Frank was good boss. One day, after Easter, he disappeared. No note, no nothing and Dixie is worried. But cops, I know they thought he ran off with another woman. They didn't know him. Mr. Frank would not leave woman to handle his business."

The sound of shuffling feet sent me outside in a hurry. Page would have a fit if he caught me eavesdropping. I made myself busy outside by picking up litter from along the barn foundation slab and depositing it in the trash barrel next to the picnic table. Twenty minutes later, I went back inside. The office door was open and no one was inside.

The phone rang. Morning Maids had been turned away by the police. Did I wish to reschedule? I wished they had called before they drove away. Perhaps cleaning crews don't carry cell phones. In any case, the lounge wouldn't be ready for the new furniture.

As though on cue, the furniture delivery truck arrived moments later. Although the store wasn't on the list the police had, Dixie produced the receipt with the delivery date on it and, after some intense conversation, the officer let the truck pass. Now that the crime scene was confined to the area behind the barn, there wasn't any reason to keep people out.

The arrival of the new furniture brought everyone into the office. I asked Brisa to touch base with her father. She answered with a pout and busied herself talking to Lori about the day's events and testing the new sofa.

By quitting time, the madness had subsided somewhat. The telephone barely rang and the clients had all departed. I made sure my desk was cleared of critical items and then I escaped the office myself, going to the back of the barn for one last look at the crime scene before I went home.

I stood in the doorway watching as the evidence technicians sifted the manure. Periodically, they would stop and photograph whatever lay on the screen. Then they emptied their findings into paper bags, closed the bags with a seal and make notes on a clipboard.

"You have a horse here?"

The activity was mesmerizing and I don't know how long I stood there watching before the deep and raspy voice came up behind me. I whirled around and found myself looking at an angular face bisected by a sharp, thin nose and dotted twice with pale blue eyes nearly hidden by black horned-rim glasses.

"No, I'm a temp."

He pointed at the credentials clipped to his shirt pocket. "Police. Know where the owner is?"

"Do you mean the owner of Bright Hope Equestrian Center or the owner of the farm?"

"They just told me to find the owner. Nobody said nothing about there bein' two of 'em."

"Ed Duran owns the farm and Dixie Villano owns Bright Hope. Last time I saw Dixie, she was out front talking to someone in a suit. That was quite awhile ago."

"Who lives in that house over there?"

"Farm hands."

He pulled a small spiral notebook from his shirt pocket. "How many?"

"I'm not sure. At least six or seven."

"Names?"

"I only know two of the men who live there. Chuck Floriak and Henry Slavin. The other guys don't come around here."

"Where's this Chuck guy?"

"A couple of hours ago he was in the barn office. I haven't seen him since."

"Anyone else?"

"Jorge Estaban works here but he doesn't live in the house."

The officer looked past me, watching the sifting activity for a moment. Turning, he went into the arena and trudged out of sight.

Thank you ma'am and don't leave town.

When I finally got home that evening, I was edgy, exhausted and embarrassed.

After dealing with telephone calls from boarders, the media attempts for interviews and various officials demanding directions or information, it was the exchange with Duran that had exhausted me. His command that I spy on Sal required examination and I had shelved the urge all afternoon. The drive home bordered on dangerous because I didn't concentrate on the road; I was haunted by how snitches usually end up face down with bullet holes in their backs.

My embarrassment was the direct result of eating nearly a dozen chocolate chip cookies all by myself. True to form, sugar and caffeine had kept me going. Now my nerves jangled as if I'd stuck a finger into an electrical socket.

I was so tired I didn't even stop for my usual post-work chat with my neighbor, Mrs. Sims. I let the car roll right past her and into the garage. Once inside, I shed my dirty clothes in the mud room, dropped the mail on the breakfast bar and headed down the hall toward my bedroom. In the spare bedroom, my treadmill called out to me. I paused and considered a run but decided an hour of pounding on the thing wouldn't work off all the extra cookie calories so why bother?

Instead, I did something for myself I've never done for anyone else. I placed lit candles on the bath tub ledge, poured myself a half glass of Shiraz and put some Danny Wright on the CD player. Then I soaked in a tub full of bubbles and let my mind drift back to Bright Hope and all that was happening there. The soothing bath clarified things a bit.

For the first time since our conversation, I remembered what Duran had implied about Sal Fabrini. Why was he pushing the theory that Sal might have dumped a body for the family? Violence had been a part of Duran's life. I did not know that to be true for Sal. Maybe the body dump was a favor for Ed Duran's old gang.

The newspaper had said the autopsy results and other unspecified evidence would be reviewed by a Lake County coroner's inquest. There wasn't any way the jury would call this accidental. People don't end up in manure piles by mistake. This was a homicide and the ensuing investigation would probably take months. I wondered how quickly, if at all, the remains would be identified. Was there any DNA left in bones that had cooked for months under mounds of rotting hay, feces and sawdust?

When I got out of the tub thirty minutes later, the water was cold, my skin was wrinkled and my fingernails were soft. I threw together a salad and sat down to tackle the mail. After pitching all the junk, it consisted of two bills, one from Commonwealth Edison and one from my insurance company. My health insurance quarterly premium had gone up again. At this rate, a new car would cost less. Maybe Nolan Grinnell could help me find some affordable coverage.

As I drifted off to sleep, I reminded myself that I'd better call my mother in the morning. By now, the dung heap dead man was the lead story on the national news. She knew I was working at Bright Hope and she was bound to be worried.

Of course, I didn't do it. I forgot to set the alarm so the morning found me making a mad dash to get to the barn on time. The phones would be just as busy as on the previous day however the weekend brought an added burden. Clients that Dixie hadn't seen since they first brought their horses in were expected to suddenly appear, just stopping by to see how things were progressing. Their new-found interest would have nothing to do with the welfare of their horse but it was a good pretext.

The benefit of all the clients coming in was that I had plenty of help assembling the furniture I had purchased. Nolan and Sal got a kick out of being handy and Sal had the tools we needed in his trunk. Between them, the tables and four chairs were bolted and screwed together in no time. Then Lori and Brisa fussed over furniture arrangement, moving the new sofa from one wall to another until finally deciding that its original placement made the most sense.

Throughout the day, I listened as clients voiced diverse theories about the skeleton. Too bad a police officer wasn't sitting in. I learned a lot from the conversations that drifted through the opening in the wall above the desk.

Bright Hope began as a backyard horse operation in a six-stall barn originally located in Green Oaks. As the Villano reputation grew, so did their need for more space, hence the move to Stable Road and then to the current location north of Gurnee. I overheard some debate about whether or not the stable was a safe place but that didn't get much play. No one volunteered that the skeleton might be Frank Villano's although someone suggested a bad end for a worker named Ramon Gutierrez.

Most people thought Dixie would have to move again because, without Frank, the business would go downhill. In addition, Ed Duran would want to develop the land and he would force her out. They pointed to the demise of the Lake County Fairgrounds and the improvement of the fairgrounds property as clear indication that agricultural Lake County was part of the past. I don't call strip malls "improvements."

Brisa gave Lori a lead on one of the vets at Arlington Park race track. Nolan pitched various insurance packages and at one point, it sounded as though he and Sal had reached an agreement on some coverage for Sal's equipment.

Lori asked Nolan if he used an accountant and if so, who. I was surprised to hear him name Greg Lacey. Small world. What surprised me even more was Brisa telling everyone that her father had just switched the farm accounting to Lacey. Something about needing a fresh perspective and that Lacey had come highly recommended.

Toward the end of the afternoon, I approached a thoroughly-relaxed Nolan. He was on the sofa, leaning back with his arms behind his head, eyes closed and his thick legs, stilled wrapped in leather chaps, stretched out before him. He looked so comfortable, I hated to disturb him.

"Gotta minute?" I asked.

"Sure." He sat upright. "Wanna talk about Dixie's liability insurance?" He shook his head. "I can't help you. The policy got yanked about three, maybe four months ago."

"Why?"

"Oldest reason in the world. Price. Dixie switched right after Frank disappeared. I guess she was trying to save money."

I took a moment to digest his news and then said, "Actually, I wanted to talk about health insurance."

"For you personally? I only do commercial but I can refer you."

"Thanks, but I want to work with you."

"Look, there are some good people in our office and I know they'd be happy to help you."

"But you don't get the business."

He smiled. "You don't really need insurance. You're trying to help me out."

"Actually, I do. I had COBRA after my old job and I converted it to a personal policy but the cost is killing me. The premiums are so high, I can barely buy groceries."

"I hear ya. It's a constant battle for me. My clients want to provide for their workers or cover their assets but they find it more and more difficult to pay for insurance coverage without affecting the bottom line."

"And it's all about the bottom line."

"Ain't that the truth!" His nose wrinkled as if he had just met up with a dead skunk. "Let me see what I can scare up for you. Somehow we ought to be able to improve on what you're paying now. I'll bring the paperwork with me tomorrow."

"That would be great. Even though I can't afford what I have, I'm afraid to be without any coverage at all. Who knows what could happen?"

CHAPTER 6

Every morning, Dixie pushed the arena doors apart at seven. On Sundays, the barn didn't officially open for business until nine and that's when Lori arrived, boxes of Krispy Kremes and Dunkin Donuts in hand. Nolan pulled into the parking lot right behind her. Now several of the regulars sat in the lounge dissecting theories about the identity of the body as they waited their turn to ride or watch their horses work.

"It's Ramon Gutierrez," said Lori, pouring herself another cup of coffee. "Who else can it be?"

She looked at me. The challenge in her eyes dared me to contradict her. Beyond that, I saw a tinge of fear, heavily veiled by Lori's frank and direct manner. The others concentrated on their hands or their cups or their feet. None of them argued with her. They, too, were avoiding the obvious alternative.

"Who's Ramon Gutierrez?" I asked as I replenished the napkin holder next to the coffee maker.

"He used to work with Henry," said Brisa. "Daddy hired him about four years ago to do what Chuck does now."

"Old guy? Young guy?"

Brisa shrugged. "Older than Chuck but nowhere near as old as Henry is."

"Henry's not old," said Lori. "He has grey hair and a bit of a pot but that doesn't mean he's old. Fifty, maybe?"

"That's old," said Brisa.

"Don't let Dixie hear you say that." I wiped up the crumbs

around the donut boxes. "Why do you think it's Ramon?"

"First of all, he's been missing longer than Frank," said Brisa. "And second, Daddy said he was dealing." Brisa sat down at the dinette across from Nolan. "And people who deal always get killed."

Nolan rolled his eyes. "There is absolutely no proof that Ramon was dealing drugs."

"Well, he was up to something," said Lori. "He was always around the barn."

"He worked here."

"At night?"

"He lived here."

Lori didn't look convinced. "I heard Henry tell someone on the phone that he thought Ramon split because it was getting too hot for him. Guess that was the truth. Looks like he's been baking for months in a manure oven."

"E-yew," Brisa groaned. "That's disgusting."

"You make it sound like Henry knew Ramon was dealing and I still say Ramon wouldn't do that," said Nolan. "Was he illegal? Maybe the heat was from INS."

"I hadn't thought of that," said Lori. She looked at Brisa. "Would your father hire illegals?"

"Of course not."

"Lots of eastern Europeans come over illegally," said Nolan. "What about Chuck or Henry?"

"Henry's been here almost nine years," said Brisa. "If he was illegal, someone would have found him by now."

"Maybe. Maybe not. Seems like a long time to be away from family. Isn't the story that he's trying to get his family over here? Maybe he's not trying that hard. If he's illegal, he can send the money home but he can't bring the family over."

"You're so sure of yourself and you don't know squat," said Brisa. "Henry sends money home but he also has a savings account here. Daddy says Henry wants enough saved so his wife won't have to clean houses. I think that's sweet."

"But if he's been here nine years, his wife has probably divorced him and moved on."

"Daddy sends Henry home for the holidays and he goes again in spring right before cutting season. I don't think he'd stay if it wasn't working out for him."

"Brisa's got a point," said Lori. "Drug running through here would be easy. That makes the most sense."

"A lot of strange things run through here and most of them are on four legs. I don't think drugs are the problem. If that body is Ramon's, he died for some reason other than pushing drugs."

Chuck came in at that moment, empty mug in hand. He stared at each client, then went to the coffee maker. "Ramon had wife and three children. Why you think he's drug pusher?"

"Good question," said Izzy as she followed him in. "Chuck, when your break's over, get Lady ready for her trip home this afternoon." She glanced at the wall clock. "When we finish our coffee, you're next, Lori. Divot should go good today. He's really comin' along."

Nolan got up, looked at me and pointed at the office. "Gotta minute? I have some information for you."

When I sat down at the desk, he handed me a pocket folder. I opened it and leafed through the pamphlets and brochures until I found the price sheet. The premiums were substantially less than what I was paying but I'd have to read the literature carefully to determine how much less coverage I would get.

"Thanks."

"No, thank you. I get a finder's fee if you buy through us so I appreciate it. A lot." He saluted. "See you later."

When lunch time rolled around, I unwrapped my sandwich and ate at my desk. All the boarders were concerned or upset by the continuing police activity and I didn't want to consume their distress with my chicken salad. But closing the office door didn't keep out the conversation because all the talk sailed through the opening above my desk.

For awhile, they compared notes about their horses' progress under Dixie and Izzy's care but as soon as Sal Fabrini arrived, the conversation returned to the mystery.

"Have you been interviewed by the police yet?" Sal asked the group.

I heard feet shuffle and then Nolan said, "I take it you have?"

"Yeah, yesterday. Some detective named Page. Nice guy but what a grilling."

"Did he take you down to the police station?" Brisa's voice was almost a squeak. "Did he talk to you while the DA watched through the one-way window?"

"Get real, Brisa. You must have seen us yesterday. Sitting under the crab tree?"

"I saw you but I didn't know he was a cop. I thought you were doing a deal with a business client."

"Only your father does deals out in the country where no one can see what he's up to."

"She's not going to dignify that with a response," said Lori, cutting him off. "Get back on point."

"OK, OK. Don't call out your dog," said Sal. "This Page guy asked me a lot of questions about the people out here, starting with Dixie and Izzy, of course. Then he went through the whole list of all of us. Asked me about each person."

"A policeman questioned me yesterday, too," said Lori. "He did the same thing. I'll bet we talked for an hour. He had a list of the boarders and the workers, probably the same one your guy had. My cop asked me about where we're all from, whether we know each other outside of here. In a way, it was kind of interesting."

"I think Detective Page liked me," said Sal. "He seemed real appreciative of all the information I gave him. He needed a boarder's insight about the routine here. I told him that sometimes I come out early in the morning and Chuck and Henry are already working. Dixie and Izzy usually are too."

"What's so special about that?" asked Nolan. "If they don't finish up the feeding before we all get here, it would never get done."

"We know that but the cops don't. I told Detective Page about how I see lights on late at night, too, even in the summer."

"Izzy works the horses at night. It's cooler. They cut hay then for the same reason."

"Listen you guys," said Brisa, her voice cracking. "Daddy's gonna make me get another horse and move to another barn."

"Your daddy's been fighting you on that forever," said Nolan. "How'd you change his mind?"

"Ed didn't just cave on this one," said Sal. "There's somethin' in it for him."

Brisa had tears in her eyes. "He did give in too easily."

"There's more. Henry asked him about Dixie moving out of here. I think Henry's afraid for his job. Wrap your head around that one, if you can."

Brisa choked. "Do you think Daddy's going to sell the farm?"

"He can't do that!" said Lori.

"Why don't you ask him yourself?" said Nolan.

"Ed planned to kick Dixie out eventually anyway," said Sal. "This land is worth millions more developed."

"You're wrong." Brisa's words were tainted with fear. "Daddy would never get rid of our farm."

"Afraid of the truth?"

I left my desk and headed for the lounge. Things were about to get out of hand and someone, namely me, should break it up. It was a good idea but Ed Duran beat me to it.

He was just inside the doorway, leaning against the jam. With the exception of the cap sitting backwards on his head, he looked like a movie cowboy in jeans, boots and a snap button shirt with the sleeves rolled up. His face was dark, his eyes shifting from Sal to Brisa.

"You're lying," said Brisa again, less emphatically. She had seen her father and now turned to him, her eyes pleading for confirmation.

"No, he's not. Not about the value of the land anyway," said Duran.

"How long have you been there?" asked Sal, straightening.

Duran focused on his daughter. "This place'd be worth a hellava lot more growin' townhouses instead of hay but Brisa, that doesn't mean I'm gonna sell it." He opened his arms and she ran to him. "Some guys just like to sound cool. Their words ain't worth much."

"Do I really have to sell Chicken and leave? Please say you've changed your mind."

He patted her shoulder as if she were six. "You talked me to death about it just the other morning. You said you wanted a better horse so you could compete at the best shows. Last night, I decided you should do what you want to do. I want you to be happy."

"Tell her the truth, Duran. I'll bet you already have the subdivision approved and registered with the county."

"Daddy, is that true?"

He didn't respond. His eyes locked on Sal and stayed there.

Sal returned the glare without flinching. "This has nothing to do with you showin' horses, Brisa. The heat is on and he wants you safely out of the way."

"Be careful," said Duran in a low and threatening tone.

"See? He wouldn't be hostile if he wasn't trying to hide something. What am I getting close to? Huh, Ed? Drugs? Still financing your operation that way?"

Duran's face flushed but he didn't utter a sound.

"Nah." Sal went on without taking a breath. "Too dangerous

these days. Must be somethin' else. Stolen equipment. That's it."

Brisa's face went white. "Don't you dare accuse my father of being a thief. Equipment is always disappearing. Daddy says it's one of the hazards of the construction business. He even found a loader on our lot that wasn't ours and we lost a backhoe just last week, didn't we? "

Duran remained quiet, still focused on Sal.

"One? You lost one? I'm out four this year!" Sal nearly screamed it. "And if you touch my new one at the Western Avenue site, I'll see you in Hell."

Before any of us could react, Sal pushed Brisa out of the way and took a swing at Duran, his fist bouncing off Duran's shoulder. Sal stumbled past his target but recovered quickly, spinning around to face his adversary. Duran circled away, his fists up. Sal advanced, pulled his arm back and swung again. Duran didn't return a punch.

"Sal, stop!" yelled Lori.

Outside, Ronig started to bark.

Nolan moved behind Sal and prepared to grab him from behind. Sal whirled, fury in his eyes.

"If you touch me, Nolan, I swear I'll kill you." Sal spun back to face Duran again. "You're going down."

As he moved in, Henry and Chuck charged into the lounge with Dixie immediately behind them.

"Hey, what's all this?" shouted Dixie. She went to a sobbing Brisa and put her arms around Brisa's shoulders. "You're behaving like animals."

Chuck stood between the men, arms out. And then, as if I had pressed the pause button on a remote, everything stopped. No one moved. The only sounds were Sal's heavy breathing and Ronig's frantic barking.

"Boss?" said Henry. "Let's go outside."

Duran straightened, brushed down first his left sleeve and then his right. He looked at Henry. "Yeah, fine."

Henry took a step toward the door. "You coming?"

Duran started after him, and then turned back to his daughter. "Brisa, we're leaving."

"Daddy, I don't want to sell Chicken."

"Selling Chicken and going to another barn is what you said you wanted. I'm just moving up the time table." He turned to Dixie. "You have a week to sell that damn horse." The door banged behind him. "Never did like that stupid animal."

Dixie looked from face to face and stopped with Sal. "We heard you all the way outside. Thankfully, the clients were too busy with their horses to notice the children fighting in the playpen. Until Ronig started barking, that is. Lori, go see to your dog."

Lori put her arm around Sal's waist. "Come on, tiger. Let's take Ronig for a walk."

The tension in the room dissolved as soon as Sal went out. Chuck gave Dixie a hard look. "Mr. Duran, he talked to you about him?"

She didn't answer.

"I got chores to do."

"Brisa, we'd better talk," said Dixie. "Go out to the picnic table and get some air. I'll be along in a minute."

The lounge was empty now except for Dixie and me. She walked over to the mantle and stared at Frank's picture. I thought she was going to cry but she didn't. She touched a finger to her lips, then to the photograph.

I went to the desk and sat down, more to give her some space than to get back to work. The ferocity of Sal's anger unnerved me. Sure, I'd watched kids go at it on the playground. But not since elementary school had I seen people resort to using their fists. I had to admire Henry and Chuck for jumping in to break it up. One of them could have been hurt. Or worse, they could get into trouble with Duran for interfering.

Dixie came into the office, sat next to the desk and put her head in her hands. After a moment, she looked up at me.

"I wonder how long that's been brewing." She rubbed her eyes. "Sal is certainly stressed to the breaking point."

"Or is it just temper?"

"He's been an angel about Sunny. Most people wouldn't wait a year for a horse to get itself together. Sal's problem is not temper."

"Was it my imagination or did Sal just accuse Ed Duran of stealing his equipment?"

"I don't know anything about the construction business but losing that much equipment must be devastating."

"Why does Sal think Ed's behind it?"

"I have no idea. You drive right by Duran Building to get here. You see all the stuff he has. If Ed needs something, he buys it. He doesn't have to steal so why would he?"

"To put Sal out of business?"

"Why? Sal's a little guy. He's got a niche carved out in the city and he does very well with it but he's no competition for Duran Building. If Ed bids jobs in Chicago, his rivals will be Pepper and that company that solved the Chicago River leak problem."

"Kenny."

"Yeah, that one." Dixie stared at her hands for a moment. "Do you suppose Sal is still sweet on Brisa and that's what this is about? All winter, he was buzzing around her like a yellow jacket near an open can of Coke. Ed told us to keep Sal away from her."

I shrugged. "From what I see, Lori's got something for Sal."

"Really? Guess I'll have to pay more attention. They look like friends to me." She stood up. "I have clients waiting for me. See you later."

After Dixie left, I turned to the computer. A couple of hours of mindless labor on a keyboard should calm me down. I began keying in the horses' medical history, the visits from veterinarians, chiropractors and massage therapists plus any medications that had been prescribed. I had a lot to do before all the information was digital.

The remainder of the afternoon was blessedly uneventful. Shadows grew longer and many of the customers departed. Lori and Sal sat nose-to-nose in the lounge. I couldn't hear what she was saying but the tone sounded soothing and conciliatory, like someone tending to a wounded puppy. I was concentrating on Sunny's file when Lori appeared at the door.

"I'm sorry," she said when I jumped. "I didn't mean to spook you." She leaned in. "What are you doing?"

"Putting data into the computer."

"Dixie's moving into the twenty-first century?"

I nodded.

"Cool." She hesitated a moment. "Look, Sal and I were talking and you never seem to go out with anyone. We're going to dinner later and doing a movie after. Want to join us?"

I wasn't sure how I wanted to interpret Lori's invitation. At first, it made me angry because it presumed I had no friends and second, it implied that since I was a social outcast, I deserved their pity. After a moment's consideration, however, I decided seeing Lori and Sal together outside the barn would be a good way to observe their interaction. Perhaps Lori and Sal were more than just barn friends or their relationship was nothing more than that. People did things together all the time without having romantic entanglements. But did that mean Sal was interested in Brisa as Dixie suspected? Ed Duran's instructions echoed in my mind however they weren't the reason I accepted the invitation. The body behind the barn was.

Most of the paper was off my desk when Jake appeared in the doorway. He was dressed down today, jeans and a pocket tee shirt the same color as his dark eyes. Cowboy boots, too, but he always wore boots. I rarely saw him in anything else.

"Oh, my gosh! What are you doing here?"

"That's not quite the greeting I envisioned." His laugh

dissolved into sincerity. "I'm here because I missed you."

"Welcome home!" I said, getting up and throwing my arms around him. "Is this better?"

"Much." He hugged me back. "You know, you could pick jobs that are a little closer to civilization. Your emails told me where you're working but it felt like I was driving to Minnesota."

I stepped away and looked at him. The first time I laid eyes on him I was struck by his chiseled features and erect carriage. The first time I got near him, my physical response to his long black hair and dark chocolate eyes nearly choked me. I was past that now, for the most part, and I had never told him how he got my juices flowing. He was so easy going around me that I was reluctant to do anything that might change that. My physically powerful reaction to him was my problem.

"I missed you too," I said. "How was the trip?"

"Better than I hoped."

"I'm jealous. I've never seen Napa Valley."

Did I see his eyes flicker? Did he just realize he could have invited me? Did I care anymore?

"Someday you will. In the meantime, how about I fill you in over dinner?"

"Drat! I already said I'd do dinner and a movie with Lori and Sal, the pair sitting in the lounge. Wanna come?"

Jake leaned back and peered over his shoulder. "I don't mind postponing an update dinner if you don't."

"I mind but I promised them."

That was true, but for two reasons I omitted that I was also on a mission. The first was that I was pretty sure he would insist that I stay out of it and the second was that I was absolutely sure he would insist that I stay out of it. I knew that because I was telling myself to stay out of it.

Inquisitiveness overruled common sense however. I had to learn something more about Ed Duran from Sal. The accusations he made during his outburst seemed to mesh with my concerns about Duran and that had me thinking it might be time to start looking for a new job. I didn't want to spend time in Dwight Correctional Center because I had been aiding a felon, however unwittingly. Perhaps the dinner conversation with Sal Fabrini would help me determine if Ed Duran was a thief, or worse, a murderer.

When Jake said he was in the mood for barbeque, Lori recommended a rib joint in Waukegan. We were an hour ahead of the dinner crowd so we had our pick of tables. Sal went directly to one by the window.

"So we can look out," he said, holding a chair out for Lori. "I like to look out."

Keeping your back to the wall. Watching for an assassin?

"Izzy raves about this place." Lori indicated Jake and I should take the chairs opposite her and Sal. "Sit, sit."

"I'm thinking of taking my vacation up here." Jake said, handing me a pamphlet for a lodge in northern Wisconsin. "Give me a chance to do some research and talk to the elders at the reservation. Maybe even check out some family members."

"You Indian?"

Jake turned to Sal. "Half Ojibwa. That's Chippewa to you."

"Thought so. Your ponytail gave it away." He gulped his beer. "Checking out your roots, huh? My old man did that. Went to Italy to meet the aunts and uncles and cousins. He came back a changed man. Said he felt connected. I was glad for him but I got a hundred cousins right here in Chicago. I don't need more connection."

"How about you, Kyle?" Lori paused to give her order to our waiter. "What's your heritage?"

"A little of this, a little of that."

"With that name, you got to be Irish," said Sal.

"Not a drop, although my dad said his grandfather is from Wales, so I am a bit Celt."

"What else?"

"I'm not sure. No one in the family has ever investigated it. My aunt told me once that Grandmamma Shirley was from France."

"Shirley doesn't sound very French," said Lori.

"Jake Prince don't sound very Indian," said Sal. "Not the way Sal Fabrini sounds Italian."

"My father is German," said Jake, "with some English thrown in along with who knows what else. My mother is full blood Cherokee. She was raised with the tribe up north. In our culture, the family matriarch must bless a name before it is given to a baby. My grandmother approved my name."

"So where's the Jake from?"

He got a sheepish look on his face. "Jack Nicholson."

"The actor?"

"Mom loves that old movie of his. *Chinatown*. Named me after the main character."

"There are a lot of Jakes around now," said Lori. "Kind of like Jennifer or Ashley."

"Or Michael. Luca's popular now," I said. "Names can tell us a lot about ourselves."

"Or nothing," said Jake. "Your name is Irish but you're not. Nolan is also an Irish name but he's about as un-Irish as a guy can be."

"Ain't that the truth," said Sal. "Look at me. Every direct descendant in my family is named Salvatore. No imagination. At least Jake here had a shot at a hip name. Too bad all he got was Jake. Why didn't your grandmother make your parents name you something cool like Running Bear or Shoots an Arrow?"

Lori gaped at him. "Sal, that's a terrible thing to say."

It was more than terrible. It was insufferable. My blood pressure rose a few points. Sal was pushing buttons but they were mine. Jake responded with no change in his demeanor or tone.

"My grandmother is named Abequa. It means stays at home."

"That's lovely," said Lori. "Was her last name Indian as well?"

"Johnson."

"That's as Anglo as it gets." Sal turned to me. "Kyle Shannon. You sure you're not Irish?"

"Positive."

Sal went quiet while the waiter put platters of ribs in front of us. Then he said, "So what do you guys think about Chuck finding them bones? Even money it's Ramon Gutierrez."

"Before you got to the barn, Jake," said Lori, "I was saying that I thought Ramon was the body Chuck found. And whether you want to admit it or not, Sal, Ed's plenty upset by all this. He and Ramon were buddies."

"If he doesn't hire illegals, he doesn't have to worry about them turning up dead on his property."

Jake looked at me. "Who's Ramon?"

"Some Mexican what used to work for Ed Duran," said Sal. "Got himself killed and buried in the horse shit behind the barn."

This time Lori slugged him. "Stop with the tough guy act, Sal. It's getting old real fast and Jake's not impressed."

Jake shot an acid look at Sal and then turned back to me. "I heard the story on the radio this morning. You OK?"

I nodded. "It doesn't really affect me. Things were tough the first day when the whole place was taped off as a crime scene. It was fine today. No police and the evidence techs keep to themselves. They're sifting the manure."

"That sounds like fun. Any sign of your buddy, Page?"

"Nope, but he interviewed Sal."

"You know that cop?"

"He and his wife helped me get settled when I moved out here. They're friends of the gal who got me my mortgage."

Jake started to speak so I kicked him under the table. Since Page was working an active case with people who were eating dinner across the table from me, I thought it would be best not to mention that I knew Ian and Liz Page so well that I had recently attended their son's high school graduation party. People questioned in a death investigation might be a little nervous around someone who could report back everything they said and did. If they complained to Dixie, she might be compelled to let me go and that would definitely not be a good thing. Thankfully, he took the hint.

"Gotcha," said Sal as he wiped his hands on one of the towelettes from the dish in the center of the table. "I know a few cops myself. They're always in the donut shop when I get my coffee in the morning. Nice guys."

"Lori, tell me about that great big dog," said Jake. "I thought he was going to come right through the window when I went over to see him."

"That's Ronig," she said. "He's my search dog."

"Like a bloodhound?"

"No. He's -."

"- now you've done it," said Sal, breaking in. "She won't talk about nothing else all evening."

Jake looked at me. "Bad question?"

"Excellent question. Go ahead, Lori. Please explain."

"I'm not sure what to say. I don't want to bore you." She glared at Sal. "I volunteer with a search and rescue team."

"That's why you always wear a pager, isn't it?" I said. "You must spend a lot of time training. Do you allow outsiders? Can I watch sometime?"

"We work in the brush. A tree is the toilet. If you're OK with that, we'd love to have you. It would be fun to have a new 'victim.'"

"You said victim, not criminal. Who do you search for?"

"Missing children, lost hunters, Alzheimer's patients that have wandered away."

"So who calls you in?" asked Jake. "The police?"

"Eventually. First they call in the Boy Scouts and the Rotary Club and anyone else they can think of. If the humans are unsuccessful, and they usually are, a police dog is used."

"That makes sense," I said.

"Unfortunately, police dogs are primarily trained for drugs and protection. If a police dog is search trained, it's a tracking dog."

"And that's bad because?"

"It's not bad," said Lori. "It's just not as effective as air scent-trained dogs. Tracking requires a scent article like a cap or a shoe. The article is often contaminated with the scents of people who are not the victim. The dog ends up tracking the wrong person and a lot of time gets wasted. It's extremely difficult for a tracking dog to hit a scent after three days and virtually impossible after five."

"So if the police dog craps out," said Sal, "then what?"

"Don't be a jerk. They don't 'crap out.' They work hard, but police dogs have to work on a lead so the dog is limited to the speed of its handler. Police teams just don't get results as quickly as we can because we work off lead. Our dogs cover ground a lot faster. Anyway, if or when the police are unsuccessful, then we get a call."

"'Bout time."

"Sadly, we are a tertiary response. We should be first. It would be better for the victim because our methods produce results faster."

Lori and Jake discussed her passion right through dessert while Sal and I talked about Sunny. Sal was clearly disappointed about not buying the horse but it was equally evident that he was struggling with real concerns about his business.

"You said this afternoon that your equipment is being stolen?"

"Yeah. And I know Duran's behind it."

"If you're sure, you should go to the police."

"I have but there's a big difference between being sure about somethin' and havin' some real proof."

"Wouldn't the police be able to get proof?"

Sal shook his head slowly. "The cops got their hands full with drug busts. Brisa was right about one thing. Everyone in construction is losing equipment. Some of us more 'n others. Losing a backhoe is a mosquito bite to Duran. It's a broken leg to me."

"If equipment is being stolen from Duran Building, then your accusation doesn't make sense."

"Izzy accuses me of stealing my own equipment. She doesn't get it. Ed Duran is stealing from himself so he won't be a suspect when he pinches from me. Everybody thinks Ed's this reformed gang member who made himself over. They're so impressed they don't believe he would do that."

"OK, let's say Ed Duran *is* stealing your equipment. Why?"

"Nobody else's got a beef with me. He wants my projects. If I can't do the work 'cause I got no equipment, he gets it. The fix is in." Sal tapped his watch. "If we're going to make that movie, we'd better get going."

We hurried out of the restaurant and drove east to the Gurnee theaters to see a 1998 art film from Argentina titled "Fuga de Cerebro," The Brain Drain. After the movie, Jake ranted about the inconvenience of subtitles.

I'm not a big foreign film fan and this one never had a chance. I watched Sal and Lori from the moment the title flashed on the screen to the last of the credits. There were no intimate moments between them. They were friends and that's as far as it went. Was Duran right? Sal had his eyes on Brisa?

Lori had driven herself to the theater so Sal could hop on the tollway and get back to the city without making a return trip to the barn. We wished them both well and then Jake and I went back to Bright Hope for my Altima.

"You sure had an eagle eye on Sal through the movie. What's with that?"

I told him about Duran's concern, his insistence that I spy on Sal and the fight that afternoon. Jake listened without interruption.

"So you decided to spy on Sal for Ed Duran? That's why you wouldn't break the dinner date with them?"

"If you think that, you sure don't know me very well."

"I don't know you well. I'm working on that." Jake glanced at me out of the corner of his eye before refocusing on the road. "So you weren't spying for Ed Duran but you still wanted to keep an eye on Sal. You got curious."

"Sal insists Ed is stealing his equipment and I wondered, if that's true, if that might somehow be tied in to the body."

"I was talking to Lori but I listened in on your conversation with him. Sounds like Sal is in real trouble, but he should be looking closer to home. He has a lousy attitude. Maybe people refuse to work with him. I would."

"Dixie said he did a lot of work for the city. She made it sound like he had connections."

"Then it's more likely that a local competitor is behind his problems. Ed Duran doesn't need to steal Sal's equipment to put him under."

"What do you mean?"

"Ed can bid every job Sal bids and undercut him. If Sal's operating close to the edge right now, losing a couple of jobs to Duran Building would push him over. There's nothing felonious about a low bid. No one goes to jail. Stealing equipment is grand theft, at the very least." Jake slowed for a stop light and glanced at me. "You don't look too good. What's wrong?"

"I really like the people at Bright Hope. It makes me sad that there's so much trouble there."

Jake was silent for a moment. "I'm sure everything will work out just fine."

"I'm sure it won't."

The light turned green. He glanced quickly at me and then pressed the accelerator.

CHAPTER 7

"I t's ten o'clock and every light in the place is on," said Jake, slowing to a stop at the Bright Hope entrance.

"Horses are in the ring. Something's wrong."

I scanned the stable yard. Spotlights cut through a thin brown-gray haze and I spotted Chuck near the outdoor riding ring gate, his hand on the latch. He craned his neck, first toward the barn and then the street. Flashing strobe lights appeared in the side mirror. Sirens drifted toward us, becoming screams as a fire engine maneuvered past us and then roared around the south corner of the barn.

Jake turned into Bright Hope and slowly rolled forward. I fumbled with my seat belt. Before his car stopped, I pushed the door open and jumped out.

Izzy came out of the arena doors leading Foggy, the horse bobbing on the end of the lead rope like a four-legged tap dancer, tossing his head as his hooves kept time with the bedlam's beat. Dixie followed with Chicken in tow. His eyes were rolled back in his head and his front end bounced up repeatedly as he did a half rear for each stride forward.

"Are all the horses out?" I yelled at Dixie, running toward her.

"Maida won't come. We'll have to twitch her." Dixie handed Chicken's lead to Chuck. "Get him in there. The others will calm him down, if they don't kick his brains out first."

Dixie turned back toward the barn. I started after her but Jake grabbed my arm, stopping me. His jaw was set, his face unyielding.

"I'll go. You stay put."

Izzy handed me Foggy's lead line. "Hold him. We can't put a stallion in with all those mares."

"But…"

"He's a good boy. He'll behave."

Jake followed as she ran after Dixie through the arena doors and disappeared in the gloom. I strained to see something. My breath caught every time the arena doorway coughed out a small grey cloud with an odor that reminded me of greasy used charcoal left sitting in a Weber grill all winter.

Foggy moved several feet away from me. I glanced at him, then watched the arena doors for Jake to come out. Beyond the barn, gray and black pillows of smoke boiled skyward. The lead line went taut as Foggy reached for the grass beneath the tree. I stepped toward him to relax the line and turned back toward the barn. Was the feed room burning?

Dread chilled my bones as thoroughly as being packed in ice. Fire belongs in a fireplace. When it isn't where it should be, loss and death become its children. Pete and Mary Penzler knew this better than anyone. I raged at Heaven, resentment rising like the smoke. It wasn't fair that someone else I cared about had to go through this nightmare.

Foggy jerked hard on the lead, pulling me to the grass under the tree. I didn't know enough about handling him to argue so I let him graze. My only real quandary was whether the grass might make him sick. Memories of Lori standing in this spot with Divot reassured me. I kept an eye on Foggy and on the arena door, switching from one to the other, as the horse mowed the lawn with his teeth.

The air was close; humidity ensnaring reeking residue like ragweed pollen. Foggy and I snorted simultaneously.

A squeal rose from one of the horses in the riding ring. Divot watched a horse trot away and then leaned against the fence, his front legs apart and his head pushed under the bottom board, straining for a nibble of grass. Raider stood near the gate, his head over Chuck's shoulder. The others moved about, occasionally challenging one another. Oscar was tied to a fence post so he couldn't run off and Chicken stood over him. Was that goofy horse defending the goat?

I called to Chuck, "Where are the cats?"

"Dunno. They need to be out, they get out."

Beyond the barn roof, beams from the firemen's work lights crisscrossed the night. Like fireflies, sparks twinkled against the night sky. I felt sick. Where were Dixie, Izzy and Jake? What was taking so long? Were they trapped inside? I strained to push my senses through the darkness beyond the arena doors but hearing nothing other than barely discernable shouts from the firefighters, unintelligible squawking from radios, high-pressure water hitting wood.

I had about decided to give Foggy to Chuck and go into the barn myself when, at last, they came through the arena doors, Dixie in the lead with Izzy and Jake, their arms clasped behind Maida's rump, pushing from the rear. Chuck's hand was on the latch handle again. When Maida was close enough to Foggy to catch his scent, she neighed loudly. Foggy's head came up and he answered her, his deep-throated call vibrating through the lead line and up my arm like an electric current. As soon as Dixie removed the pinching chain restraint from Maida's nose, the mare bolted forward and then cut sharply left, toppling Jake, who tucked and rolled away. Dixie let the mare swing around on the lead, deftly turning her so that the frightened horse would go through the gate into the riding ring.

Maida pushed her way through the other horses to be near her stall mate. Foggy stretched his neck forward until they touched noses and then went back to nibbling. Maida stayed close to the fence and I reached out to stroke her neck. Her ears moved continually, forward to Foggy, back to the other horses.

Izzy came toward me. "I told you he'd behave. You OK with him?"

"We're fine. How are the others?"

"Mom's checking now."

Dixie shooed the horses away from the gate and went into the riding ring.

"One, two, three." She walked slowly through the agitated horses, patting them and cooing in low pitched tones. "Eleven, twelve...Everybody's here," she called out when she reached the far end of the ring. "Chuck, if it's safe, can you get into the feed room for some hay?"

"Are any of the horses injured?" I asked as Dixie ran her hands over each horse, her touch reassuring it and checking for wounds simultaneously. "Is anyone hurt?"

"My nerves are shot but the horses seem fine. We'll have to go over them again in the morning when we can see but so far, so good."

Chuck returned from the barn with three hay bales balanced precariously on the wheel barrow. As soon as he dropped a bale on the ground, Dixie slit the twine with a pocket knife and broke the bale into segments. She set some near Foggy and then divvied up the remainder for the horses in the riding ring. The milling around ceased, their heads lowered and their nervousness dispelled. I felt my shoulders come down and I breathed normally again.

Izzy said something to Chuck and the two of them went into the barn. Dixie walked over to us and leaned against the fence, mopping her forehead with the bottom of her tee shirt.

"Thanks for your help," she said to Jake. She looked at me. "What are you doing here?"

"We went to dinner with Lori and Sal. We came back to pick up my car."

"Lucky for us."

"Izzy told me the barn isn't burning," said Jake. "What is?"

"The out building beyond the barn. The one we call the garage. We moved the horses because of the smoke. I don't think they were in any danger from the fire."

"It doesn't hurt to be cautious," said Jake.

"True, but we had to get them out anyway, especially those near the back door. They were scared and might have hurt themselves in their stalls. Chicken was a total basket case."

"And poor Maida," I said, reaching for her. "What was that thing you had on her nose?"

"It's called a twitch. The chain pinches so they focus on their nose instead of whatever is frightening them."

"It looks like a medieval torture instrument."

"Yes, it does." Dixie patted Maida's neck. "But if you rub her nose, you'll see she's fine."

Izzy returned, set down four pails and dropped the water hose from the crook of her arm. Chuck followed her with more buckets and some S hooks.

"Where's Henry?" Izzy asked suddenly, whirling toward her mother.

"In back," said Chuck. "Near garage. He tried to save tractor."

"Oh dear lord." Dixie took off in a run and disappeared around the corner of the barn.

Izzy aimed at a bucket and twisted the hose nozzle. Water exploded out, sputtering as air cleared the hose. The coughing and popping attracted the horses. They jockeyed to be first in line near the gate.

The hose barely reached the riding ring so Izzy filled buckets and then Chuck hoisted while Jake secured them to the rails with the big hooks. As soon as they hung a bucket, the horses emptied it.

There were minor skirmishes as the barn pecking order manifested itself. It was clear that Maida held top spot. She moved from bucket to bucket and from one hay pile to another without any interference from the other horses. As she approached the bucket from which Sunny was drinking, her ears flattened. The gelding backed away immediately and moved to another bucket where he bullied Divot.

"Kind of like people," said Jake, leaning against the fence after filling a bucket for Foggy. "Look at that. They leave the water they're drinking to check out another bucket. It's the same water from the same hose, but they think it's better."

I watched Maida return to the bucket where she started. Izzy had just refilled it.

"Maybe it is better. Just of out of the hose, there may be more air in it or it's colder? Their taste buds might be able to detect a subtle difference."

"These horses suffer from 'the grass is greener' syndrome." He gave a half chuckle and pointed at Divot who had left the hay and was back at the fence trying to eat the grass on the other side. "I'll bet that's where the saying comes from."

I patted Foggy. His muted hay-munching chomp-chomp was a pleasant background to our conversation. "Maybe that's why humans and horses go together so well. Neither species is satisfied with what it has."

"Whoa, that's too deep for me," said Izzy. She glanced toward the barn. "I wonder what's keeping Mom. I hope Henry's all right."

"Go check on them," said Jake. "I'll keep an eye on the horses."

Izzy looked at Jake for a moment and then ran off.

"Thank goodness the fire wasn't in the barn," I said, watching Izzy until she was out of sight. "Some of the horses would have died for sure."

"I wonder what started it," said Jake, looking beyond the barn roof and pointing. "They've got it under control now. There's hardly any smoke. Probably be completely out soon."

I shivered. Jake's gesture reminded me of one Page had made over a year earlier.

"You're cold? I've got a jacket in the car, I think."

He was back moments later and hung a windbreaker over my shoulders. He watched Foggy for awhile and then looked at me.

"You're remembering the Penzler fire, aren't you?"

I nodded.

"I knew it." He sounded put out. "Well, stop thinking about it. This isn't Penzler's. Everyone is fine, the horses are fine, and you're fine."

We were quiet after that. Jake was absolutely right. This wasn't Penzler's and there was no reason to believe that this was anything other than an unfortunate accident. But his words had hurt. I needed a hug and he issued commands. He hadn't been there; he hadn't seen the Penzlers' life go up in smoke. He had no idea how I felt about it and had no right to presume he did.

Wrapping Foggy's lead around my hand so I'd know instantly if he moved, I rested my chin on my arms and watched the horses flow from one end of the ring to the other, churning slowly like lingerie in the delicate cycle of my washing machine. Ten feet from me, leaning against the fence under the oak branches, Divot was asleep, one hind leg cocked. If he wasn't worried, why should I be?

I yawned.

Jake looked at me. "Do you want to lie down in the car? I'll wake you if something happens."

I shook my head.

"You're going to tough it out."

I nodded.

"Sorry about what I said earlier. You didn't like it but it was what you needed to hear. Am I wrong?"

How did I answer that? He wasn't wrong about what he said. It was how and when he said it.

He reached for me then and I shrugged him off, moving away.

He didn't pursue it and we were still miles apart when Izzy returned from behind the barn.

"Everybody OK?" she asked, hurrying up to Jake.

"The horses are fine," he said. "How's it going back there?"

"It's out. The fire trucks are packing up. They'll leave soon."

"Find Henry?" I asked.

"That maniac. He went into the garage to save the tractor and almost got himself killed. The paramedics want him to go to the hospital to get checked out. He's refusing."

"Did he get burned?"

"Smoke inhalation."

"Did he rescue the equipment?"

Izzy nodded. "I guess so. I was so mad at him I didn't ask."

"Ed should be happy if he did," I said. "Tractors must cost thousands of dollars."

"There's no reason for Henry to risk his life to save a stupid tractor."

"We men are crazy that way," said Jake.

Izzy smiled. "Yeah, you are."

Dixie reappeared a short time later. "I turned on the fans. The barn is airing out nicely. We should be able to put everyone to bed in another hour." She rubbed Foggy's neck. "Tough night. Guess you're glad you don't work on Mondays. You can sack in tomorrow."

"I'll be here if you need me."

"No, take your day off. We're officially closed on Mondays so there won't be any clients and we'll let the calls go to voice mail."

"Is Ed here?"

"He and Brisa went back home this afternoon. Now that I think about it, he hasn't called. I'll bet he doesn't know about the fire." She pulled her cell phone from its belt clip. "Guess I'd better make sure he does."

She got into her truck and, as the dome light went on, I saw her put the cell phone to her ear.

Izzy said, "I'll check the barn. The sooner we get the horses put back, the sooner we can go home and get some sleep."

By the time Izzy returned, Dixie was out of the truck, her conversation over.

"Ed's on his way," she said. "No one called and he's not happy about that."

"Too busy to call," said Chuck.

"Ed knows you were with me and what a help you were. He's mad that the fire department or the police didn't call him but he's very happy with you."

"Did you tell him about Henry?" Izzy asked.

"Let's just say he's very unhappy about that, too."

"Pitched a fit, didn't he?"

"Yeah. Well, time for another check on the barn." Five minutes later, Dixie had a smile on her face. "Nice clean air throughout and the circus in the back is gone. Let's get to it."

Putting the horses back took an hour. Jake manned the riding ring gate while Chuck confirmed that each stall was ready for its occupant's return. They started with Raider and returned the horses to their homes in order; Dixie and Izzy making sure each was settled and calm before bringing in the next horse. When Izzy took Maida, she told me to follow with Foggy. He walked beside me, head down and lead line slack, calmly entering his stall when Izzy took the lead from me and walked him in. After every horse was in place, I dragged Oscar inside and Chuck shut him in the stall near the tack room.

Then Dixie took my arm and led me to the feed room. "Thought you'd want to see this."

Neiman and Marcus were curled up together on a hay bale as if nothing had happened. Now I could go home and sleep.

Jake followed me to my townhouse but he did not stay. He didn't even get out of his car. I pulled into my garage a few hours before dawn and, as soon as I flicked the porch light, he pulled away.

We hadn't been incommunicado however. We talked on our cell phones all the way from Bright Hope to my driveway. Jake tried to sell me on the idea that the fire was an accident caused by the decaying manure's heat. He pressed the point that the fire could have smoldered inside the garage walls for a long time without anyone noticing. I wasn't so sure however I conceded that the outbuilding didn't have anything of value in it after Henry got the equipment out so it probably wasn't arson.

Fortunately, we did not end the night still talking about the fire and as I watched him pull away, I recalled his face when I had started into the barn to help with Maida. That look covered a lot of emotional territory, his and mine.

*   *   *   *

Somewhere in the distance, I heard bells ringing. When they didn't stop, I left the dream world, propped myself up on one elbow and fumbled for the cordless telephone.

"Hello?"

"Good morning, sweetheart. I woke you, didn't I?"

"Hi, Mom. Yes, you did."

"Well, you should be up and at 'em by now. You'll be late to work."

"I don't work on Mondays for this job."

There was a pause, long enough that I managed to plump extra pillows behind my head before she spoke again.

"Sorry, honey. I have trouble keeping track of my own schedule, let alone yours. You were going to call me today and tell me all about the dead body at the farm, weren't you?"

No mention of the fire. Maybe it hadn't made the news. I decided not to mention it. Mom sounded plenty worried and I didn't want to add to it.

"I was going to call," I said. "Really."

"Sure you were." She giggled. "And your brother will be president some day." Mom paused. "Your father's worried sick. Are you all right?"

"I'm fine. This has absolutely nothing to do with me. They think it's some guy who worked at the farm long before I got here. Probably a drug deal gone bad."

"That's terrible."

"It is, but at least I can assure you and Dad that there's no maniac running around stables killing people."

"Have you seen your policeman friend?"

"No, I haven't. That's even more proof that I have nothing to do with this. If I was involved, Ian would have talked to me by now."

"Well, I guess I'm reassured." She didn't sound convinced. "Your niece's birthday is coming up. Shall we do a thing here?"

We talked about Valerie's wish list and Mom decided I should get her back-to-school clothes. That meant Grandma would get the toy. Gee, I wonder who Valerie would like best. Six-year olds aren't crazy about clothes. They aren't wild about money in the college fund either but I always made a contribution on Valerie's birthday and for Christmas. I started the fund the day she was born and, although small, it would be there when she needed it. Based on the rate of rising tuition, I figured college would cost her half a million dollars or so. At least my few thousand would pay for a textbook or two.

Mom and I settled on a date and I was assigned the Jell-O mold as usual. That was because Great-Aunt Lucille's Jell-O mold-laden recipe box now sat on my kitchen counter plus I managed to get the salads unmolded without either melting them or smooshing them. Jell-O molds are fine but once in awhile it would be nice to do a salad or vegetable dish. At least Jell-O requires more creativity than the relish and vegetable tray, which is what my sister-in-law always had to bring.

It felt good to have had a conversation about something so normal. How do mothers and grandmothers and best girlfriends know just when to call? For that matter, sometimes dads and brothers and boyfriends do too, although usually not so often and perhaps not quite as timely. I leaned back against the pillows and let my eyelids fall.

When they opened again, the sun was higher in the sky but I wasn't in the mood to get out of bed. So I didn't.

It felt deliciously self-indulgent to spend extra time snoozing; however by mid-morning, I was too hungry to stay in bed any longer. I padded out to the kitchen for coffee, some fresh fruit and the newspaper.

The fire at the barn got several small paragraphs on page three of the newspaper. The accompanying photo showed only the burned out roof of the garage, visible beyond one of the fire trucks. I wondered how much was actually left.

I resisted the urge to go out to the barn to see for myself and instead tackled some of the mundane tasks of daily life – like laundry. I hate laundry. It isn't the washing and the drying I dislike. It's the folding. A complete waste of time and effort. I carefully smooth out all the wrinkles, use the side of my hand to sharpen the fold and lay the tops or jeans neatly into their respective drawers. And yet, when I remove a garment to wear, it's full of wrinkles. How does that happen? Just what are my clothes doing when I'm not watching?

After the laundry was put away, I had a sandwich and examined the mail now in front of me. The catalogs went into a pile on the corner of the breakfast bar for future perusal. Two of them were Christmas catalogs. After all, Labor Day was right around the corner so it was time to start thinking about the holidays.

The solicitations from charities I don't support and the plain old junk mail were in another pile ready for the recycling bin. What was left, other than two bills, was the newsletter from the Cedar Creek Homeowners' Association.

Being part of an association was a new experience for me after owning a small single-family house on the north side of Chicago. I paid my monthly assessments and otherwise went about my business. I hadn't been in the townhouse long and had been so busy getting rid of the purple chickens in the kitchen that I had given no thought at all to the association as an organization.

The newsletter was primarily reminders and helpful hints. It suggested homeowners with fireplaces have the chimneys professionally cleaned before using the fireplaces in the fall. Good idea. I pulled my planner from my tote and made a note for the next day. Then I returned to my reading.

A paragraph recommended that residents use black plastic bags rather than white ones for the garbage. Black is less attractive to crows. In Chicago, I had trash cans in the alley and I worried about raccoons, not crows. Another segment told me the landscapers would replace diseased or dying shrubs in October. I gave that some thought. Did I have any diseased or dying shrubs? Yes, I did. The yew at the end of the driveway looked dreadful. But why replace it? The snowplows and salt from the road guaranteed no shrub could survive in that spot. Was I allowed to make suggestions to the board? I read further.

The board of directors requested volunteers to serve on a rules review committee. They also sought people to serve on the board as the terms of two of the board members were expiring and they were not seeking re-election. I pondered both notices. I had skimmed through the rules and regulations when I received my copy at the title company during the closing on the townhouse. In all honesty, I had never closely read them and I confessed a complete ignorance of the process of self-rule as controlled by the Illinois Condominium Act. I wasn't sure I knew where my rules and regs were hiding.

A search of my office file cabinet revealed them right where I'd put them, in the file labeled Rules. I flipped through the spiral-bound yellow booklet. Lots of tiny type that looked mind-numbing. Still, I probably should know if I was violating any rules before I alienated my neighbors and got myself a bad reputation or a fine.

I spent close to an hour reading and rereading the rules and regulations that governed my residency at Cedar Creek, learning a lot about communal living I didn't know. As near as I could tell, I didn't have any rules violations but I had to go out to the patio and count birdfeeders before I felt sure the grounds committee wouldn't haul me away in handcuffs.

I mulled that over. Rules and regs can only go so far in controlling human behavior. What had made Frank Villano desert Dixie, if he had? What had caused someone's death? Who had buried the skeleton? What had started the fire? Had farm employees been dealing drugs? Were any of the clients involved? So many questions and no carefully organized set of rules controlled how they would be answered.

Those questions bothered me even as I lay in bed that night waiting for Mr. Sandman to clunk me on the head and put me to sleep. He showed up eventually, although I did not sleep well at all and the problem with being clunked at night is that morning tends to come the same way. When I woke, my sinuses felt stuffed with cotton, my head was the size of a basketball and my temples thump-thumped to the beat of my heart. I thought I'd been hit by the equivalent of an Evander Holyfield left hook. Too much air conditioning, too much barn dust and way too little sleep.

After I forced myself to do fifteen minutes of stretching exercises, I got ready for work and hurried out to the garage. The best cure for my sinus headache was a cup of hot coffee and a freshly-made cinnamon roll from Penzler's. I couldn't get there fast enough.

CHAPTER 8

I arrived at Penzler's after the worst of the morning rush and waited patiently for the two people in line ahead of me to order their grande lattes with two shots, soy milk and extra syrup. In other words: expensive, great big, very strong coffees with hot milk and plenty of sugar. Me, I like coffee black. To my mind, good coffee doesn't need milk or sugar. It should be smooth with plenty of body and well within its shelf life so there is no bitter or sour taste. Penzler's has coffee that good. It is perked, not dripped or pressed or steamed, in a coffee pot older than I am.

Pete saw me and poured my coffee without waiting for my order.

"What if I'd wanted a mocha espresso with sprinkles this morning?"

He snorted. "That'll be the day. Mary, how about one right out of the oven for Kyle?"

Mary opened the glass case, extracted a cinnamon roll from the rear of the tray and placed it carefully on a plate. Then, signaling me with her eyes, she walked purposefully outside to one of the tables and sat.

I would follow one of her rolls right into a dark alley in the middle of the night. So, after I paid at the register, I was just steps behind her.

The roll lay before me, enticing me to be very, very naughty. This was at least an extra hour on the treadmill but it was worth the sacrifice. My headache felt better already.

Pete came outside moments later and slid onto the bench next to his wife. They waited quietly, side-by-side, watching as I savored a forkful of fluffy, spicy pastry. I let the bite melt in my mouth, washing it down with coffee before I looked at them.

"You want the scoop on the fire," I said before filling my mouth again.

"We've got time," said Pete. "No one's in the store right now, but talk fast."

"Please tell us no one was hurt," said Mary. "We saw the news story in yesterday's paper and it said there were some minor injuries so we want to hear from you. Are you all right, dear?"

"I promise we're all fine and none of the animals was hurt. Not even a cat. One of the workers inhaled a lot of smoke saving some equipment, but that's the only injury I know about and he didn't go to the hospital."

"Was it the manure?" asked Pete. "Too close?"

"I don't know. I suppose they'll figure that out today."

"Poor Dixie," said Mary. "She's had a tough time of it lately. First Frank, now this."

"Yeah," said Pete, "but she's a hardy one. Even in the dead of winter she used to ride over here, tie up to the hitchin' post and watch the sun come up."

"You had a hitching post?"

"In front of the old store," said Mary. "You never saw this area when it was all farmland and pasture so you can't imagine how it was. When Dixie and Frank started out, they had a place a couple of miles up Stable Road. She used to ride over here every morning."

"Got to be a habit," said Pete. "She'd come over early, before I opened up. At first, she stayed on the horse and I brought coffee out to her, but after a couple of times of that, I put in the post. Hard to get in a good visit when the person you're talking to is six feet in the air."

"It was her quiet hour, her special time for reflection and

meditation. She used to tell me that, by the time she rode back to the barn, she was ready to face the day."

"I don't know about that, but she sure set stock by it. For a couple of years, she never missed a morning. Weekday or weekend, didn't matter. In the winter, though, I let her sit on the stoop by herself. My old bones won't take the cold."

"I wonder how long it's been since she had a morning ride." Mary pushed herself up from the bench. "I'll be right back."

She walked briskly to the house, mounted the wooden steps up to the porch and went inside. The white clapboard farmhouse stood about fifty yards east of the store. A long gravel driveway led to a garage in the rear and separated the house from the store parking lot. Overlooking a two-story weeping willow with leaves now the yellowish tint of late summer was the wooden front stoop. An overhang sheltered the front door. As I watched Mary come down the porch steps, I noticed she had a black book in her hands.

It was a photo album. After Mary sat down next to me, she flipped past several pages until she found what she wanted. She propped the book up so I could see it without having to put down my fork.

"There's Raider tied up," she said.

It was the buckskin all right. The reins were looped around the cross pole and his head was down, probably wishing he had some hay to munch while waiting for Dixie to return. Whoever had taken the picture of Raider at the hitching post and the cars parked in the small lot beyond the store's west side had captured the perfect image of the changing times – the juxtaposition of horse powers in a Lake County I had never seen.

I moved out to Lake County well after the expansion boom had taken hold so there was little left to remind me that it had once been mostly farmland. Much as I loved the townhouse development where I lived, I was sure that there were people, like my grandfather, who thought about earlier times with longing. Did

Dixie?

"Pete had to take out the hitching post when Raider almost got hit by a car that was backing out." said Mary, turning the page so I could see another photo with several horses tied in front of the store. "Too many cars and too much traffic. Riders stopped here all the time, especially on weekend mornings. It became quite the meeting place."

"Like the old Highland House restaurant used to be for the Harley Davidson crowd," said Pete. "Even that's gone now."

Stable Road's name took on new meaning as I looked at the photos. Had it been like a country lane in Lexington, Kentucky, with miles of brown rail fence and acres of green pasture dotted with grazing horses?

Examining the riders' faces, I pointed to one I recognized. "This looks like Brisa Duran. Do you know her?"

"Her father stopped in whenever he had a project in the area," said Mary. "Ed's had Brisa in tow since she was old enough to toddle. Always bought her a Tootsie pop. How are they, dear? I haven't seen Brisa since she was, oh, twelve, thirteen."

"They're good. Dixie says Brisa is a very talented rider."

"Hey," said Pete. "Remember that kid, that football player from Waukegan High, who worked for Ed and used to come in all the time in the summer?" Pete's face screwed up and he drummed his temple with his index finger. "What was his name?"

"Don't hurt yourself, dear," said Mary. "You're thinking of Nolan."

"Am not. I'm thinking about that kid who was the tight end."

"The only football player I remember who worked for Ed was Nolan Grinnell."

Pete slapped his forehead. "You're right, as always. In the paper all the time. Good prospect for college ball but his knees gave out."

"Nolan's got a horse with Dixie," I said. "A beautiful gray

Arabian named Foggy."

"He always talked about getting a horse," said Mary, "so this is a life-long dream come true."

"But we don't know how long his dream will last." I picked at the crumbs on my plate. I shouldn't have said anything but talking to Pete and Mary was like talking to my parents.

"Having money troubles, is he?" said Pete.

"Now, dear, don't go talking out of turn."

Pete flushed. "I'm not. Nolan was in here last month trying to sell us some insurance."

"That's right. He was. He did seem a little anxious."

"Desperate is more like it. Pushed me hard but we already got plenty of insurance. Don't need more, not even to bail him out."

Mary looked troubled. "You said you don't know how long he will have a horse at Dixie's. How bad is it?"

"She may have to take ownership of Foggy and sell him to cover the unpaid board and training."

"She won't like doing' that," said Pete, "but I don't think she'll have to. As I remember, Nolan was a go-getter. Once he set his mind to somethin', he made it happen. He'll cover his butt somehow."

"That's true," said Mary. Her soft lips lifted. "Anyone who can work with Ed Duran, summer after summer, knows how to handle tough situations. Nolan'll find a way. You tell Dixie to go slow. Nolan will pay his bill, one way or another."

Two cars pulled into the lot and Pete rose.

"You stay out here and visit," he said, patting Mary's shoulder. "I'll take care of these customers."

I stood up and hugged each of them. "I gotta get going myself. I don't want to be late to work."

As I drove out to Bright Hope, I thought about what Pete and Mary had said about Nolan. Their faith in his ability to get things turned around was reassuring and I wanted to share that ray of hope with Dixie.

When I arrived at the barn, Izzy was fumbling with the coffee pot. She was clearly asleep on her feet, moving at half her usual pace, her face droopy.

"You didn't get any rest yesterday, did you?" I said, taking the pot from her and filling her mug.

"Horses still need care, even if we're closed. Then I had some prospects here until nine last night. I just couldn't get them to leave. They musta asked a million questions about the fire and the skeleton. At first, I thought they were just being' nosey but their son has a reining horse. They brought a video so I can see what he does." She drank some coffee and winced. She blew on it and tried again. "The horse stops mid-spin and their son goes airborne every time."

"And they want you to fix it."

"I used Divot to demo what horses are supposed to do. If Lori ever wanted to sell him, I think they'd be very interested."

"Anything special planned for today?"

"Naw, just the usual." She let me refill her mug. "We're leaving early today, by the way. Mom and I are going over to the saddle shop to check out some equipment. She wants my opinion since Dad's not around."

I heard the catch in her voice. My heart ached for her but I couldn't think of anything to say so I just nodded.

Izzy went out to the barn, leaving me feeling totally inadequate. I've experienced other people's grief and I've been to plenty of funerals but I never know if I am saying the right things at the right time. I stared at the spot Izzy had vacated, wondering about Frank Villano and the kind of father he was. If Izzy was any indication, he'd been a good man.

After glancing through the mail, I checked the telephone messages. There was only one. Ed Duran wanted me to get a worker's compensation incident report completed for Henry. I pulled a blank form from the drawer, looked it over and set it aside. Then I took a walk through the barn.

Sparrows filled the rafters as if nothing had happened the night before. Was this apparent forgetfulness another part of being a prey animal? Past dangers were put aside in anticipation of new ones? Maida stood quietly in her stall; Divot and Chicken were calmly eating breakfast. Even Sunny complimented me with a look when I stopped to check on him.

I pondered his beating again. People did what they did for specific reasons. Human behavior is never random. Even serial killers have motives for what they do. They may not make sense to the rest of us, but the reasons exist nonetheless.

Considering all that had happened lately, I attached a great deal of importance to the fact that someone wanted to keep Sunny riled up. Unfortunately, I wasn't able to go beyond that. I couldn't fathom motive. Was it directed at Dixie and Izzy or Sal? Or was there a lunatic out there who just liked battering horses? Was there any connection between that and the fire?

When I got to the barn's rear door, I looked for Henry and saw him heading toward his tractor.

"Henry," I yelled, hurrying toward him. "We need you to come into the office sometime today, to fill out some paperwork about your injury."

He shook his head and cupped an ear. The chugging engine swallowed my words as quickly as I shouted them, making it impossible for him to hear me. I pointed at him and then pretended to write something. Next I pointed toward the office and myself. He looked at me blankly. I was about to try my charade again when he suddenly nodded and wagged a thumbs-up.

It was shortly before noon when Henry stood in the office doorway, cap in hand. "You need me for something. Is now OK?"

"I have a form to fill out about your accident."

He entered the office, leaned over the desk and read some of it.

"I not go to hospital. Why we need form?"

"Mr. Duran wants it in the file in case you have to go to the hospital later, for an infection or if another problem develops with your breathing that you don't have now. Let's go out to the lounge where we can both sit down. No one's in there right now. We can work on this together."

We went through all the basics on the form; name, address, social security number. He wrote the answers in neat, precise penmanship. When we reached the section requesting a description of how the injury occurred, he stopped and looked at me.

"How do I do this part?"

"Tell me about the fire. I'll take some notes and then we can decide what to put on the form."

Henry shifted slightly in the chair and cleared his throat as though preparing to recite his catechism.

"I just get in for late coffee with others. Chuck runs into kitchen shouting about smoke. He goes back out to check horses. I call fire department, then go to see for myself what is what."

"And you saw smoke?"

"Much smoke. I go into garage to remove tractor and spreader. It is hard to breath but I save them." He pointed to his chest. "Firemen give me oxygen. No problems."

"Any ideas how the fire started?"

He shook his head. "No. We are all very careful in garage."

From Henry's brief description, I wasn't sure what should go on the form so I told him we'd leave it blank and just clip my notes to it. If we ever had to turn it in, we'd decide then what to write. I thanked him for his time and he rose to leave.

"Henry, has the new ring come yet?"

He looked at me quizzically.

"For your birthday?" I pointed at the one naked finger. "Izzy told me you get a new ring each year?"

"Oh. Yes. Ring come but I will not wear until birthday."

"When is that? I can't wait to see what she sent."

"A few days. I will show you then.

"Thank you. And if there are any problems with your breathing, you let me or Mr. Duran know right away."

Henry bobbed his head and left, the screen door banging into place behind him.

The day slipped by quickly. I had a lot of office work to do and Dixie and Izzy stuck to their training routine. The police were in and out but I never saw Ian Page. In fact, I was beginning to wonder why no one from the task force had interviewed me. As a temp, I was accustomed to being a phantom, the worker who has no identity and who is outside the general sphere. But in this case, I was very much inside.

I argued with myself about calling him. If I did, would I appear nosey? Surely if he wanted to speak to me, he would have. And yet, if I didn't contact him, would I be in trouble when he found out I was here and I hadn't called?

I took a quarter out of my wallet. Heads, I would call; tails, I would not. I flipped the coin, and flipped it again and then again until it came up heads. But before I could dial Page's number, Ed Duran came in.

"I stopped by to thank you for handling the worker's comp thing," he said. "Henry said you helped him with the form. Anything I need to do?"

"Nope. The form is in the file as an incident report."

I got it out and passed it to him so he could review it.

Duran gave it back. "My rates will go through the roof if we ever have to send this in. Stupid move trying to save that tractor. A new tractor would cost a lot less than a new Henry."

"But he did save it."

"Yeah. The spreader got singed but the tractor's perfect. You'd think that tractor was his, he worries about it so much."

Duran muttered all the way out the door, leaving me to wonder about people's priorities and how many times it has been shown that people do not behave logically in a crisis. Henry should have let the tractor burn. If he was worried about what the loss of a tractor meant to his boss, he must know by now that Ed Duran was far more concerned about Henry Slavin than he was about a John Deere.

Dixie and Izzy drove off together shortly after three. It was almost quitting time when Dixie telephoned.

"You're on your way out the door, aren't you? We're running late. Can you stay until Sal gets there? We're meeting this evening."

I checked the calendar. "Of course, I'll stay. I didn't know you had an appointment."

"I didn't until two minutes ago. He just called and he sounded so stressed I didn't want to turn him down."

I set Sal up at the table when he arrived. He didn't speak to me other than to acknowledge my greeting and wave away my offer of a soft drink. His dark eyes were dull and a grayish tinge lay beneath his tanned skin. After seeing him this way, I decided I preferred his short temper. At least there was vitality in that.

I wandered down the barn aisle. Foggy's stall was empty. I hadn't seen or heard Nolan but that didn't mean anything. He probably checked out the fire damage and then entered the barn through the rear. Still, I was surprised I hadn't heard him in the tack room. It wasn't normal for him to be at Bright Hope on a weekday. He must be out on the bridle path getting in a few more rides before he had to relinquish ownership.

Next door, Maida opened one eye, looked at me, nodded once, and then closed it again. I took that as permission to enter and went in slowly, being careful not to startle her. Her black mane flopped against her brown neck as she shook off a fly. She didn't open her eyes. Apparently she didn't feel I was anything to be concerned about.

I leaned against the stall door and slid down, folding my legs under me, settling onto shavings that were still clean. Musk and the coal-tar oiliness of creosote blended into an eau d' horse barn scent that had become familiar. Most people assume that barns smell bad. That wasn't true of Bright Hope. There was something earthy and genuine about its olfactory goulash.

Maida put her head against her foreleg and rubbed her nose. I watched in fascination as she solved the simple problem of an itch. Then she stepped forward, placing one hoof near my right knee, and lowered her head into my lap, nickering softly. I scratched her forehead.

"Life is pretty simple for you guys, isn't it? Nice stall, lots of good feed, no predators."

Maida pushed her head against my chest. I continued scratching.

"Granted, ending up in a dog food factory probably isn't the best way to go out but a lot of humans don't have a pretty exit either. I'll bet that somebody didn't want to end up fermenting in a manure pile."

She snorted and pulled away. It had been impolite to make the reference to dog food. I deserved the mucus that now covered my knee.

"I wish I'd known Frank," I told her, using some shavings to soak up the muck from my jeans. "Seems like everyone liked him. Well, obviously not everyone if those are his bones at the morgue. But most people. Mary says Dixie hasn't been the same since Frank disappeared. How could she be? Even if the authorities haven't confirmed it yet, the skeleton has to be Frank's. You know for sure, don't you girl? Think I've put the last yellow rose in that vase on the mantle?"

Maida looked at me briefly, then pawed under her feed bin. Using short bursts of air from her nostrils, she blew shavings away from buried pieces of leftover hay. Soft pops echoed in the stall as her ample, velvety lips flapped together; vacuuming up hay bits no thicker than a business card.

She should be outside in a pasture. Nature designed horses for grazing. In the absence of that, lipping tidbits of alfalfa from the shavings was the next best thing? How did she keep herself occupied? Do horses get bored?

I was about ready to leave when I heard Sal's voice, so I stayed put.

"Look, Dixie, you can show me Sunny all you want and I know you're doing your best but I'm just can't do it. I've got too many things going on and I don't have time for a horse. Draggin' me out here to look at Sunny sleepin' in his stall isn't going to make me go all soft in the knees and change my mind. Brisa may go for that but I'm no girl."

"If you didn't want to see him, you wouldn't have driven up here. You wouldn't have spent the last twenty minutes listening to me talk about how he's almost ready for you. You would have called me on the phone and been done with it."

"Like I said, I owe you a face-to-face."

"I've put a lot of money and time into Sunny to make sure he's what you want. We have a contract, Sal, so I need a better explanation of why you're backing out of our deal."

The footsteps stopped.

"Look at that sky. Ain't it beautiful? Nolan had me believin' that I could be riding on nights like this. He says it clears his mind, keeps him sane in this insane world."

"All the more reason…"

"Jeez, Dixie. They got another backhoe last night. I'm losing my shirt. Don't you get it? Thousands of dollars worth of equipment is drivin' off my work sites."

"Your insurance must cover the loss. What's the problem?"

"The problem is my insurance company said the loss of one or even two is normal. Five in six months ain't. They won't cover."

"Insurance companies have to cover unless they can prove

illegal activity."

"Yeah, well, they're draggin' their feet until they complete their investigation and I still need to replace what gets stolen. That's out-of-pocket, Dixie. This last backhoe tapped me out. Damn Ed anyway."

"I don't believe Ed's the one."

"My equipment didn't start disappearing until this year. And this is the year Ed starts bidding business in the city? I ain't no fool."

"Maybe you didn't have anything worth taking until now?"

"One of Ed's goons applied for a job at my site. Handed me some bull about how Henry sent him. Like I'm stupid or something."

"Maybe the man needed work."

"He didn't need a job; he has a job. With Ed Duran. I sent the guy packin'."

"Sal, you just looked at that horse like he was a La-Z-Boy and you hadn't sat down in a week. Sunny's coming along beautifully. He's gorgeous and you're going to look great on him. He's just exactly what you said you wanted."

Silence for moment.

"Stop pulling on me, Dixie. I don't want to see him."

I thought about slipping out but there was no way to do it without them hearing the stall door slide. Since I hadn't immediately announced my presence and left, it would be obvious that I was eavesdropping. I waited.

More silence and then Dixie spoke. She sounded angry.

"Don't you shake your head at me, Sal. We've got a contract."

"Blood from a turnip, Dixie. Suing me would cost you more than Sunny's worth." Sal paused. "Ah hell, I'm outa here."

I heard heavy, quick footsteps go away from me down the aisle. Seconds later, tap, tap, tap.

"Wait! We're not finished."

Sal's voice was farther away. "Yes. We are."

A banging screen door told me Dixie was outside or in the office. I stood up, brushing sawdust from my rear. Poor Sal. Backing out on the deal had to be agonizing.

I didn't want to return to the office just yet. Better to give Dixie and Sal some space.

Outside, the yellow crime scene tape was still up, although the perimeter had been pulled in substantially so that the tape surrounded only the tent and the manure remnants beneath it. I wondered how long it would remain in place. There didn't seem to be much left to sift. I walked out to the carcass that had been the garage.

It appeared smaller than I recalled but with Mt. Manure gone and the building a specter of its former self, my perceptions were probably off. Massive fire truck tires had mashed thousands of gallons of water into the dirt, pushing mud up like the waves from a great belly flop. There were deep furrows in the ground and I nearly tripped in one as I went to the far side of the garage for a better look.

A cloud passed over the sun. Scattered storms were in the forecast. One good rainstorm would wash away the ruts along with the soot and the remnants of the manure pile. No one would be able to tell that any of it had ever been there.

Sal's Corvette engine roared. I went back into the barn to find Dixie.

CHAPTER 9

Dixie's truck was gone and only my Altima remained parked in front of the barn. I locked up and went home.

Television reruns provided little distraction and I lay on the sofa contemplating ways to help Dixie and Izzy. Plenty of businesses fail when the owners collapse under emotional loads that don't include disappearing spouses or fires. The Villanos were hanging on. By a thread maybe, but neither woman had given up. I admired that. However, high regard for my bosses wasn't the only motivation. There was also the look on Pete Penzler's face when he recalled taking early-morning coffee out to Dixie.

The next morning, I skipped my walk and spent some time on the Internet, searching for Bright Hope information and reading archived newspaper articles about Ed Duran's company and Fabrini Construction. I didn't learn anything new but I felt better for the effort.

Bright Hope looked like a car dealer's lot when I pulled in. Lori's SUV sat under the oak tree and several official-looking vehicles, including the fire marshal's red and white Crown Vic, were parked near Dixie's truck at the office entrance. I'd seen the Crown Vic after the Penzler fire. The memory sent a nervous ripple across my shoulders. I parked by the south door of the barn and entered the barn near Raider's stall.

A weighty boom-thud drew me to the rear of the building. Chuck, sweat dripping off the end of his nose like water from a leaky faucet, banged a sledge hammer against the bottom of the uncooperative barn door. After squirting lubricant on the rollers, he tried again, pressing his back against the door and swinging the hammer between his legs. He repeated the maneuver, uttering Polish expletives. Whether oil or cuss words provided the grease, this time, the door slid back, creaking and moaning like a Loop elevated train on the Wabash Avenue turn.

Beyond him, evidence technicians still shifted material into buckets. Mt. Manure had been reduced to a pitcher's mound. It looked like they'd be finished and gone before the end of the day. Those people had earned their pay – straining horse dung through a sieve for days on end in the August heat. I wondered if they had found anything of significance. I had the same thought about the fire marshal.

I checked the arena. No Dixie, no Izzy, no horses. Odd.

Because the animals' care required adherence to a schedule, they were fed, watered and their stalls were mucked out early in the morning. By the time I arrived at eight-thirty, Izzy was usually working her second horse of the day in the indoor arena while Dixie had one outside. Those habits had shielded us from the effects of the chaotic events of the last few days. This morning, all the horses were in their stalls and the barn, with the exception of Chuck's hammering, was still. Even the dozens of sparrows that lived in the rafters seemed quieter. There was no evidence of the morning routine anywhere.

I turned back to Chuck. Now that the door was open, he pulled to close it. It didn't budge. Before he had a chance to increase my collection of swear words, I asked him, "Have you seen Dixie or Izzy?"

"With police. In office."

More questions they didn't want to answer or bad news they didn't want to hear. Either way, it was a lousy start to the morning. I dawdled, visiting Foggy and Maida before walking to the front of the barn. When I entered the lounge, I found Lori sitting on the sofa, a tissue pressed against her nose. The next thing I noticed was that the shrine to Frank was gone.

"Lori, what's happened?"

"It was Frank. Oh God, it was Frank."

I sat next to her, putting my arm around her shoulder. "Tell me. How do you know it was Frank?"

She pointed to the closed office door. "The coroner's in there with Izzy and Dixie. They've ID'd the skeleton."

"They told you?"

"They were standing out here getting the bad news when I walked in."

I considered things for a minute as Izzy's sobs drifted out the pass-through.

"Look, I have to buy stamps. Why don't you come with me? It'll keep us both occupied and give them some privacy."

Lori nodded agreement and twenty minutes later, we were standing in line at the post office. With the exception of an occasional hiccup, she was silent during the ride into Wadsworth so I was surprised when she finally spoke.

"Frank was a great man, you know." Lori's tears had dried but she spoke like her lips were numb from Novocain. "He was gentle and loving and very talented. He even got along with Ed. That's hard to do because Ed's so..." Her voice trailed off.

I paid for the stamps. "Ed's a strong-minded kind of guy."

"Yeah."

When we returned to my car, I fumbled with my purse and hunted for misplaced sunglasses. Lori sat rigid beside me, her arms wrapped tightly around herself. My heart hurt, for her and for all of us.

Mary Penzler had said that finding Frank would be a relief for Dixie. I hoped she was right. Was this kind of loss ever a blessing?

"It was murder, you know," said Lori so quietly I thought she might be talking to herself.

No kidding. A body in a manure pile is a pretty good indication.

"Probably," I said.

"Absolutely! The coroner said that there was a bullet hole in his head."

I leaned across her, pulled the packet of tissues from my glove compartment and handed it her.

"I'm very sorry you overheard that. No wonder you're so upset." I watched her dab at her eyes for a minute. "You OK?"

"No."

I started the car. Lori turned away from me and looked out the passenger window, silent for several blocks. When she spoke again, her voice was soft and hesitant.

"When Frank disappeared, we all just went with the flow because Dixie is the one who does the training anyway and a man running off with another woman isn't that big a deal." She paused. "It ought to be, but it isn't. And everyone thought that skeleton was Ramon's so no one got upset by that either because we all figured he was dealing drugs and he got what he deserved. I don't know how things will be now. They killed Bright Hope when they killed Frank."

"I don't understand. What do you mean?"

"Dixie will have to close. Clients will refuse to come to her."

"She's the best at what she does, isn't she? Why wouldn't they want her?"

"They'll be afraid to come because they might get killed, too."

"That's ridiculous."

Lori slowly shook her head. "No, it's not. We're all afraid, Kyle. All the time. If we don't buy the latest gadget for our kids, we're afraid they won't love us. If we're late to work, we could be fired so we're afraid we won't be able to pay the mortgage. If we don't buy a pill, we're afraid we'll die of some disease. If we get on a train, a terrorist could blow it up and we're afraid because we don't want to die."

"I don't see how that keeps people away from Bright Hope."

"Maybe it won't. I only know how I feel. My one safe haven isn't safe anymore. Before all this, I could go to Bright Hope, be with Divot and forget about the fight with my sister or the reduction in my benefit package. I can never feel that way about the place again."

Lori was right, although my personal fears were more mundane than terrorism. I was always concerned that I wouldn't have enough temp assignments to pay the bills or that I would say or do something that would alienate my mother or that Jake would decide a petite, perky blond was more to his taste. Did my concerns qualify as fears? Where was my haven and how would I feel if it was destroyed? Lori's lament gave me a lot to think about.

"I see you agree with me," she said, watching me closely. Tears trickled down her cheeks again. "Where will I take Divot? I don't want to leave but if Dixie closes, I won't have a choice."

"I pass other barns on my way out here. What's wrong with them?"

"They're private, built for two to four horses, tops. They look big because they have small riding arenas inside. Almost every public stable in Lake County is gone. There are a few around Libertyville and more north of Gurnee but development has pushed most of them across the border. The land is too valuable so people sell it and retire to Florida. It grows houses now – rows and rows of houses." She hung her head. "I really don't want to move to Wisconsin."

"What about your job? Wisconsin would be a heck of a commute."

"I work out of my house so I could live anywhere, but I've been here my whole life. Lake County's kind of in the middle of my territory so I can get to wherever I need to go." Lori wiped her eyes. Once she began talking about work, the tears stopped. "But that's not what has me so worried. Who will train Divot? There's no one left around here, besides Dixie, who understands working trail horses."

I thought she might start crying again she looked so sad. I wasn't sure how to respond to her. As a former city gal, I was amazed by the number of horses in Lake County. The fact that this number might be vastly reduced from earlier days had not entered my mind until Mary Penzler brought it up. Now Lori referred to it.

"Perhaps the opposite will be true," I said, more to offer an alternate perspective than because I really believed it. "People who didn't know Dixie existed are calling to ask about what she does. Some of those callers could be serious prospects."

"They're drawn to a place they saw on the news. They'll be gone as soon as the thrill is."

"Or as soon as they get their first bill."

Lori gave me a lop-sided smile. "That will scare them away for sure."

"Say, what were you doing at the barn this morning? You don't normally come around until Friday."

"I was supposed to meet up with Doc Lemmer. We have a new Lyme disease medication that works pretty well and I wanted to give him the literature about it. He wasn't in the barn so I went into the lounge to see if he was in there. That's when I walked in on the coroner talking to Dixie and Izzy."

"Worming day." I snapped my fingers. "Guess I'll need to reschedule that."

When we got back to Bright Hope, things were quiet. The coroner's car and Dixie's truck were gone. A note on my desk asked me to call Dixie on her cell phone. Our conversation was short. Dixie's tension and grief were audible through the lousy cell connection as she confirmed that her husband was dead. She and Izzy were at the funeral home making arrangements and she didn't plan to return to the barn until late afternoon.

With Frank Villano's identification, I expected the level of the investigation to step up a couple of notches. I still hadn't heard from Ian Page but that was sure to change now that the victim had officially been identified and the cause of death was a bullet to the head.

The afternoon went slowly and I had a hard time staying focused on work. I tried some computer input but after entering Chicken's data, I lost interest. I fielded a few phone calls and then opened the mail, placing the payments from clients into the bank envelope and the vendor invoices into my accounts payable folder. Normally I paid bills and did payroll on Friday. Would Dixie be around this Friday to sign checks?

Her bank balance was pretty good right now but Lori's words about clients leaving troubled me. The continual fear about not having work raised its head like a cobra. I pushed the fearful snake back into the basket of my mind, refusing to let myself dwell on what-ifs. That would be living my life in fear and I wasn't going to give in to that. Tomorrow maybe, but not today.

I decided to prepare the checks to pay bills so they'd be ready whenever Dixie was available to sign them. Commonwealth Edison, AT&T, Ericksen's Feed, Doc Lemmer. I typed the payee and amount into the computer. Northwest Mutual. A premium notice for Frank Villano. For a half a million dollar policy.

Hokey smokes!

Appalling plots sprang to mind: Dixie killing Frank for the insurance money, Izzy killing Frank for the insurance money, Dixie and Izzy killing Frank for the insurance money. That made no sense. Neither of them would get the money until Frank was declared dead so, under those scenarios, it would have been wiser to leave Frank out in a hay field where someone would find him.

If Dixie killed him, she would hardly insist that Chuck and Henry remove the manure that hid the body. However it had been several months since Frank disappeared. Had Dixie waited to make her act look good? To ensure that people would look elsewhere for the killer? Was the mantle memorial a well-staged play on our sympathy so she wouldn't be a suspect?

Who were the suspects in this homicide? Had the task force developed a list? If so, who was on it? Did the police know about Sal? What about Uncle Ed? Or Jorge, Henry and Chuck?

Ian Page must know that I was working at Bright Hope and yet he hadn't been in touch with me. Why not? Was he avoiding me? I could think of no reason he wouldn't take advantage of our friendship. And at the very least, I should have been questioned along with everyone else.

Finally I could stand it no longer. I dialed the Vernon Hills police station, identified myself and asked for him. After being on hold for about a minute, I heard a voice.

"Page."

"This is Kyle." I counted to ten. No response. "Kyle Shannon?"

"Yeah, Kyle. What's up?"

Nothing much. Just a dead guy with a half million dollar life insurance policy.

"Are you aware that I'm working at Bright Hope stables?"

Complete silence.

"You're kidding."

"I'm not."

"When did you start working there? Before or after they found Frank Villano?"

"Before."

"Son of a …! Hold on."

I waited as a digital voice advertised the next citizen's police academy class. The message started again before Page came back.

"Sorry. I checked and your name isn't on any of the lists. Shouldn't you... Ah hell. You're a temp. Of course you're not on the lists. Hold on."

He didn't hit the hold button this time so I heard him yelling at an officer named Zucker about the woman who works in Bright Hope's office and had anybody bothered to interview her.

"What woman in the office?" asked a distance voice.

"The one with brown, shoulder-length hair and bangs. The one who probably gave you the list you've been using. You gave us the employee and client lists, didn't you?"

"Nope, not me. I suppose Dixie or Izzy did."

"OK, you're off the hook on the lists," Page called out. "She says she didn't give them to us."

"You want me to go interview her?"

"No. This is her on the phone." Page snorted. "Where you at? Can you talk or shall I see you later?"

"Whatever works for you. I normally leave about four-thirty but I'll stay if you want me to."

"I'll meet you at your place at five. Liz and I are going to dinner. Want to join us after we talk? I'll call her and let her know. See you in about forty-five minutes."

I drove home as fast as I dared and then dashed around making sure that the kitchen sink was empty and that there were no magazines on the living room floor. When the doorbell rang, I was pouring iced tea.

"Let's go out to the patio," I said as I let Page in and led him out through the kitchen. "It's not bad in the shade and there's a decent breeze."

Page is taller than me by about three or four inches. His face is clean-shaven and his short brown hair is almost a buzz cut. He works out routinely so he's lean from running and buff from lifting weights. "Vernon Hills Police Department" was embroidered on the pocket of his navy polo shirt. His belt supported a phone and his service weapon.

"Liz will meet us at Max and Erma's in an hour," Page said, stirring a teaspoon of fake sugar into his iced tea. "So?"

"I figured out that the reason you didn't know I worked at Bright Hope was that after he called the police, Ed Duran sent me home. He said the bones were from a deer and there was no reason for me to be questioned because I didn't know anything. He also sent Jorge home."

"Why would he do that? Does he think you know something?"

I shrugged. "Ask him?"

I explained how I came to be at Bright Hope, how long I'd been there and what I did for them. Next I recounted what I'd seen the day Frank Villano's skeleton was discovered.

"I understand he was shot in the head," I said when I'd finished my narrative.

"How'd you hear that?"

"Lori Boc overheard the coroner telling Dixie and Izzy."

"Well, it's true, not that it's any big help. There's no bullet, no gun, nothing to guide us. The only thing we're pretty sure about is that it wasn't suicide. Position of the hole makes it doubtful. However, in all our interviews no one gave us the smallest hint of a motive."

"How about a $500,000 insurance policy? How's that for motive?"

"On Villano?"

"The premium notice came in today's mail."

"That's serious money. People have killed for a lot less."

"You would know, but I don't think Dixie killed Frank and certainly not for money."

"So you buy the memorial bit?"

"Yes, I do. Sal Fabrini tried to convince me that Frank ran off with another woman but Dixie always said he was dead."

"Maybe she knew he was dead because she killed him."

I ignored his comment. "Speaking of Sal, he has quite a temper. He and Ed Duran got into it on Sunday."

I told him about the fight.

"Could that have been an act?"

"No. Sal was really hot. They weren't faking." When Page stopped writing, I asked, "Was anything important found in the manure pile? It sure took long enough for the evidence technicians to sift through it. I thought they'd be there forever."

"So did we. Still, as crime scenes go, it wasn't bad. Those guys have seen some really ugly stuff."

"You didn't answer my question. Did they find anything?"

"All kinds of things. Buttons. Probably off of Villano's clothes."

"What else?"

"I haven't seen the full list yet."

"And you don't intend to share it when you do."

"Not unless there's a good reason. You're just curious."

"I'm human."

"Yeah, well, you know sharing the list might jeopardize the case."

"Whoever killed Frank Villano should go to jail, go directly to jail and not pass go. I don't want to get in the way of that."

"I know. Anything else you want to tell me?"

"You want to have a chat with the Penzlers," I said. "Did you know there was once a hitching post in front of the store and they took it out because a truck almost hit Dixie and her horse?"

"I remember the hitching post. I didn't know she was the reason Pete took it out."

"They also told me that Nolan Grinnell used to work for Ed Duran."

"You'd better tell me everything you remember from that conversation."

I did my best. After that, we covered what I knew about Bright Hope's clients. By the time I finished, we were late leaving for the restaurant so Page had his cell phone to his ear as I pulled out of the driveway to follow him.

Elizabeth Page was accustomed to delayed or canceled meals. That was part of the deal when you married into law enforcement. She had once told me that having her husband come home alive was the most important part; the exact time he came through the door was secondary. Perhaps her wholehearted acceptance of that was the reason he tried so hard to get home on time. She kissed him hello as I slid into the booth across from them.

Wheat color hair framed Liz's face and set off her soft brown eyes. She was a great cook and I made a point of accepting her dinner invitations whenever they were extended. One might assume that she was easily overshadowed by her husband. After all, he wore a gun. However, in her quiet, forthright way, she was as commanding a presence as he was.

I enjoyed their company immensely. We met at a Sierra Club fundraiser that I had been forced to attend by a well-meaning friend who thought I needed more of a social life. Her ploy had worked to the extent that I ultimately moved out of Chicago and into the northern suburbs. However, that had disconnected me from my city pals. They rarely included me in their lives now and my efforts to maintain the link had not yielded results. The Pages were the only people with whom I currently socialized with any regularity.

"Ian said you're working at Bright Hope." said Liz, picking up the menu. "Didn't Mary Penzler introduce you to Dixie Villano at the store last November?"

"Actually, it was Izzy." I put down my menu. Mushroom Swiss burger, no bun, broccoli. "How's Tim?"

"Off to college next week." Page stopped while we placed our orders. "I'll drive him down next Sunday."

"U of I, right?"

"Engineering. Nowhere better to get the degree than U of I."

"How's your family?" asked Liz. "Everyone OK?"

I told them the latest family news. Everyone was in good health, thankfully, and my oldest cousin had just had her second child. My brother was debating going back to school to get his master's degree and I was still trying to get settled in my townhouse.

"That takes awhile," said Liz. "In another year, it will feel more like home."

"Speaking of my townhouse, here's a key." I passed her a copy of my house key. "I'd like someone besides me to have one."

"I'll add it to my collection." She dropped it into her wallet. "How's Jake?"

"Good. He was on the West Coast at a convention. Got back on Friday and we had dinner Sunday night. He's leaving on vacation in a couple of weeks. Heading up north to do some research at the reservation."

"Are you two getting serious?"

I felt myself get red. "We're not serious serious. I'd call it seriously committed to continued dating."

Liz groaned. "That sounds exciting."

"You just heard his schedule. We don't have time to do more than that. We—"

"Make time."

Page elbowed her gently. Their eyes locked and then Liz smiled at me. "OK, new subject. Do you still like temping?"

"I do, but sometimes it's hard being a non-entity." I winked at Liz. "No one interviews you at murder scenes."

"Hey!" Page had been reading a text message but was obviously listening to the conversation.

Liz laughed. "And did you shed any light on their investigation?"

"Actually, she did," said Page, closing his cell phone and clipping it onto his belt. "Thanks to Kyle, I have some angles to work that didn't come out of the sheriff's office."

"Meaning?" I asked.

"Normally a police department lets the task force take the lead on a homicide investigation but, if it happens on the sheriff's turf, they maintain control. Instead of the task force making the work assignments to its members, the sheriff does."

"So you interview who you're assigned to interview."

"Pretty much."

"And that's bad."

"That's politics." He gave us a grim smile. "And you know how I love politics."

Liz wrapped her arms around her husband and planted a kiss on his cheek. "No worries, darling. The radio said there was a triple outside Hainesville. The sheriff'll be so busy with that, he won't bother about your little horse pucky investigation."

"From your lips." Page pointed toward the ceiling. "Trouble is, Duran is big in the county and there's an election in November. It helps if the voters can see you doing your job. The Duran case is perfect for that. That's why there are so many news conferences with all the elected officials standing around the podium. Still, if that triple is more than a domestic, they'll focus on that for a while and I can have the team work on these new leads."

"Do I know any of these Bright Hope people?"

I listed the clients for her.

"Nope. Not a one, except Ed Duran, of course. The newspapers say he's expanding into Chicago."

"And not everyone is happy about it."

I told her about the scuffle between Sal and Duran on Sunday afternoon. It was the second time for Page but he listened intently, no doubt hoping to hear a new detail. When I finished, Liz looked thoughtful.

"So Sal Fabrini thinks Ed Duran is stealing equipment," she said. "That's very interesting."

"Why?" asked Page.

"Remember that news story about that ring of construction equipment thieves they busted in the south suburbs? Could this be part of that?"

"Maybe. Heavy equipment theft is a growing problem. The auto theft task force just arrested four guys and recovered a stolen front end loader."

"How does someone hide a stolen front end loader?" I asked. "It's not the kind of thing you can shove inside your garage or throw a tarp over."

"You see graders or loaders hauled on trailers all the time, right?"

Liz and I nodded.

"Did you ever once think one of them might be stolen?"

We shook our heads.

"Construction equipment moves around a lot normally. Contractors share it amongst themselves. Ralph has a bulldozer; Sam has a backhoe. They share. That way, neither has to put out for both pieces. Plus, the stuff gets moved around from job site to job site. Unlike your car that's supposed to be somewhere specific, equipment can be almost anywhere. It's not uncommon for the owner to lose track of it. So, the best place to hide stolen heavy equipment is in plain sight. The bad guys put the equipment on a trailer, haul it to another job site or to another state, and no one gives them a second glance. Then they lease it or sell it. Pure profit."

"And," I said, "if it's stolen from the company that is leasing it, it's no loss to the bad guys because they didn't pay for it anyway."

"Exactly."

"But how do you steal a front end loader? Do you jump start it?"

"That's the hard way. You use a key. They all use the same key."

"Wait a minute," said Liz. "What do you mean they all use the same key?"

"You know that big yellow grader that's parked over by the new school construction on Aspen Drive?" Page said. "That's a

Caterpillar. The key that starts it also starts a Caterpillar loader or a Caterpillar back hoe. Same with John Deere or Komatsu."

"But you have a vehicle ID number," I said. "You can check it against a list or a hot sheet."

"Big equipment doesn't have VIN numbers. It has PIN plates. PIN plates are stolen as often as equipment is. A missing PIN plate doesn't mean much anyway. They fall off on their own all the time."

"You've been researching this."

"Sal's accusation got me thinking. Equipment theft wasn't really a problem until the low interest rates caused the construction boom. In the old days, there weren't as many construction projects or companies doing them. So, there wasn't that much equipment. Now all kinds of shmoes have become contractors and they can't afford equipment so they lease it or help themselves to it. "

"Do the bad guys use the money for drugs?" I asked.

"I suppose they use the money to live the American dream. Nice cars, nice clothes, nice women."

Liposuction, nose jobs.

"Is the money financing terrorism?" asked Liz.

"God, I hope not but who knows? I don't think there's *that* much money in it. The thieves turn a good profit but I haven't heard anything about it being in the billions like drugs."

"That's good," I said, finishing off my burger. "Anyone for dessert?"

"I thought you were on a diet when you didn't order a bun."

"A bun makes me too full for ice cream and if I come to Max and Erma's in the summer, I want a sundae."

Page laughed. "I can't argue with that logic. I'll join you."

When the waiter came to our table, Liz made it three and we spent the rest of our meal talking about more pleasant things.

It wasn't until I was home and reading the paper that I remembered that I had not told Page about the attack on Sunny. Maybe, with the information he had as a result of all their interviews and investigating, he could figure out how it fit in. It had to be related somehow.

I told myself I'd tell him about it in the morning. It was a nice thought but I didn't remember to do it. Maybe if I had, things would have turned out differently.

CHAPTER 10

It was noon when I first heard about Page being on the premises. Chuck told me he was out by the picnic table near the house talking to Jorge. An hour later I saw him myself. He and Ed Duran were leaning on the riding ring fence watching Dixie work Divot. When Page came inside, I was inspecting Henry's new ring.

"It's amazing," I said, examining the scrolled sterling band that encircled his ring finger. The setting held a square-cut piece of amber the color of aged paper, white with tinges of yellow gray around the edges. "I thought all amber was orange."

"Baltic amber is many colors. Yellow, green, white. All amber."

"When you bring your family here, will your daughter come or will she stay in Poland?"

"She come. All come. Whole family."

"How many are in your family? You make it sound like a big one."

"Wife, daughter, daughter's husband, daughter's children, two sons, sons' wives, sons' children."

And the second cousins twice removed.

In all the conversations I'd had about Henry bringing his family to the United States, I had never stopped to consider what that meant. Somehow I had pictured a wife, a child or two and a couple of suitcases. More assumptions drawn from movies and television. Good grief. When would I get over that?

"Having your family here will be the best birthday present of all."

"Yes. Not much longer now. All arrangements made."

"That's wonderful news. I'm sure your daughter will do well here. Lots of stores would love to sell her beautiful rings."

Page appeared in the doorway. I looked up and Henry turned around, following my eyes. He immediately stepped aside and dipped his head.

"Hello, Henry," said Page. "I don't mean to interrupt."

"Time to get into fields. Sorry I talk so long."

He sidled past Page and out the door. For a moment, Page watched him and then approached my desk.

"I gather his daughter is a jeweler?"

"Craftsperson might be a better description."

I explained what Izzy had told me about the rings and how Henry had been waiting for the new one.

Page settled on the stool. "I forgot to ask you how Dixie and Izzy took the news about Frank."

"Like you'd expect. They were both upset but I think Izzy took it harder because she had remained hopeful. Dixie always suspected Frank was dead. She had steeled herself for the eventual bad news. How did you finally make the ID? DNA?"

"Dental records. The forensic pathologist confirmed the bones were human and gave us the sex and height. That ruled out Ramon because our skeleton was too tall. Bacteria in the composting manure destroyed all of the surface DNA. Maybe the crime lab could have used DNA from the bone marrow but that was probably degraded too. Since we had a pretty good idea it was Frank Villano, it made sense for the pathologist to go right to the dental records. The lab has plenty of other cases to work on where the DNA is viable."

"I saw you talking to Ed. Did heavy equipment come into the conversation at all?"

"You know it did."

"Brisa said Ed lost a backhoe recently."

"He's losing more this year than last. Supposedly he's reported it all so we'll check the records. He also told me that, if Fabrini was being honest and not just spouting off for effect, Fabrini Construction is in serious trouble. Losing that much equipment will put Sal under." Page turned to go. "Thanks for the tip about the insurance policy."

"Any time."

That reminded me. I'd been so focused on telling Page about the policy that the invoice never made it into the computer nor had a check been issued for the premium. I pulled the invoice from the payables file. Balance due: zero. That didn't make sense. OK, reread it from top to bottom. Balance due: zero. I set the invoice aside so I could ask Dixie about it later. If she had paid it, I needed to record the expenditure. If there was an error, I would have to follow up.

Jake called near the end of the day and offered to buy me dinner. Things had been a little tense since the fire and I welcomed the opportunity for a quiet meal together. We agreed to meet at an Italian restaurant in Libertyville at six. Since that was only a half hour drive and I didn't have any errands to run, I delayed my departure from the barn.

As I strolled past each stall and watched the horses munch their dinner, I felt myself relax. Lori's comment about Bright Hope being a safe haven made sense. The animals were therapeutic.

It wasn't in the plan for me to stay at Bright Hope permanently but for the first time, I was sorry about that. Ed Duran wasn't going to foot the bill forever and Dixie couldn't afford a full time office clerk. If I did the job for which I'd been hired, a part timer would be plenty. Still, if income and benefits were no object, Bright Hope would make a terrific work home. I patted Foggy and Maida, ending my tour in the restroom. When I came out, I heard Nolan Grinnell. He was in the lounge and he didn't sound very happy.

I'd had enough eavesdropping lately but I did take a quick peek inside as I scurried past the door. Nolan was nose-to-nose with Ed Duran and they were arguing about Foggy's unpaid bill.

Jake was already in a booth, a glass of red wine in front of him and one waiting for me, when I arrived at Lino's. He was in a suit and his raven hair was tied back. Must have been a corporate kind of day. I wanted to throw myself into his arms but I slid into the booth across from him and settled for giving his hand a good squeeze. After we ordered, we chatted about his work and the problems at the barn. Over dinner, we compared notes on the books we were reading and by the time the cannoli was served, we had covered all the safe topics.

"You've been kind of distant lately," Jake said. "What's buggin' you?"

One of the reasons I like him is his ability to instantly get to the meat of an issue. That is also one of the things that drives me nuts. No preamble, no lead-in. Straight to the guts of the thing. Makes it hard to avoid topics you don't want to discuss.

"Nothing like coming right to the point," I said.

"You're dodging my question."

I didn't say anything.

"I should have asked you to come with me to California?"

My index finger flew to the tip of my nose before I could stop it.

"And just why would I invite you to do something I know you can't do? You'd feel left out and disappointed."

"That's what Mary said."

A spark flickered in his dark eyes. "You'll talk to Mary when you're bugged but not to me?"

"Apparently you talked to Mary or you wouldn't know why I was upset."

"We're talking to Mary and not to each other? What sense does that make?"

"None."

He threw up his hands. "I surrender."

I didn't know what to say. The whole thing seemed as silly as when Mary and I talked about it. Still, I couldn't help the way I felt.

"It's my problem. I'll get it worked out."

Jake leaned in. His eyes flashed and his voice was tight. "That is not how I do a relationship. We're in it together or not at all."

His words cut deep. It took me several seconds to push my panic away. I played with a hangnail.

"You want to break up?"

"Hell no, I don't want to break up. But I am not going to beat my head against a wall either. It's real simple. Something I did bothered you. You have to tell me what that is if I'm going to change my behavior or at least explain it to you. Our future, if we're going to have one, is all about communication. If, after six months of being together, we can't talk about this little thing, how we will be able to talk about the big things when they come along?"

"I hate it when you're right."

"I know."

I looked up at him and took a deep breath. "OK. Yes, you should have asked me to go to California with you."

"But you wouldn't have come."

"That's beside the point."

"There's logic in there somewhere but damn if I can find it."

I shrugged, then reached across the table and touched his hand. He didn't pull away.

"I don't fully understand it myself. Maybe it's a girl thing. I needed to feel wanted, that the trip to Napa wouldn't be good for you if I wasn't along."

"That makes no sense."

"I didn't say it did."

He leaned back against the booth and was quiet. I finished my cannoli and felt like an idiot. I honestly didn't know why I felt as I did. Somehow, that invitation was important but I couldn't explain it. Not even to myself.

"It was all right for me to go to California to a conference. It's the Napa part that's the issue, right?"

I nodded as I pushed cannoli crumbs around with my fork.

"OK," said Jake. "Simple solution. From now on, I don't tell you about those things. I leave them out."

"When you put it like that, it sounds ridiculous."

"That's because it is ridiculous." He leaned forward again. "Someday we may take trips together. That day isn't here yet and it has nothing to do with how we feel about each other. It has to do with our schedules and our lives. I promise, next time I'll ask you to go along and you can refuse." He sipped his espresso. When he looked at me, his eyes were gentle. "There's one more thing. The times you need a hug seem to be few and far between. I missed one of those times at the fire, didn't I?"

I didn't answer.

"Look, I'm just a man. Sometimes you have to tell me what you need."

I had to smile. "Well, thanks to this conversation, we know I'm a girl and you're a guy and sometimes that's enough to really mess things up."

"Amen." He grinned for a moment and then turned solemn again. "It doesn't matter to you if we don't hold hands all the time and it's no big deal if I don't put my arm around you at the movies, is it?"

I shook my head.

"But I do care about you and you need to know that." He paused, rubbing the bridge of his nose where glasses would sit if he wore them. Then he lifted a gift bag from the seat next to him and passed it to me. "Maybe this will help."

I pushed the tissue aside and lifted out a green velvet box. There was jewelry inside for sure. My eyes got moist as I lifted the lid and saw a silver heart, adorned with tiny diamond.

"This is a symbol of something Chippewa?"

"A grain of wild rice would be a more appropriate icon. Many of my people died fighting the Sioux to preserve their claim on the beds of rice at Mole Lake. However, I didn't see any gold-dipped rice kernels at the store so you'll have to settle for this. I assume you're OK with that."

Like I said, he's always right. His gift helped a lot and after we left the restaurant, I tried to demonstrate how much.

*   *   *   *

Going to work the next day was easier. I was up on time without the clock radio pulling me out of bed. Although it was supposed to be another hot one, the previous night had been cool and I had slept solidly. After a brisk walk through the neighborhood, I had breakfast and drove out to the barn, singing loudly to oldies blasting on the car radio.

Izzy was in the riding ring with Divot when I pulled into Bright Hope. I waved and went to the arena door to greet Dixie. Sal stood in a corner, arms folded across his chest. Dixie hitched Sunny to the sulky and adjusted the check rein. I decided not to interrupt and headed to the office.

"Good morning, good morning," called Izzy as she banged through the screen door. Tension crept into her high-octane greeting the way dirt sneaks under my welcome mat.

I heard clacking at the coffee maker.

"Is there coffee or do I need to make some?"

"There's plenty here. Practically a full pot. Sal got here early and made it himself. Where is he?"

I turned on the computer and went out to the lounge. Izzy poured a mug and offered me one.

"Your mother's in the arena getting Sunny ready. Sal's with her."

"Mom's going to demonstrate? Good idea. Hard to talk about Sunny Disposition if you can't see what that disposition has become. I know. Bad pun." Izzy sank into the couch. "Mom said she almost lost Sal the other night. He wanted to drop the whole thing."

"She talked him out of it?"

"She convinced him to watch Sunny work this morning. The whole deal will be screwed up if Sal doesn't see some serious flash today."

"Thanks to you, Sunny seems to have recovered from the beating he got last week. You spent a lot of time with him."

"He's worked great every day since then so he should be good today, too." She paused, long enough for me to see a powerful anger lurking in her beautiful dark eyes. "I'd love to get my hands on the SOB who did it. We've got a lot invested in that horse. If Sal doesn't take him, we'll have to start all over to find another buyer. We're talking hours of time and the thousands we paid for him." She drained her mug and slammed it down on the table. "And I can't ignore the cruelty. I'd kill the bastard just for that."

Izzy hoisted herself upright and stared for a moment at the empty mantle. She went over to it and caressed it. Suddenly oblivious to me, she bowed her head. After she patted the empty space, she faced me, pushing away the gloom that had filled her eyes.

Whatever she was about to say never passed her lips because Sal pushed his face against the screen door. "Izzy, if you're coming, let's go. I gotta get back to the city."

I followed Izzy and Sal to the center of the arena and watched as Sunny went around us at a slow jog trot. The horse appeared relaxed in his harness; no tossing head, no mouthing the bit. Dixie pulled back on the reins slightly and Sunny downshifted to a walk. She turned him, letting him walk a few paces along the wall. With a cluck-cluck of her tongue and a slight shake of the reins, she pushed

Sunny into an easy trot again. Once around and then Dixie clucked again. Sunny responded, ears forward, picking up the pace with each hoof pounding out a perfect rhythm. I could have sworn he was smiling.

Sunny looked pretty classy pulling the training sulky and I could see why Dixie chose him for Sal. He was flashy, like Sal's Corvette. His chestnut coat glistened as he floated through patches of sunlight, his mane and tail flying behind him. I felt my chest swell with pride for this horse that had come so far. It was hard to equate this beautiful animal to the one who had charged me just days before.

The demonstration ended with Sunny pulling the sulky to the center of the ring, stopping and standing quietly for a full minute. When Dixie relaxed the reins, Sal clapped with the enthusiasm of a parent who had just watched his child perform in the school play. Sunny bobbed his head as if acknowledging the accolades.

Dixie left the cart and went up to Sunny's head, patting his cheek gently and putting her pleasure in her voice. Sunny leaned into her and she hugged him, stroking his neck.

"That was fabulous!" said Sal. He started forward, then checked himself.

"Come on over," said Dixie. "Talk to him as you approach. Look him in the eye as a friend, not an aggressor."

Sal followed her instructions and soon found himself patting the gelding's neck.

"You were great, boy." He looked at Dixie. "Can I do that? Drive that rig, I mean. Nolan told me he loves driving. Man, I can see why. This guy moves out just like my 'Vette." He turned to me. "Get out the paperwork, lady. I'm gonna buy me a horse today."

"Are you sure, Sal?" asked Dixie. "Tuesday night, you wanted to back out."

"That's before I saw this. Man, this guy is too cool. You were right; this horse has my name on him." When Dixie continued to hesitate, he said, "I gotta have him, Dixie. Never mind what I said before. I'll find a way."

"If that's what you want." She turned to me. "Go on, Kyle. Get some paperwork pulled together."

I left Sunny, Dixie, Izzy and Sal in a huddle. The last thing I saw was Sal, his palm flat, feeding his new horse a bit of carrot. Too bad Izzy crumpled Sunny's stall sign. Looked like I needed it after all.

An hour later, Sal Fabrini had stuffed the bill of sale into his briefcase and was standing by Sunny's stall, cooing. I was happy for him. He seemed genuinely thrilled by the prospect of working with his own horse.

Dixie's next meeting filled us with dread. I had hoped Sal would be gone before Brisa and her father showed up but he was reluctant to leave Sunny. At least he was out of sight in the back of the barn. It would be best if Duran and Sal didn't run into one another for a while but there was no disguising a yellow Corvette. Duran would know instantly that Sal was on the premises.

Brisa preceded Duran into the lounge, went directly to the table and sat down, setting her riding crop in front of her. She looked down at her folded hands as if she were in prayer. Perhaps she was. From the sour look on her face, it had not been a good morning.

Duran stood behind his daughter, feet apart, his hands resting on her shoulders. He wore a similar expression so I gave him a nod and escaped to the office. He started talking the moment Dixie entered the room.

"Sneaking my daughter over to some fly-by-night outfit in McHenry stops right now. Makes me look cheap and I am not cheap. If my girl needs special training, she gets it. But I won't pay another barn room and board. You work it out so that she gets her training but the horse stays here. Nuff said?"

"But Daddy," said Brisa, "you don't understand. I need to be with other people who have the same goals I do. You want me to be the best, don't you?"

"Dixie Villano is the best. When I wanted to pull you out of here after Frank turned up dead, you insisted on stayin' put. Now you tell me that you need to move on. You're makin' me crazy." He threw up his hands. "I could use some help here, Dixie."

"You have a point, of course," said Dixie. "Brisa, I appreciate your loyalty but you can't have it both ways. Keeping Chicken and staying here doesn't make sense if you want to compete at Class A shows."

"OK," said Duran. "Let's say I cave and buy her a new horse. I never thought much of that Dalmatian thing anyway. Too skinny and too weird lookin'. But the new horse stays here. Brisa doesn't need anyone else."

"Oh Daddy," said Brisa. "You—"

"Brisa, you listen and learn. You working with anybody else is a bad investment and I don't make bad investments."

From the sound of his voice, this was just another business transaction to him and he expected others to view it the same way.

"Here's the deal, Dixie," Ed went on. "Brisa's been after me to get her a better horse and I found the perfect horse for her right here. That gray one in the back. He'll do just fine. He's purebred, he's show quality and he's available."

"No, Daddy -."

"It's a done deal," said Duran.

"I think you'll find Foggy's a poor choice for Brisa," said Dixie.

Her tone was measured and it didn't sound like she was bowed by Duran's statements but I couldn't see her face. Was she surprised or angered by what Duran had just done?

"I paid off Nolan's bill and now the horse belongs to Brisa. Like I said, it's a done deal."

This was news to me. I had not received a check nor had Dixie mentioned getting one. Duran must have paid Nolan directly.

"Ed," said Dixie, "I think—"

"But Daddy, he's the wrong breed," Brisa moaned. "Besides, Nolan loves him. You can't do that to Nolan."

I stood up and went to the doorway just as Nolan charged in, a piece of paper in his hand.

"I've changed my mind. Foggy is *not* for sale. Take back your check."

"We have a deal," said Duran, emphasizing the last word. "Are you trying to hold me up for more money? Is that it?"

"You've known me a long time. I don't do that kind of thing." There was a slight pause. "Sorry, Dixie, but I just can't part with him. I've found another way to pay my bill."

"Dixie's got no part in this. You sold the horse to me because you had to and she'll honor the sale because she has to."

At that, Nolan tore the check into little pieces and hurled them into Duran's face. "I've got a week. Right, Dixie?"

"You've got as much time as you need," said Sal, entering the lounge. He glared at Duran. "This is one bidding war you're not going to win, Ed." He turned to Nolan. "Like I told you, I'll loan you the money. You can keep your horse."

"I'm sorry, Mr. Duran," said Nolan. "I know we go way back but Foggy isn't for sale. I found some financing."

"Look at his face," said Sal. "Hah! For that, it's no loan. It's a gift."

That proclamation was followed by silence. Duran's jaw tightened, his fists clenched. Sal adopted a balanced stance. I held my breath. The moment passed.

"I know you're caught in the middle on this so don't worry about it," said Duran, looking at Dixie, his eyes softer. "This isn't your battle. I have complete faith in you. But unless you get the money from Nolan or Mr. Macho here by the deadline, the horse belongs to Brisa. Understood?"

Duran kissed his daughter on the cheek and walked out of the lounge.

After a pause, everyone began talking at once. I dropped coins into the vending machine and helped myself to a cold can of caffeine. I'd have helped myself to something a lot stronger if I could have but I don't think beer is sold in vending machines yet.

"Well," said Izzy as she came into the room, "that went pretty well, I thought."

Dixie looked at her. "You heard?"

"I wondered what had happened to you. When I caught Uncle Ed's tone and the topic of conversation, I decided it was safer to wait outside."

Nolan looked at Sal. "You're a lifesaver, man. Foggy's everything to me."

Sal's eyes were downcast and he moved a clod of dirt around with the toe of his boot.

"I shot off my mouth," he said, "because Ed drives me crazy but, man, I don't know how I'm going to pay for my own horse, let alone yours."

"Oh, Sal," said Dixie. "I wish you hadn't done that."

"Done what?" asked Lori, entering the lounge and looking from one face to the next. "What's wrong? Why does everyone look like the Cubs just lost the home opener?"

"Come on," said Izzy, steering her back toward the door. "Let's go see Divot and I'll explain."

"I don't want Foggy, Nolan. He's your horse," said Brisa. "I'll convince Daddy. It'll just take me awhile."

"Thanks, but I don't have much time."

"Nonsense," said Dixie. "I don't plan to enforce the contract."

"You'd better plan on it," said Sal, "because Ed'll make you."

"That's true," said Brisa. "With Daddy, it's a matter of principle. Nothing makes him crazy like athletes who don't honor the contracts they signed. He'll insist that you put that awful clause into effect and that Nolan respect it."

"Is he like that with everything?" I asked. "Any loopholes you might know about?"

Brisa shook her head. "Nope. He's even that way with the guys that live in the house. They get to live there rent free while they work here. Daddy has a contract with all of them, so many hours of free work in exchange for the rent. Then he pays them the difference."

"Henry told me working here was a good deal for him," said Nolan, "but I didn't know there was a signed contract. That sounds rather complicated for such a simple thing."

"It's new. Daddy says it keeps everything business-like. Henry, Chuck and the others know the deal and everybody gets what they need."

"And the workers can't complain about their pay or file unemployment or otherwise cause problems," said Sal. "Pretty smart."

"Daddy's a good businessman."

"If he's so good, why does he have to steal from me to keep me from beating him out on the bids?"

"He doesn't steal! He says you beat out yourself. He says he gets headaches because of you."

"Good!"

"That's enough, you two," said Dixie. She turned to Nolan. "Looks like you need to do some serious thinking about how you're going to pay off your bill. And Sal, you apologize to Nolan for making promises you can't keep and then figure out how you're going to pay me for Sunny."

"Man, I am outa here," said Sal. When he got to the door, he looked over his shoulder at Nolan. "Sorry about the loan, big guy."

Sal banged out of the lounge.

Nolan punched his fist into his hand. "Damn. Now what am I going to do?"

Brisa put her hand on Nolan's broad shoulder. "We'll figure

something out. We have to. I don't want Foggy any more than you want to give him up. I could just kill Daddy for doing that to you."

"None of that talk," said Dixie, dropping onto the sofa. "Your father worships you and he's trying to do what he thinks is best,"

"He's running my life and I've had enough. I am not taking Foggy."

Dixie rubbed her eyes. "You two go get some air or some lunch or something. I want to think about this."

Nolan and Brisa looked at her and then at each other. Finally, Brisa picked up her crop and the two of them went outside.

"Whew," I said. "That was an interesting meeting."

"That hothead, Sal. He's got a stick up his butt about Ed and it just hit the rest of us. Frank warned me about him. I should have paid more attention. Sal's going to stiff me on Sunny now. I can feel it."

"Frank warned you about Sal?"

"He warned me about Ed." She looked up at the empty mantle. "Frank said something was going on with Ed and I have to admit that Ed's been unusually edgy and preoccupied lately. Frank thought Ed was on the verge of sticking his nose into Bright Hope business and then the next thing I know, he's talking about scouting new locations for Bright Hope. When Frank disappeared, Ed was great. He helped if I asked for it but he didn't act like some men would have. He didn't rush in to take over my life. Now that Frank is officially dead, Ed's everywhere. Dictatorial, controlling." She sighed. "I don't recognize this Ed. He's like a ..."

"A gang leader?"

Dixie went pale. "The phone's quiet. Walk with me."

I followed her to Foggy's stall where she stopped briefly, mumbling softly. She reached through the bars and patted the stallion's neck.

"Even Henry knows you'd be a bad fit, right fella?" She turned to me. "He told me the other day that Brisa would look good on

Sunny."

"But Sunny is for Sal."

"Only if Sal can pay for him. Henry's right. Sunny and Brisa would look great in the show ring. Of course, if Ed bought Sunny, Sal would go ballistic."

"But you intend to suggest it."

"I might. I'll give Sal a week and then we'll see."

Dixie walked past the feed room and toward the front of the barn. Divot was in his stall, his eyes closed as Jorge rubbed him down. Chicken's stall was empty. We went through the screen door to the outside.

Izzy had Chicken in the riding ring and I heard her tell him to walk. He moved forward, slowly at first and then with more confidence.

"If Ed has his way and Foggy goes to Brisa, Chicken will be up for sale faster than you can say checkbook. Izzy will concentrate on vocal commands so he'll work for little kids."

"You anticipated this?"

Dixie faced me. "When we went out the other day, we didn't go to the saddle shop as planned. Izzy insisted we go to the attorney instead. She wanted to see how things stood with the business and Ed and all. Turned out, that was a better way to spend the afternoon than buying new tack." Dixie watched her daughter with pride. "Afterwards, we went to dinner and had a long talk about Chicken. Izzy's evaluation of his potential matched mine exactly. Brisa eventually gets what she wants so Izzy said we should get Chicken ready to sell." She paused. "Neither of us thought of Ed buying Foggy. That came out of nowhere."

We watched Izzy for awhile longer and then went around the south side of the barn, staying in the shade of the building. The sun had baked the soil into brick, the cracks in the ground like mortar lines. It wasn't a drought year but we could use some rain.

The charred framework of the garage looked bleak. Littered

with debris and gouged by deep tire ruts, the ground nearby made the moon's surface look inviting.

Manure was once again piling up behind the barn. While the original dumping spot was off limits during the sifting process, Chuck and Jorge heaped the stuff on the north side of the barn. It was a long haul, going out the front and around with the wheelbarrow. As soon as the evidence techs released the area, Chuck and Jorge went back to the routine of dumping directly beyond the back door.

"Where is everyone?" asked Dixie, shielding her eyes from the sun and doing a slow three-sixty.

"Lunch?" I pointed to the picnic table next to the farmhouse where several men were seated.

"Ed scared the hungry right out of me. You don't have to keep me company if you want to go eat."

I shook my head and stayed with her as she moved toward the shed.

"That garage burning down might be a blessing in disguise. If I can talk Ed into it, I'd like to put in a small pen back here. It would be nice to have a place away from the road to turn the horses out."

She walked forward another few paces and then turned around and looked at the barn. I followed her eyes.

"If we come out to about here...aiyee."

I had been looking at the barn's back door and did not see Dixie go down. She was on her butt, legs splayed out like a ladybug on its back. I reached out to help her to her feet.

"Are you hurt? What happened?"

"I wasn't watching where I was going. Stupid ruts."

The mud ridge Dixie tripped over was close to six inches high.

"I hope Ed's insurance is paid up," said Dixie, brushing the dirt off her hands and laughing. "Let's see, if I limp back to the barn, think I can work up enough sympathy to get him to drop the whole Foggy thing?"

Dixie kept on talking, to herself now, waving her hands and hobbling around the proposed turnout area, practicing an exaggerated limp. She was several yards away when a metal object, imbedded in the top of one of the ruts, glinted in the sunlight and caught my eye. Bending down, I dug it out and turned the thing over in my palm. It was brass, about an inch long and roughly the diameter of a straw. A shell casing.

"You found something?"

Dixie started toward me. I immediately closed my hand around the shell.

"A quarter," I said. "Finder's keepers."

"Lucky you."

She turned away and resumed her pacing. When her face was toward the barn, I wrapped the casing in a used tissue I had in my pocket and stuffed the little package back into my jeans.

CHAPTER 11

A s I stood up, Dixie pointed toward the barn.
"Time to head back," she said. "We both have work to do."

Some of the spring had left her step and, as we walked past the reborn manure pile, Dixie looked at it and shuddered.

"Do you think they'll catch whoever killed my Frank?"

"Those evidence techs wouldn't spend all that time sifting through horse shit if they didn't think it was worth the effort."

I took her arm and gently pulled her into the barn. When we reached the tack room, she patted my hand, gave me a weak smile and went in. The lounge was empty; owners were with their horses. It looked like I had time to tackle some computer input that required concentration. Shoeing records lay in a neat stack ready to go but it was several minutes before I stopped thinking about Dixie and focused on horse feet.

I was worried about her. Dixie wore a good face but her emotional exhaustion was evident in the circles under her eyes and the powdery look to her skin. If she didn't have the business to run, would she collapse in a heap?

When Sal stuck his head into the office two hours later, it was time for me to pack up and go home.

"Izzy wants you in the arena before you go home," he said.

Was he teasing me? Something about his tone that made me uneasy.

"Why?"

"Got me."

Sal turned away but not before I saw a smirk on his face.

What was Sal up to? What could Izzy need so late in the day? Did she really want anything at all or was I about to be the brunt of some practical joke? I suspected the latter but the only way to find out was to follow Sal so I bumped the file drawer closed with my hip and headed for the arena.

The office had been bright with afternoon sunshine. There were no windows in the arena so even with the doors open at either end; the corners were shrouded in shadow. I paused just inside, waiting for my eyes to adjust.

Izzy stood in the middle with Chicken. Lori, Sal, Brisa and Nolan grouped around her like pups at a food bowl. They parted as I approached revealing Maida in western tack.

"Done for the day?" asked Izzy, patting Chicken and passing his reins to Brisa.

I nodded, warily. Lori tried unsuccessfully to smother a grin and Sal wouldn't look at me. Clearly something was up.

"Good," said Izzy. "You're taking Maida out for a ride."

"Pardon me?"

"I said you and Maida are going out for a ride."

I had been set up all right but I couldn't tell who was behind it. No one would look at me except Izzy and the corners of her mouth twitched.

"You chicken?" she asked.

"No. He's Chicken," I shot back, pointing at the gelding.

"Ha ha. Very funny. Look, she's all ready for you." Izzy extended her arm, pushing the reins at me. "Take an hour and get reacquainted with horseback riding."

My youthful passion for all things equestrian was long behind me. Horses are magnificent as a species but now I loved them best from the ground. Some of my reticence was the realization that there is absolutely no way to completely control anything that has a brain. I don't even have power over my computer and its brain is just copper and silicon. Riding horses is not like riding a bike. I didn't remember how and I sure didn't want to fall off.

"Go on," said Izzy, thrusting the reins at me again. "It'll put you in touch with your inner self."

"Pul-leaze!"

"It will get you in tune with our clients?"

"I don't buy that one either but it's better than the inner self argument."

"How about your boss is insisting?"

Laughing, Izzy placed Maida's reins into my hand and closed my fingers around them. Then she turned her attention to Brisa and Chicken. Chuck stepped forward, took the reins from me and led Maida through the back door to the outside. After he gave me a leg up and I hoisted myself into the saddle, he adjusted the stirrups.

"Neck rein her," he said, laying the reins in my palm. "Lay left rein against neck to go right. Like steering car."

I nodded, afraid my trembling voice would betray how accurate Izzy had been when she called me chicken. I remembered how to rein, but long ago lost the inner thigh strength required to maintain a good seat. I clutched the pommel. Now I knew why Maida was in western tack. There was more for me to hold on to.

"You know where trail is?"

I shook my head.

"Come on," said Nolan, leading Foggy. "I'll show you."

He mounted and turned toward the gravel drive that cut through the barnyard. I lifted the reins and Maida followed behind. We'd walked only about fifty feet when raucous applause and shrill whistles spooked her. She shot forward, her butt tucked and ready for a serious gallop. I reined her in then twisted around in the saddle to see what had startled her. Sal whistled through his fingers. Brisa, mounted on Chicken, clapped enthusiastically.

"You go, girl," shouted Lori, jumping up and down.

How nice of all them to line up and see me off. Dixie wasn't in the group and I wondered what she would say about all of this. I almost turned Maida around.

"I can't blame you if you want to go back." Nolan smiled warmly. "Izzy has a way of making us do things we didn't know we wanted to do."

"I probably shouldn't be riding one of Dixie's horses."

"Maida belongs to Izzy and this is her idea."

We left the audience of smart alecks behind and Maida quickened her pace until she walked next to Foggy again.

The trail to the bridle path cut through the hay fields. Nolan pointed toward the tractor and we both waved at Henry, chugging down a row near the line of trees that separated the field from forest preserve easement. A multi-pronged hoe-like contraction followed his tractor, turning the soil over and burying the leftover plant stalks.

"That guy is always working," said Nolan, admiration on his face. "He has a goal and he's going to get to it. I don't know how he can stand being away from his family for so long. My wife may have a hissy about our animals but I'd miss her if she wasn't around to nag at me."

"People will sacrifice a lot to get what they want. Look at Chuck. All he talks about is his wannabe racing stable. That much determination is bound to pay off."

"Where you headed?" asked Nolan. "Up the river trail?"

"Is that what you'd recommend?"

"It's real pretty that way. The north trail is straight. Wide, too. Izzy and I hope to try a sleigh on it this winter if we get enough snow." He paused. "If I can figure out a way to keep this guy."

"Dixie doesn't want to take him. Ed surprised everyone with his announcement."

"I know. Ed can be mean when it comes to business. He's always been like that."

"You worked for him once."

"Yeah, and I learned he won't back down if he thinks he's right. But he was always fair so I don't get this thing with Foggy. Must have something to do with Sal offering to front me the money."

"Are they honestly big rivals?"

"Don't see how they could be. Sal's blowin' smoke about Ed stealing his equipment. Sal's probably stealing it himself."

"You're kidding."

"A skid loader's worth an easy fifty thousand and the insurance claim is free money. No income tax. If Sal's business is hurtin', a couple of big insurance payoffs would be a hellava boost."

"Sal said he's lost four."

"Two hundred thousand. That's no chump change. What's a Corvette cost these days? More than I can pay. And Sunny may be a bargain but I know exactly what it costs for a horse's upkeep. Sal's crying poor but he always has the toys he wants. Kinda makes ya wonder, doesn't it?"

"Could Ed's attitude have something to do with Brisa?"

Nolan thought about that a moment. "Maybe. She and Sal had a thing about six months ago. Sal told me Frank wanted him to cool it. I guess he did because he stopped bein' around her until lately."

"You've been with Dixie quite awhile. Izzy said they're trying to convince you to show Foggy?"

"Foggy's fully recovered and he never did have any real training problems. I should probably make room for someone else but Foggy's real happy here. So am I. I got no interest in being anywhere else or doing anything else. This suits me just fine." He paused. "And Foggy's a stallion. A lot of barns won't let us in unless I cut him."

"And you plan to breed him someday?"

Nolan shrugged. "His bloodlines are good. He's young. If I have to sell him, keeping him a stud prospect is good business."

"So it all boils down to money again, doesn't it?"

"It does, but I can't be like Sal. I have to keep emotion out of it or I'll make bad decisions. Ed's right about one thing. If I can't pay, Foggy has to be sold."

"Did you turn in my insurance papers? What about the referral bonus?"

"I'll give it to Dixie as soon as it comes in. It won't be much, maybe a few hundred."

"That should hold Ed off for a while."

"I doubt it, but it's worth a shot. I owe Foggy that much. At least Brisa will be good to him. I have that to hold on to."

"You could still come out to visit him, couldn't you? Maybe she'll even let you ride him?"

Nolan's painful stare at the trail ahead told me my attempt to cheer him had been a complete failure. We rode the rest of the way to the trail in silence.

I kept a watchful eye on Maida. Her excited call to Foggy the night of the fire still rang in my ears. How would she be when he and Nolan turned south?

As we reached the trail head, Nolan said, "Do you want me to go with you?"

"No thanks. I don't plan to go very far. Frankly, pardner, I doubt my legs can handle too much time in this here saddle."

He laughed. "I don't mind, Tex. Really."

"I'd rather you go figure out a way to hang on to your horse. I'll be fine."

Nolan didn't protest. He nudged Foggy with his heel and they jogged down the trail toward Gurnee. I turned Maida left and she clopped along without a backward glance at her stable mate.

The Des Plaines River Trail and Greenway runs the entire thirty-one mile length of Lake County from the Wisconsin state line on the north to the Cook County border on the south. Portions of the trail are heavily used by cyclists, runners and equestrians but at the north end, where Maida and I were, there was little sign of activity. No mountain bike tire tracks and no discarded plastic water bottles. Maida moved along at an easy pace, her walk rocking me gently in the saddle.

After leaving Nolan, we went through a patch of oak forest, tall straight trees with a bit of low-level vegetation clustered in patches where sunlight came through the leafy canopy. An area of sumac came next with its thin, spreading branches encroaching on the trail like tentacles. Beyond the shrubs that bordered the trail and invisible to those not five feet off the ground, wheat-colored prairie grass waved in the breeze. The stalks leaned to and fro as the wind pushed through them. Tall grass prairies must have had the same rolling wave-like appearance when covered wagons carried the pioneers into Kansas and Nebraska. Here, on the restored prairie of the forest preserve, the effect was beautifully appealing. If I were a buffalo, it would look good enough to eat. As it was, I had a glimpse of how Illinois must have been two hundred years before Maida and I arrived. Perhaps it was moments like this that drew Jake to his heritage.

Somewhere in the trees, a cardinal chip-chipped. It was answered by the cantankerous caw of a crow. Overhead, a hawk circled, riding the updrafts as it watched the ground for its dinner. Bunny ala carte? They sat fearlessly at the edge of the trail, munching on bunny food as Maida walked by. How do bunnies know that horses won't eat them? Were they aware of the circling doom overhead that would?

Sunshine pushed through breaks in approaching storm clouds and painted leaves a radiant yellow before spattering the ground. I looked at my watch. Forty-five minutes out, a bit less to return. That should get me back to the barn before Maida and I got wet.

One of Maida's ears pricked forward and back like a scanning radar dish. I looked around, seeing nothing until she twitched violently, nearly unseating me. She twisted her head around and thrust her nose against her shoulder. A gigantic black fly took flight from her neck. Where had that come from? I hadn't seen it land on her. It buzzed back and I swatted at it. It circled away and then the beastly thing returned. I stood slightly in the stirrups to bat at it again.

"Go chew on a deer," I yelled, flailing at the fly with one arm.

It was a battle of wills now. The fly dove toward us, determined to have its dinner on Maida's neck. I was equally resolute that this flying parasite would dine somewhere else. After nearly throwing myself out of the saddle, I connected, giving it a good smack. The fly took off.

At that moment, something leapt from the bushes and ran directly in front of Maida. She bolted left. I sailed off to the right, hanging in mid-air for several seconds. Then gravity took over and I came down. Hard. My left ankle turned toward Los Angeles. My right hip hit the ground. I bounced once.

*   *   *   *

When I opened my eyes, I felt like I was on a Tilt-A-Whirl with three corn dogs and a couple of waffle ice cream sandwiches in my stomach. I slammed my eyelids down and waited for the wave of nausea to pass.

Thunder rumbled in the distance. Had it rained? Was I wet?

I remembered Maida's dodge and my unceremonious exit from the saddle. Hitting the ground was crystal-clear. Things after that were a blur. I had the feeling that hikers had passed by because I thought I remembered someone talking. But that could just as easily have been a dream. The harder I thought about it, the more insistent the throbbing inside my head. I stayed still, kept my eyes closed and made myself breathe evenly. After a couple of minutes, the pounding eased.

How long had I been unconscious? I didn't have a sense of

being out for very long but I'd never lost consciousness before. How would I know?

Still reluctant to open my eyes, I listened intently. Birds seemed to be everywhere, including right above me. Where was I?

It was time to open my eyes again. This time, my vision was clear and I wasn't dizzy. I lifted my head. Surrounded by sumac canopy, I couldn't see the trail. Had I bounced right into the bushes?

This portion of the prairie was near the river-fed wetlands and probably never really dried out. No wonder I felt wet. I'd landed in a mosquito block party and if I didn't get out soon, I would be the buffet meal. Mosquitoes carry the West Nile virus and people died from West Nile every summer. Ticks carried Lyme disease. Either could make me very, very sick. I needed to get moving. Quite literally getting back on the trail could be a matter of life and death.

I started to rise. Birds scattered, the noise of their angry lift-off drowning out my scream. Easing back into a prone position, I wiggled my toes, as much as toes can wiggle when they are stuffed inside cowboy boots. My left ankle was on fire. Even if it wasn't broken, it was seriously sprained. What about the rest of me? Before I did anything I took inventory, moving first one body part and then another. My fingers and hands were fine. Everything moved with no problem. Same with both arms, although my right shoulder was stiff. OK. I would use my right leg to hoist myself upright. I gritted my teeth and rolled onto my right hip. Tears ran down my cheeks. Damn. Was it broken?

I rolled back onto my stomach and took several deep breaths. With no pressure on it, my hip reminded me of the way stereo speakers sound if you put a pillow over them. The ache was there but muffled. My ankle was another matter. I had to get the boot off. But if my ankle was broken, keeping the boot on was best. It would provide support. I forced myself to breathe again. The sweet taste of blood was on my tongue. I must have bitten my lip when I rolled onto my hip.

I thought of Maida. I didn't hear her but, left to their own devices, don't horses always return to the barn? Or was she trained to stay by her rider? Was she nearby grazing? If so, I might be able to ride back. If she was long gone, her return to the barn without me would surely signal the troops that something had happened to me.

I tried to stand up but my ankle wouldn't support me. As day faded into dusk, the mosquitoes appeared. I had to get out of the wet grass. Without a chain saw to carve my way through the thicket, I had to maneuver around the trunks. That meant crawling east before I could turn back west toward the trail.

Using the sumac trunks, I pulled myself a few inches, rested briefly, and then hauled myself forward again. Finally, nearly delirious with exertion, I made it onto a dry patch of ground east of the sumac. Mosquitoes tortured me with their buzzing as I lay still, regaining some strength. Periodically, I slapped my cheek. Blood smears covered my palm and I rubbed it against the grass.

Wet with sweat, my bangs clung to my forehead as if soaked in glue. My tongue was so thick I couldn't swallow. My determination dissolved like bouillon crystals in hot water. I was even too tired for tears.

Why didn't...? Where were...?

My eyes closed.

When I woke up, darkness shrouded me. There was little light pollution here; no streetlights with their pink sodium vapor glow tainting the night's beauty. Above, resplendent against the ebony sky, stars twinkled encouragement.

An owl hooted in the distance. Grasses rustled to my right and signaled the stirring of the nocturnal inhabitants of the preserve. Fox, raccoon, coyote. Oh great. Predators on the move. They didn't represent any real danger but their activity was a reminder. It was time to get moving if I didn't want to spend the entire night in the woods being eaten alive by bugs.

I hoisted myself into a crawling position. With a little experimentation, I discovered that if I bent my legs, keeping both ankles in the air and "walking" on my fists and knees, I could move forward. It was slow going. I stopped every few steps to brush insects from my arms. Eventually I made it to a patch of grass that stretched up the rise to the trail. I was finally out of the scrub and the trail, a ribbon of gray in the dim light, was only about ten feet to the west. After I rested a minute, reaching the trail would be my next goal.

The grass rustled again. Whatever it was, it was big. Coyote? I listened intently. It was coming right for me. To protect myself, I curled into a ball, ignoring the screaming protest from my hip.

Something pushed at me with a wet nose. The creature went away. I stayed curled up. I could hear it in the grass. After a few minutes, it was back and rammed me again – hard, like a closed fist. I stayed curled up.

It lay down next to me and shoved its nose past my elbow, burrowing toward my face. Then I was wet with slobber. The animal pulled away and let loose an ear-shattering bark that was so loud the kids on Great America's roller coasters must have heard it.

Ronig? Hallelujah! It was Ronig!

CHAPTER 12

The outside world bored into my brain like a surgeon's drill. One eye opened and I immediately closed it again. *This definitely is not heaven. Dead people don't hurt.* I remained still for moment and then opened both eyes. It was morning; the sky beyond the window baby blanket blue, midday's harsh brightness still to come.

As the nearby thrup-beep of a monitor pulsed steadily, lucidity seeped under my brain's closed door. The experiences of the night before flooded my consciousness. But with clarity of mind came a wave of nausea. My eyes squeezed shut. When it passed, I ventured a look at my surroundings.

Someone had been in to visit. A variegated philodendron in a modest brown wicker basket sat on the chest of drawers opposite the foot of my bed. Shouting its Get Well Soon message in neon green, a Mylar balloon drifted toward me. I lifted my hand to it.

Ye-ouch!

The ache in the rest of me was immediately superseded by a sharp stab in the back of my hand. My IV cord was caught on the bed railing. I reached out to release it and something grabbed my ankle, the pressure increasing as if it were in a vice. I let out another yelp. Biting my lip, I took several deep breaths, forcing bile back down into my stomach where it belonged.

Cheerful chatter drifted in from the corridor and I moved my eyes toward it. If I held still, I was only aware of a dull headache but there was no sharp punch of pain. How badly injured was I? I vaguely recalled asking myself the same question the night before. Doing a physical inventory then had not been very reassuring. It made sense to do one again.

No respirator. I was breathing without assistance. I wasn't in traction or a body cast so my hip wasn't broken. Did it hurt? I touched it.

Of course it hurts, you idiot.

Something encased my ankle. A cast? I rose up so I could see.

"Don't move again. You'll regret it."

Ian Page stood in the doorway. I turned toward him...and shrieked.

"You're pretty banged up. I'll have the nurse bring you something for the pain."

He disappeared before I could answer and returned with a petite brunette wearing a Winnie-the-Pooh smock. Suspended on a beaded chain around her neck, a pair of reading glasses bounced on her ample chest as she walked in. She handed me a little paper container. Inside lay one round white tablet.

She smiled warmly. "How do you feel?"

"Like a horse danced on me."

"Your doctor said you can have something stronger if you need it but pain killers can tear up the tummy. If you can handle the pain with just this, it'll be better in the long run."

I took the pill. She checked my pulse and my temperature. Apparently all the numbers were where they should be because she nodded and left the room without saying anything else.

Page found the controls and raised the bed so I could see without moving. I sank against the pillow.

"I fell off my horse."

"Yup." Page pulled a chair to my bedside, positioning it so he was in my line of sight. "Tell me about it."

"This is all Izzy's fault. She insisted I go for a ride. Maida got spooked and I flew through the air like Supergirl. Only without the cape. The next thing I remember, I was lying in a bunch of wet bushes and Maida was nowhere to be seen. Ronig showed up eventually and so Lori must have come, but I don't remember seeing her. And Izzy brought a cart and there was an ambulance ride. You were with me in Emergency." I looked around. "You were pretty grumpy. Did you demand a private room near the nurses' station?"

"What spooked your horse?"

"You didn't answer the question."

He smiled at me. "What spooked your horse?"

"Something charged out of the brush. Maida sidestepped left and I went off to the right." Like a slide presentation, the events replayed in my mind, one picture at a time. "I remember it in slow motion, me suspended horizontally above the trail, like I was flying. I hit the ground with my right hip. I came to in the bushes."

I yawned.

Page frowned. "That painkiller's kicking in already, isn't it?

The twanging pulses in my head dulled. My eyelids start to droop but I didn't want to sleep. There were so many questions to ask.

"Who called you?" I asked, stifling another yawn.

"I got to Bright Hope, maybe thirty minutes after you took Maida out for your ride," said Page. "I wanted to ask you some questions so I decided to stick around until you came back." He paused. "It wasn't wasted time. I chatted with Governor Blagojevich and then I watched Lori Boc work her dinosaur."

"Hmmm."

"I'll be back in a couple of hours and we can talk then."

"Hmmm. Did you say dinosaur?"

"Go to sleep."

I wasn't groggy or nauseated the next time I woke up. The IV was out of my left hand and the thrumping monitor was silent. Freedom had been bestowed on me while I slept. Lifting myself up slowly, ever so carefully, I navigated to the bathroom where I tried to clean off some of the dirt, gently wiping my face with a washcloth and scrubbing my hands. There was a shower but I wasn't able to negotiate anything that complicated at the moment. The bed was a mile away and I wanted nothing more than to return to it.

My bruised hip was on the opposite side of the bum ankle and cast so neither leg worked well. Maneuvering onto the bed took awhile. When I leaned over the mattress, my bare butt hung out of the hospital gown, flashing the nurses' station. Instinctively, my hand clutched at the fabric edges to hold them closed. My desire for propriety thwarted my efforts to heave myself up. Either I had to spend the rest of the day upright or I had to let people in the hall see my naked backside. Comfort or modesty? Releasing my hold on the gown, I hoisted myself into bed.

The room temperature hovered near zero but beads of sweat dotted my forehead. Pulling a blanket up to my shoulders, I lay still for a minute but in my relaxed state, a new sensation surfaced. As prickles beset me, I noticed dozens of red welts dotting my arms like swollen freckles. Resisting the urge to scratch off the top layer of skin, I rang for help.

It was mid-afternoon when a tap-tap at my partially closed door roused me from another nap. Jake stuck his head into the room.

"Visitors welcome?"

When people come to visit you in the hospital, you are instantly aware of how disheveled you look and how dirty you feel. My brain knew Jake wasn't looking at my messy hair or my lack of makeup but at this particular moment, my heart wished he hadn't come. Lying in muddy grass for a couple of hours was a good excuse for my appearance but we all prefer to have others see us at our best and I was a long way from that.

"You are," I lied, finger-combing my hair.

"I was here earlier but you were out like a light." He struggled unsuccessfully to hide a grin. "You snore."

"I do not. It's the drugs."

He shoved the door aside with one foot while he balanced a happy bouquet of lavender, pink and white dahlias in his hands. Pushing the basket over, he set the vase on the dresser.

"Those are stunning," I said.

"I only take partial credit. They're from Mary's garden. She cut them and I took them over to the florist for the vase and the arranging. Mary sent some cookies, too."

He looked like he wanted to hug me but wasn't sure how to do it without hurting me. After taking in the air cast on my ankle, he settled for a soft kiss on my forehead and then set a small tin on the night table.

"OK if I stay awhile? Are you watching the Cubs?"

"I started to but I fell asleep."

Jake looked up at the television and then back at me. Two red spots appeared on his cheeks and he looked away again. I wondered what he wasn't saying. Considering how delicious things had been the last time we were together, his discomfort was a surprise.

He drew a chair alongside the bed and sat down. After a minute, he sighed and took my hand. "What should I do to fix this for you?"

"There's no way you can fix my ankle." I gave him a sympathetic smile. "It will have to fix itself."

"That's not what I meant and you know it. Can I get you anything? You must need something."

"I honestly can't think of anything right now."

He was silent for several minutes after that. Stroking my hand, he watched the Cubs leave two men on before he turned to face me.

"When do you get out of here?"

"Tomorrow morning. I hope."

"I'll take you home."

"Thank you. I hadn't given any thought to that."

He gave a nod as if my response had somehow settled something and, my hand still in his, watched the game until the next commercial break.

"We'll have breakfast."

"OK."

"You'd better rest now. I'll see you tomorrow. What time?"

"I don't know. I'm sure the doctors will tell me after I see them. Of course, it's a weekend so I could be here until Monday. Shall I call you?"

Jake shook his head. "I'll be here at eight. If they haven't sprung you by then, I'll put the war paint on."

I laughed out loud. It hurt like crazy but it felt great. I reached for him and he came back to me so quickly I was wrapped in his arms before I realized it. Then he was gone.

As girls will do, I had a good cry and then spent the rest of the afternoon trying to decipher the encounter. It was a ridiculous waste of time but I really didn't have anything else to keep me occupied. The cable movie channel, which was no doubt part of my room charge, aired a professional boxing match, not a movie. I checked on the Cubs and wished I hadn't. As usual, they lost. By the end of the game, my stomach was growling. Sure that my gastro-intestinal symphony had more to do with hunger than with the Cubs, I pushed the call button.

When Page reappeared, my room was in shadow, the sky outside my window turning a mellow gold with the approach of dusk and a summer storm. The television was still on but I wasn't watching the three contestants banging their buzzers. Playing along had given me a headache and I had other, more serious activities before me. A dish of green gelatin and two packages of soda crackers had my complete attention.

"That looks appetizing," said Page. He set down his briefcase.

"How do you feel?"

"What's in there?" I looked pointedly at the floor. "You never carry a briefcase."

"Answer the question, please. How are you feeling? Have you seen a doctor this afternoon?"

"The doctor said they're keeping me one more night for observation. They think I had a concussion since I was apparently unconscious for awhile. I can go home in the morning but he recommended a day off before I go back to work."

"That doesn't look like much of a meal."

"They want to make sure this stays down before they bring me real food."

"Will it?"

"Round one did. This is round two. I was just about to beg for a hamburger."

Page opened his briefcase and lifted out a Penzler's bag. "Chicken salad on wheat, coleslaw, two cookies. Mary sends her love."

I touched the folds of the familiar brown sack. Almost as good as a hug from my mother. "Did Maida get to the barn all right? Was she hurt?"

"She got back just fine. She went right into the barn and stood quietly by her stall door waiting for someone to put her inside. We're not sure how long she stood there but boy was Chuck mad that you hadn't told him you were back. He didn't want Izzy or Dixie to think he doesn't take care of the horses so after he explained to them how he found her, cleaned her up and fed her, he told Dixie that she should fire you. Dixie didn't know what he was talking about but Izzy went absolutely crazy. She started screaming about something being wrong and I should put out an all points bulletin. Thankfully, Lori kept her head. She explained why Maida coming back without you was a big problem."

"I knew help was on the way when Ronig showed up. You told

Lori to search for me."

"Not exactly." Page sat. "It was more like she insisted I let her. She said time was critical and the sooner we got going, the sooner you'd be found."

"She needed permission to look for me?"

"Without an official request for aid, she can't call for help."

"So you asked."

"Lori had her cell phone in her hand as soon as I opened my mouth. After contacting her team, she took Ronig out of the truck, got him ready and the next thing I knew, we were looking for you. There's only one path out to the forest preserve so she and Ronig spent some time searching the hay fields along it."

"I was out on the trail. Why waste time in the fields?"

"You could have fallen off Maida on the return trip. How were we to know? Anyway, after Lori cleared the area, we got to the river trail."

"Did Nolan tell you which way to go?"

"He wasn't around. Guess he left before Maida returned." Page paused a moment. "We made our decision the old fashioned way. We flipped a coin. By that time, someone else from the search team had arrived so Lori told them to work the trail to the south."

"You weren't with Ronig when he found me. Where were you guys?"

"Behind him by a hundred yards or so."

"That far? How did you know where he was? What if he'd circled behind you?"

"After she gave him the 'go find' command, he was off ranging. That's what Lori called it. As we walked along the trail, Ronig ran from side to side in the brush."

"Lori tried to describe the process to me once."

"It was a weird ballet. Most of the time we couldn't even see him. He would come back every now and then, but he never stuck around. He wears a bell and a bright orange vest when he's working. I'd catch a glimpse of orange in the brush and sometimes I could hear the bell. Lori knew right away when Ronig caught a human scent. His whole attitude changed."

"How long before you found me? It was just after five when I left the barn and dark when Ronig got to me."

"A couple of hours, at least. After Lori and Ronig did the hay fields, she and I were on the trail for at least an hour and let me tell you, I had very unhappy feet." He lifted a foot. "Loafers are not designed for hiking. Lori was moving at a much slower pace than she would have liked just to accommodate me."

"She could have left you behind."

"No, she couldn't. I have the gun."

I closed my eyes and remembered. The rustling grass had terrified me and when Ronig first bumped me with his nose, I wasn't sure what to think. Once I realized that the night creature was Lori's dog, I had reached out to him. I wanted him to curl up next to me like Lassie or Benji, to warm and comfort me until Lori arrived. Instead, he let out a piercing, stabbing yap that I thought would lead to permanent hearing loss.

"You were crying when we got to you."

"I was relieved."

"You were afraid?"

"I was terrified."

We were both silent for a minute.

"Lori radioed that we had you but you were hurt and we'd need transport. Izzy came with a cart. Good thinking on her part. Faster and easier to get you out."

"Horse power still's the best, I guess." I pushed at my bangs. "I have only bits and pieces of memory from last night. The jostling cart, being put into the ambulance. Wanting to sleep."

"Adrenaline let down coupled with the pain." Page rubbed his forehead. "Do you remember how you ended up on the ground?

He waited quietly while I ate part of my sandwich. It gave me time to think about what had happened. What did I remember and could I trust what I recalled? Were some of my memories simply pain or drug-induced dreams?

I told him why I went for the ride, how the whole barn had stood outside to tease me, how Nolan and I had waved to Henry and that Nolan had turned south at the trail head. The first part of the ride, the quiet scenery of the forest, was a pleasant memory and I enjoyed reliving it.

After I finished the second cookie and dusted the crumbs off my hands, Page said, "This morning you said something charged at you from the brush. What was it? A deer?"

"It was definitely a person. With flapping wings."

Page scowled.

"Obi-Wan in the original Star Wars movie. He wore a brown caftan. Remember how he raised his arms to scare off the Sand People who were looting Luke's hover craft? That's what comes to mind. A dark, hooded person flapping his winged arms and making a weird noise."

"No wonder Maida bolted." He pulled out his notebook and pen. "So you think this was deliberate?"

"You know it was." Hunger satisfied, I was suddenly very tired. "But was it a bratty kid looking for a cheap thrill or was it someone specifically trying to hurt me?"

"Let's assume the latter. The next question is why would someone want to hurt you? Are we getting close to some answers?"

"You might be. I'm not." I scratched my arm. "Look, if whoever killed Frank Villano felt really threatened by me, I'd be dead myself. This had to be someone trying to get me to go away for awhile."

"Or maybe this was Frank's killer and he or she just didn't want to bring more heat down because this case is hot enough. Our bad guy must know that killing you would tell us that we're on to something."

"But if I have a riding accident, then there's no connection?"

"Exactly."

"There's something else. I didn't end up in the bushes by myself. Someone dragged me out of sight. If I had rolled there myself, I would have been on the trail side of the thicket, not the river side. Where I was...that was no accident either."

Page gave me a long look. "You must have done or said something that would call attention to yourself. What did you pick up on?"

I sat up quickly, wrenching my ankle. "I am such an idiot! Damn. Where are my clothes?"

"You're not going anywhere," said Page, a look of alarm on his face. "You're as white as your sheets."

"Check my pants pockets!"

Searching the dresser, he found my mud-caked jeans in the bottom drawer. As he pulled them out, I realized I should have given Jake my key and asked him to bring me some clean clothes. Page saw my expression.

"Liz is over at your place getting you something clean to wear. I got chewed out but good for not bringing you stuff this morning." He blushed. "I thought it would be better if she did it."

"Thank you. Now check the pockets."

Page slipped his hand into each one, thoroughly examining even the corners. "Nothing. What was I supposed to find?"

"A shell casing."

Page put my jeans back in the drawer and went into the bathroom to wash his hands. When he had returned to his chair, I told him about finding the casing, how I had wrapped it in tissue and then slipped it into my pocket.

"Someone saw you do it."

"But there wasn't anyone with me except Dixie."

"Obviously there was. Or Dixie is our suspect. At least now we know why Obi Wan made an appearance. He, or she, got what they wanted. The shell casing." He tapped his pad with the pen several times. "I'll bet you that casing is connected to Frank Villano."

"I'm not taking that bet. I'm sure you're right."

A bolt of lightning cut through the sky illuminating storm clouds. Thunder rumbled outside my window.

Page activated his Nextel. "Liz, you on the road?"

"I'm about ten minutes from the hospital. Hi, Kyle. Do you need food?"

"She's been fed. I picked up Penzler's." He looked at me. "Need anything besides clothes?"

I shook my head.

"We're good here. Drive carefully."

"I will."

She clicked off. Page went to the window.

"It's raining in sheets. Wish I'd known about the shell casing sooner."

"Would that have made a difference? I only saw the one."

"Where, exactly, did you find it?"

"In the ruts by the shed."

"What ruts?"

I shrugged. "The fire truck ruts. The treads on the tires squished the mud and that exposed the casing?"

As another roar of thunder rattled the windows, he said, "This rain will wash stuff away but it may also unearth new evidence. I'll have the techs go out there tomorrow with metal detectors and check the area again, just in case. Show me exactly where you found that shell."

He drew a rough map of the area behind the barn, an oval representing the manure pile and three squares for the burned garage, the shed and the farmhouse. Then he handed me the pad and pencil.

"Show me."

I did and handed it back. "X marks the spot."

"Cute." He studied the drawing for a minute. "And the shell was down inside one of the ruts?"

"Yes."

"How did you spot it?"

"The sun. Dixie was pacing off a possible turn out area and a shiny thing caught my eye. At first, I thought it was a coin."

"And then you picked it up. Putting your fingerprints on it."

"Sorry but I didn't want Dixie to see what it was. If I'd used a twig like they do on television, it would have been pretty obvious what I'd found. Besides, it was full of mud. I couldn't have stuck a twig in it even if I'd thought of that."

Page stared at the map. "How far down in the rut was the casing?"

I reached for the pad and he passed it to me.

"Like this," I said, doing my best to put two-dimensional form to a recollection. I drew the rut pattern, a series of spikes reminiscent of the blips on a heart monitor, and then put an X where the casing had been, inside and near the top of one of the ridges.

Returning the notebook, I said, "Does that make sense?"

Page looked at it for a solid minute. "It's not what I expected. You didn't draw crisscrosses like tire tread. So what you saw wasn't tire tread. It was track tread. Like from a bulldozer." He flipped the page to my first drawing. More silence. "And you placed this X north of the garage, near the shed. The fire trucks weren't up there. They came and went around the south side of the barn." He went quiet again. "No fire engine tire made those impressions."

"If that's track tread, where's the equipment that put it there?"

"You were out there. Did you see any?"

"Nothing but the tractor and the manure spreader. They both have tires."

We didn't have time to consider other possibilities because Liz Page arrived. She kissed her husband, then examined my face closely.

"You don't look too bad but you sure look tired." She turned to Page. "You've been questioning her, haven't you?"

"Of course."

"Well, that's enough of that. I'm going to help her get cleaned up and then she's getting some rest."

I started to protest but Liz held up her hand.

"You two can talk more tomorrow." She pointed at her husband. "You're going home," then turning her index finger toward me, "and you're going to take a shower and go to sleep."

She laid clean clothes in an empty dresser drawer, put a small suitcase in the closet and then lined up toiletries on the bathroom sink like plastic soldiers. After turning off the television, Liz pushed her husband out the door. Then she helped me into the shower stall to wash off the events of the previous night while an aide put clean sheets on the bed. I had to admire her loving efficiency. Weeks from now, over a fabulous dinner, she would want all the details. But for now, she focused on healing. Later, as I yawned myself to sleep, I was thankful for both sides of my friend.

The next morning, I was up before the sun, pestering the nurses about when the doctor would arrive to release me. There isn't much to do in a hospital at five in the morning so, after I got a garbage bag from the nurse's aide and stuffed my dirty clothes into it, I was ready to leave. The confines of modern medicine had held me long enough. Although grateful for the care I had received, I was past ready to go home. The doctor finally appeared, pronounced me fit and sprang me just before eight.

While I received continuing care instructions and signed my financial life away at the desk, Jake carried my belongings out to his car. The aide wheeled me to the hospital entrance and I was officially released.

The hospital breakfast, delivered at seven, consisted of soupy oatmeal, orange juice and skim milk; all perfect for someone with a bad stomach or no teeth. Since neither applied to me, I subsisted on the last of Mary's cookies. By the time Jake pulled to a stop in the Egg Harbor parking lot, I was ravenous. Thankfully, we were ahead of the post-church stampede. My being in a cast probably helped a bit, too, because we were seated after just a ten-minute wait, unheard of for any popular restaurant on a Sunday morning.

"How you doing?" he asked after the waiter left us. "You look exhausted."

"Every time I nod off, I roll onto my right side and my hip wakes me up."

"Bet you're glad to be out of the hospital."

"For now. When I get the bill, I'll probably have a heart attack and have to go back."

Jake looked stricken. "You don't have any insurance, do you?"

"I just signed a new policy with Nolan Grinnell's company. He calls it 'hit by a bus' insurance. The only way to make it affordable was to have a huge deductible. I haven't had time to set up one of those health care savings account things and the policy won't cover anything but major expenses."

"Like falling off a horse."

"Yeah, like falling off a horse."

He leaned in and lowered his voice. "Seriously, how much is this going to cost you?"

"I have no idea. I don't want to think about it."

He snapped his fingers. "You're OK. This was worker's comp."

"How do you figure that?"

"You were at work when the accident happened."

"No, I wasn't. I was on a trail riding a horse."

"But it was your employer's horse and you wouldn't have been on that horse if Izzy hadn't insisted."

"But it was on my time."

Jake thought about that. "But Izzy insisted. She told me that she said it would be good for your relationships with the clients."

"You forget. I'm an independent contractor. I don't think I get worker's comp. And even if I did, I wouldn't file. Not under these circumstances. It wouldn't be right."

"OK, OK." He sounded like a kid who had been ordered to clean his room because he was grounded if he didn't. "I agree with you but I thought it was worth exploring."

I wished he hadn't brought it up. The bill was going to be in the thousands. I had a standard eighty-twenty policy with a four thousand dollar deductible. That meant I paid four thousand plus at least twenty percent of the balance. It was going to be a lot of money. Oh well. The Altima would just have to hold out another couple of years. The money put aside for a new used car was now earmarked for the hospital... and the doctor... and the lab.

Our meal, when it came, was absolutely delicious. Over three-egg Denver omelets with pancakes, Jake and I talked about his upcoming trip to the reservation and his on-going desire to know more about his Native American heritage. He was paying the bill when I remembered.

"My car."

"What about it?"

"It's at the barn. How do I get to work on Tuesday?"

"I'll take you."

"Maybe we should go get it now?"

"You're going home. You're yawning. No way you're ready to drive."

"Tomorrow then."

"Can't. Tied up all day. Maybe tomorrow night. We'll see but worst case, I'll take you to work on Tuesday morning."

The restaurant was near my townhouse and it was barely ten minutes later when Jake turned onto my street.

"Damn," he said, scowling.

Ian Page was parked in front.

CHAPTER 13

S eeing Page was a surprise. Somehow I thought further
questioning would wait. Sunday is supposed to be a day
of rest and after my heavy breakfast, I could barely keep
my eyes open.

Although polite, Jake was as prickly as a thistle when Page
followed us through my front door As soon as I was safely
ensconced in my recliner, my ankle on a pillow, Jake said, "I'll check
the refrigerator while you two talk. You probably need some
things."

Page watched him leave the room. "I upset your boyfriend."

"He thinks your questions will keep me from resting."

"Can't stay that long. I just wanted you to know that the
evidence techs are at the farm with metal detectors." He went to the
door. "I gotta get home. You take care of yourself. Bolt the door
behind me."

Extricating myself from the chair, I gimped to the door and
flipped the dead bolt into place as soon as Page was gone. When I
turned around, Jake was standing next to my empty chair, concern
clouding his eyes.

"You can't stay down for five minutes." He pointed to the
chair. "That ankle is supposed to be elevated."

"I was being polite."

"He would have excused your lack of manners"

"He told me to bolt the door."

"You know, maybe, just maybe, if you kept your nose out of

police investigations, you wouldn't have to deadbolt the door."

"That's not fair. Up until Friday, my nose wasn't anywhere but on my face. Other than normal curiosity, I had no interest in their investigation."

Jake snorted. "Sounds like you cracked your skull instead of your ankle. You're damn lucky you're not dead. Someone scared your horse on purpose and I don't think they were all that worried about what happened to you. I went out and looked at the spot. You didn't end up in that sumac by accident."

"It was kids," I said.

"Yeah, right. And I just won the lottery."

"You don't gamble."

"My point exactly."

No wonder he looked so solemn. He knew I had help falling off Maida and that someone dragged or rolled me into the shrubs. Did that explain his insistence on bringing me home? Come to think of it, Page could have telephoned me about the metal detector search.

We were silent for several moments, staring at each other. Finally, Jake came toward me, opened his arms and invited me into them. For a brief time, the world stopped, murderers were of no concern and nothing on my body hurt.

He gently turned me around so I faced the Indian medicine wheel he had given me as a house-warming gift. It was almost two feet in diameter, quartered by two crossed arrows and adorned with a leather dream catcher and a carved wooden peace pipe. Crafted by one of the Plains Indian tribes, I first saw it hanging in his work cubicle. Now it hung over my fireplace.

"The medicine wheel is about the choices we make," he said. "How one decision leads to another and then to another. It represents the cycles of nature and the flow of life. All things are interconnected and each affects the other."

"May the Force be with you."

"Sort of." He squeezed my shoulders. "Each tribe brings its own look and interpretation to it. Our wheel is more colorful but I liked the simplicity of this one the minute I saw it. Like most people, I used to think medicine wheels ward off evil spirits but that's really not it at all. The wheel is a teaching device. It tells us that different groups are part of the whole, that all directions lead back to the beginning, that there is always a new path open to us."

"Sounds mystical."

"All of life is mystical." Jake wrapped his arms around me, pressing my back to his chest. "We learn from studying the wheel that a question begets an answer that only begs another question."

He paused and the silence expanded until I heard his heart beating. When he spoke again, his words made me shiver.

"Something you did set you on a path. Someone else was on a path because of a decision he or she made. You collided." Jake pointed to the wheel, his index finger following an arrow shaft to a junction with the outside rim. He paused. "Now another decision will change your direction and send you somewhere else. Your decision may separate you from this person or keep you on the same road." His finger led my eyes around to the other arrow. "You must consider your next move very carefully."

"You want me to stay away from the investigation."

"I don't think that's possible now. No, what I want is for you to consider what has happened and think about what you will do next, how it will impact the others involved. Look at the wheel. There are no breaks in it and no matter which way you go, whether right or left, you come back to the beginning."

He let that settle for a moment before he said, "Whoever spooked Maida did not kill you, but they could have. They made a choice. Will you be as lucky if there is another encounter with this person?"

"That's why Ian told me to deadbolt the door? That's why you're hanging around this morning? You two don't think I'm safe in my own home?"

"I don't know what he thinks but I'd say you're all right. For now. If you were supposed to be dead, you would be. Like I said, the next move is yours and what you do will certainly influence someone else's behavior."

I tried to go over it in my mind, recalling who might have seen me pick up the casing. It didn't take long to realize that anyone could have watched me but no one could have known what I'd found unless they already suspected there was something there to be discovered. Or maybe the reason I wasn't dead was that the person, whoever he or she was, merely wanted to learn for themselves what I'd found and when they took it from me, they thought that ended the matter. Even though I would tell the police about the casing, there was no proof and no evidence.

Jake didn't let me spend much time mulling it over. After making me take a pain pill, he left so I could rest. Dutifully throwing the deadbolt, I returned to my recliner to snooze rather than going to bed. The chair kept me properly positioned; ankle elevated and hyper-sensitive hip straight. I drifted into a drug-induced dreamless sleep.

The doorbell woke me several hours later. Jake was on my doorstep with Sunset grocery bags in his arms. He bustled around the kitchen while I stood in the doorway watching him put canned goods in the cupboards and load up the refrigerator with cheese, vegetables and fruit. Then he did the one thing guaranteed to make me truly happy. He didn't fuss; he didn't try to make it all better. He kissed me softly, made sure his cell number was programmed into my phone and – he left.

In my experience, people who are managers of time or staff or projects in their business lives usually attempt to control the people and the events in their personal lives. It has nothing to do with whether that manager is in a glass tower executive suite or in an auto body shop. If they're in charge of their work life, they want power over their love life as well.

How did he know that that wasn't a good tactic with me? Had I told him that I prefer to be alone when I'm sick? Had he been taught to be so sensitive to others or was it instinctive?

Jake Prince wasn't perfect. I certainly wasn't either. Would our foibles screw things up or bring us closer together? I looked up at the medicine wheel but didn't see any answers. Maybe a Crazy Eight ball would have some.

After a light supper of apple slices and peanut butter, I returned to my recliner and drifted off, my sleep punctuated by dreams that would have delighted Jung and Freud. When I awoke the next morning, I was so stiff I could hardly toddle to the bathroom. A long hot bath, with my ankle carefully propped on the tub ledge, helped but the doctor had been right. My body needed a day off.

After I joyfully discovered that crop pants were designed for people in ankle casts, I hobbled into the kitchen for some tea and returned to my chair. It was time to telephone my mother.

The problem with long distance family is the lack of support when you need it. The benefit of long distance family is they can't breathe down your neck or intrude when you don't want them around. Mom was far enough away to make hovering inconvenient but she was close enough to help out during emergencies. I debated how much to tell her about my injuries. My ankle was in a walking air cast. The doctor had told me that the hairline fracture was minor and would heal quickly. The only reason I was in a cast at all was to protect the ankle from possible further damage.

Typical Mom, the first question she asked was if the horse had been injured.

"Maida is fine, Mom." I paused. "I spent the night in the hospital though."

"I'll be there in three hours," she said. "I'll just call your father and then I'll come."

"That's not necessary. They only kept me for observation."

"Of course it's necessary. Observation means they were worried about something, probably a head injury."

"Look, I'm going back to work tomorrow. I won't even be here for you to fuss over."

She let out a heavy sigh. "We worry about you, you know."

"I know."

"We love you."

"I love you, too."

Mom was rather pragmatic about the whole thing once I convinced her that I was going to live. By the time we finished our conversation, the mail had arrived and so had lunchtime.

I felt pretty good after lunch and since my work ethic forbade me any more leisure time in the recliner, I paid some bills and stared at my computer trying to decide how to invoice Duran Building for the previous week. The advantage to being on a company payroll is that you simply report your hours and someone else decides whether or not you are entitled to sick pay. As an independent contractor, I knew I wasn't going to get sick pay but I wasn't sure when my work time ended and my personal time started. I finally decided not to bill Duran for the time I spent with Ian Page on my patio. Although the conversation would be considered work-related if it had occurred at Bright Hope, I didn't want Ed Duran to know about it. And, as I had explained to Jake over breakfast, the ride and its aftermath were on my time as well.

By mid-afternoon, northern Illinois was as steamy as a rice cooker. My patio, sheltered by mature trees, was reasonably comfortable however. Lying on the chaise, my ankle propped up on cushions, I leaned back and closed my eyes. Next door, bumblebees buzzed around Mrs. Sims' purple cornflowers and sparrows splashed in the birdbath nestled between two clumps of black-eyed Susans.

"Excuse me, excuse me," called a high-pitched voice. "Are you sleeping?"

Not anymore.

I roused myself from the nap that had enfolded me, turned and saw Mrs. Sims standing at the edge of her patio. Slightly stooped, she used a cane to steady herself but only her legs were wobbly. Blue eyes, under carefully coiffed, gun-metal gray hair, reflected a sharp and active mind. Today, she had on a flour-smudged apron over a light-weight pink cotton dress and the yeasty aroma of freshly baked bread drifted out her patio door. Had she not roused me, the smell would have.

"I'm awake." I waved to prove it. "How are you?"

"Just fine, honey. How you doing? I'm sorry if I woke you. I couldn't tell if your eyes were closed or not. Do you have a minute? I would like to talk to you about something."

"Sure. I'll come over."

"You will do no such thing. You just sit right where you are. I will come to you."

And she did. She even brought her own iced tea and a small plate of butter cookies. Taking a moment to arrange herself, she hung her cane on the arm of the chair and smoothed her apron.

I sat up. Not only could I see her better from that position, it was easier to reach the cookies.

"How are you, first of all?" she asked, examining my cast closely. "You know, sometimes technology takes all the fun out of things. If you have to wear a cast, at least it should be one people can sign."

I didn't tell her how thankful I was for the technology that kept half a ton of plaster off my leg. As annoying as it was, I couldn't imagine lugging around one of the old style casts.

Mrs. Sims' smile pushed her wrinkles up toward her eyes. "Your policeman friend was here. Were you in a car accident?"

"I fell off my horse."

"I'm so sorry. Please tell me it wasn't connected to that awful skeleton thing. You and your policeman friend were out here the other afternoon. I know he's working the stable case and you two were nose to nose about something. I see him on TV. He's never the one doing the talking but he's always there, standing in the background. Doesn't look like he likes being on television much."

"He doesn't. They make him attend the high-profile press conferences so the public sees lots of manpower."

"Yes. Well, perception is everything, isn't it?" She leaned forward. "So he was here about that case, wasn't he?"

"Yes. I work at Bright Hope."

"You know, I don't usually pay much attention to the news but this story is different. Ed Duran got his start working for a friend of my late husband's."

I struggled to swallow the tea in my mouth. Of all the things I was prepared to hear Mrs. Sims say, that wasn't one of them.

"Really? That must have been years ago."

"Oh, it was. Ed wasn't married to Brisa's mother yet." Mrs. Sims pushed the cookie plate closer to me. "Don't hurt yourself straining, honey."

"So he had quit the gang?"

"He was out of jail but I don't think he was out of the gang. I remember my husband saying his friend was impressed with Ed's work but he was worried about the gang causing problems for the business."

"What happened?"

"Nothing. Ed got married, went out on his own."

I studied her face. "But?"

"There were rumors. Lots and lots of rumors. I shouldn't repeat them."

"Yes, you should." I tried to be receptive but not too eager. "I've heard drug money was the seed for his business."

"That was one rumor. It might be true. Who knows? After Ed left, my husband's friend heard that the reason there'd been no gang problems was that Ed killed off anyone who threatened him or anyone around him."

I thought about that. "That doesn't fit the Ed Duran I know. I've seen him get angry but he didn't lose his temper. "

"True or not, that follows Ed wherever he goes. His old tattoo doesn't help his cause. People say he had to have a special one to belong to the gang."

"There's no tattoo now. He had it removed. You know, some people don't like body art of any kind and it doesn't matter whether it's a dagger or a flower."

Mrs. Sims' eyes twinkled. "I've always fancied a little butterfly, right about here." She touched her left hip. "In my day, ladies did not wear tattoos."

I didn't want to think about Mrs. Sims' secret desires so I switched the topic back to Duran's past. "I understand Ed was very happy with Brisa's mother."

"Oh yes. She was the reason he worked so hard. It's sad she died so young."

"Cancer, wasn't it?"

"He nursed her himself."

"That sounds more like the Ed Duran I know. Her death must have been hard on Brisa."

"His angel child. He would do anything for her. I hear Brisa will have a new mother soon. Ed's going to propose to the woman who trains the horses. He's been in love with her for quite awhile."

"Really? Where did you hear that? From your husband's friend?"

"Heavens no. He's been dead almost as long as my William. I'm pretty sure I heard it at church from Pete Penzler."

I stared at her.

"You look so surprised. Lake County is still just a bunch of small towns and you know everyone tells the Penzlers everything. They're much better than the newspaper."

She took hold of her cane, pushed herself upright and then sat again. "Goodness, I am forgetting why I came over in the first place." She pulled an envelope from her apron pocket and thrust it at me. "You have read this, haven't you?"

I took the envelope from her, withdrew the contents and skimmed through a letter from the homeowners' association board of directors about a special assessment for sealing the driveways.

"Is there a problem?"

Mrs. Sims grimaced. "You bet there is. Why do they need a special assessment? There's supposed to be money saved up for things like this."

I'd paid no attention at all to the letter when it came. Driveway sealant ranked near the bottom of the things I wanted to think about. If I needed to worry about something besides murder, I had hospital bills coming soon. The special assessment was just one more check to write.

"I'll get to the point." Mrs. Sims looked me squarely in the face and pointed at my cast. "That is not a good enough excuse to miss the association meeting. You simply must come. We have to start asking questions about how that board is spending our money."

"I haven't been to any of the meetings so I don't have any background on the issues. You go and tell me all about it. I'll vote whatever way you tell me to."

She looked disappointed. "It's your duty to get involved. If you live in an association, you have to help govern it. You think about it and let me know. We have a couple of hours before the meeting and it would be worth a loaf or two of homemade bread if you'd drive. If you're feeling up to it of course."

"I'm afraid I can't take you, whether I feel up to it or not. I don't have a car."

She winked. "No problem. We'll take mine."

Mission accomplished, Mrs. Sims took up her cane and shuffled back to her place, leaving me with another headache and an awful lot on my mind. Ed Duran planned to marry Dixie? What else was in Ed Duran's plans and did Dixie know about them? Was Equestrian Escapades more than a passing fancy? Was that why the arbor had been trimmed back? What exactly had Pete heard and from whom had he heard it?

For a moment, I considered calling Pete and asking him those questions but then I remembered what Jake had said about considering my actions. If talking to Pete would set someone off, Page should be the one doing it. I dialed his cell and left him a voice mail.

That decision was some sort of magic tonic because I drifted off to sleep and awoke feeling renewed. There was no throbbing in my head or ankle. I contemplated the homeowners' meeting. Should I go? Was I up to it? I decided I was and called Mrs. Sims.

The meeting was held monthly in one of the conference rooms at the public library. I could almost walk the mile and a half but two major highways ran between my townhouse development and the library so if I did, I would be road kill within minutes. I drove Mrs. Sims' dusty old Buick and parked in the handicapped spot courtesy of the special plates on her car.

When we entered the conference room, three men and two women were seated behind tables at the front of the room. No one was in the audience section. I propped the cast on a chair in front of me as Mrs. Sims shuffled off to chat with the women.

After exchanging a few words with her, a man came over, flipped one of the chairs in the row in front of me and sat down. He had a teddy bear quality, chubby but huggable, a look accentuated by big dark eyes, large ears and a great smile filled with the teeth one sees in whitening toothpaste commercial. He extended a hand.

"Greg Lacey. Mrs. Sims tells me you're Kyle Shannon. Glad to meet you."

I took his hand. His palm was dry and my fingers were intact when he released me. I'd guessed correctly about the mustache. It was neat but thick. He huffed in person, too.

"Are you the accountant for Cedar Creek?" I asked.

"I'm your board treasurer."

"No kidding. You're a neighbor?"

"I rent the unit out right now. When my wife and I retire, we plan to move in." He pointed at my cast. "What the heck happened to you?"

"I fell off a horse."

"No kidding? So you're at Bright Hope? Guess your temp service was right not to take the work order." He paused briefly. "Are you involved in that skeleton thing?"

"Not by choice. Say, can you answer a question for me? What makes a person switch accountants?"

"That's like asking what makes people switch doctors. There are lots of reasons. I'd say the biggest is that the existing accountant gave the client bad news and the client wants a second opinion."

"Like when your mother said no so you went to your father to get a yes."

"Exactly like that. Why? You planning to leave so soon? I haven't done anything for you yet."

I laughed. "No. I heard Ed Duran switched the farm accounting to you and I thought it was a small world. Then I wondered why he made the change."

Lacey didn't respond.

"You can't talk about it, I know. But I have a question I think you can answer. If I have a business and someone steals my tractor and the insurance pays off on the claim, is the insurance money taxed?

"Nope."

"That's very interesting. Thanks."

One of the men banged a gavel, Lacey joined his fellow board members and the meeting got under way. Mrs. Sims sat next to me and together we listened as the board reviewed various bids and discussed the action they wanted to take to seal the driveways. For the benefit of the few homeowners in the audience, Lacey explained that the rising price of oil-based products had increased the cost of driveway sealant substantially. All the contractors had re-bid the project at a higher price and that was the reason they didn't have enough funds. They also explained that they were using the small special assessment to avoid dipping into the reserve fund that was earmarked for new siding.

"I did a bit of sleuthing for you," said Mrs. Sims as we walked out to her car after the meeting. "Ethel's the secretary of the board. The one in the yellow dress?"

I nodded while I concentrated on getting behind the wheel.

"Ethel's daughter works for the village police department."

I started the car.

"Ed Duran had a long talk with the police today and he went there himself. He wasn't brought in."

I didn't put the car in gear. "He talked to the Lincolnshire police?"

"He went into the sheriff's office in Waukegan. Ethel's daughter doesn't know what was said but she told me that after he left, there was a lot of activity."

"I'll bet." I wondered what, if anything, Ian Page knew about it.

"What do you suppose he told them? Do you think he confessed?"

I pulled onto Half Day Road and headed for home. "If he had, he wouldn't have been allowed to leave the station."

During the night, the humidity evaporated like my paycheck during the holidays. The oppressively hot weather was gone and, according to the weathermen, we would have a day or two of perfect temperatures before the next wave of hurricane-spawned clamminess floated up from the Gulf States.

Sleep was still elusive. My hip didn't bother me much unless I touched it; however my ankle cast was beyond frustrating. I spent the night shifting from one uncomfortable position to another. At five, I gave up, got up and had coffee on the patio.

Sitting quietly invites contemplation. The chipping cardinal, the rustle of birch leaves, the distance hum of increasing traffic. Yet, no matter how hard I tried to focus on the sounds of dawn and the gray sky dissolving into purple and blue, I wondered what Ed Duran had told the police. Inside, the medicine wheel, barely visible against the dark wall, haunted me. Ed Duran had chosen a course. What had he set in motion?

CHAPTER 14

When Jake picked me up the next morning, I filled him in on the homeowners' association meeting but I didn't tell him I'd been mentally hashing over the Bright Hope case. So, as I sipped the gunpowder green tea he brought for me from Caribou Coffee and listened to the morning news on the radio, I felt a twinge of guilt.

"Are you sure you feel all right?"

His question pulled me from my thoughts. "I feel fine."

"No residual strain from your evening?"

"None. You think I should have stayed home last night and rested."

"At least you picked an activity that involved sitting."

"I put my cast up on a chair."

Jake smiled. His teeth matched the pearl snaps on his denim shirt. No big time meetings today. He was in black jeans.

"You be careful," he said as we approached Bright Hope. "And don't overdo on that ankle."

It was a bit before seven when Jake dropped me off and sped off so he could get to work on time. Now, as I shooed Oscar away and unlocked the door to the lounge, I thought about possible "persons of interest," the current and politically-correct term for suspects. No matter the label, someone connected to Bright Hope had put me in the hospital and I was determined to be on guard.

Inside, sunlight ladders stretched from the desk to the window. Dust particles floated up and down the steps for a moment before I pushed the sash up and let in the outside.

From the distant clank and clatter, I knew Chuck and Jorge were somewhere in the barn. I began my own chores by starting the coffee maker. I had just turned it on when the chug of a diesel engine reached my ears, followed by Izzy's staccato voice. She bounced into the lounge, snapped her cell phone closed and then stopped suddenly.

"What are you doing here so early?" She stepped forward and took a close look at me. "You shouldn't be here at all, should you? How's the ankle?"

"In a cast."

"Smart ass." She looked me in the eye. "You didn't take any time off."

"I took yesterday off. That's all the doctor said I had to take. I promise I'm fine."

"You were really out of it the other night. Do you remember anything about what happened?"

"Bits and pieces."

"You didn't answer my question. Why are you in so early?"

"My car was here. Jake brought me."

"Oh yeah. He called about it." Izzy poured a mug of coffee. "Mom will be here any minute. I tried to get her to sleep in but no luck."

"Is she sick?"

"She was out late last night rescuing another horse. Baby animals are so cute everyone loves them. But then they grow up and they're not so cute and they require a lot of care. People are so selfish. They take no responsibility for the animals they have. They just dump them."

"How do you dump a horse?"

"Let it loose on the highway."

I felt my eyebrows go up. What people will do continues to astound me.

"Good morning." Dixie came into the office and glared at me. "You should be at home in bed. What are you doing here?"

"Leave her alone, Mom. She promised me she's OK."

Dixie went to the desk. "Do I need a doctor's release or something?"

"I don't think so."

"Well, it's good to see you. I can sure use the coffee this morning." She paused and then looked at her daughter. "The final arrangements are made with the funeral home. We can have the service whenever you feel up to it. How about next Monday? If I notify family today that gives them almost a week to get here."

A cloud passed over Izzy's face and blocked out the sun that had been shining there. Her bottom lip trembled. She set her coffee mug down hard, the brown liquid slopping over the rim.

"How could you do that? How can we expect Dad to rest in peace with his murderer still lose?"

Izzy stormed from the office and Dixie looked at me. She had just aged ten years.

"I suppose some of that is my fault. My little shrine probably didn't help matters. I was so wrapped up in my own grief I wasn't paying attention to hers. She was giving off distress signals and I ignored them." She paused and looked at the mantle. "After Frank disappeared, Izzy took to wearing that awful knife. If they ever catch the guy that killed her father, I don't know what she'll do."

Dixie headed to the riding ring and I followed her outside like a peg-legged pirate. The barn didn't officially open for two hours and I wanted to watch her work a mare I had never seen out of the stall.. Training horses appeared to be the same as training oneself. Lots of repetition coupled with love and patience.

As I approached the riding ring, Chuck turned the horse over to Dixie and went into the arena. I leaned on the fence, putting all my weight on my good foot. Dixie placed herself in the center of the ring and started the horse circling counter-clockwise at a walk.

As the horse went around her, Dixie let out more lunge line until the horse was about ten feet from her. After the mare had walked around her several times, Dixie clucked and the horse picked up speed, trotting in circles with Dixie in the center. Ten rotations later, she slowed the mare to a stop, then turned the horse so the circles would be in a clockwise direction. She was just about to start when we heard shrieking. Moments later, Chuck, shouting in Polish, stumbled outside, waving his arms frantically.

Dixie tied the horse to the fence and hurried toward him. I followed; hop skipping as quickly as I could, cutting across the arena and into the aisle on the south side of the barn.

The door to Sunny's stall was open. Izzy, on her knees before it, held herself, rocking back and forth, gasping convulsively.

Dixie hung back, almost as if she knew what she would see. I moved cautiously around her to Izzy. I wanted to squat down, get to her eye level but my cast made that impossible. I took her biceps in my hands and lifted up. She rose without resistance.

Dixie advanced. "What's in there?"

I turned Izzy toward her, blocking her path. One glimpse of the grim scene was all I could stand and I already knew that picture would be in my head forever. No reason for her to be haunted by it too. The horror on Izzy's face told the story.

I pushed the stall door into place with my elbow and then herded both women ahead of me through the arena. About half way to the lounge, Izzy stopped suddenly, bent over and retched. As she coughed and cried, I turned away, suppressing my own gag reflex. Finally spent, Izzy straightened and, with her leaning heavily on her mother, we made it back to the lounge.

As soon as Dixie and Izzy collapsed onto the sofa, I hurried into the office and pulled my cell phone from my purse. I shook so badly I could barely press Page's speed dial number on the keypad. He didn't answer. I sent a 9-1-1 page to him and then dialed Doc Lemmer's cell phone number. Sunny's legs were covered with blood and there was no way to know if any of it had been his. Finally, I dialed 9-1-1.

It took a few minutes but eventually the local dispatcher figured out what I was trying to tell her. She wanted me to stay on the line but when my cell phone rang, I hung up

"Ed Duran. Dead."

I didn't wait for a response. Clapping my cell shut, I hobbled quickly to the restroom and promptly lost my breakfast as the abdominal earthquake hit. The last time I was this sick I was eighteen and had just polished off one too many vodka and Cokes at my first frat party. Now, as another spasm washed over me, I thought of Ed Duran and would have traded almost anything to be this sick because of a hangover.

Approaching sirens blared. My stomach still roiled and my knees quaked. I wanted to be sick again but there wasn't anything left and I didn't have time. Additional upchucking would have to wait.

I stumbled across the arena sand to stand in the open doorway where I could be seen. Two sheriff's squads bounced into the parking lot and skidded to a stop. One of the officers hurried toward me. His lips were moving. Death's stench remained in my nostrils. When I opened my mouth to talk, I choked. Finally, I gave up and just pointed at the south door.

Pulling his weapon, the deputy proceeded slowly through the screen door and into the stall aisle. The second officer told me to stay put, undid the strap on her holster and moved cautiously into the arena.

I leaned against the door jam and looked beyond the flashing lights. The brown mare was still tied, although she had stretched the lead line to the breaking point. Somehow she had put her head between the two bottom rails and now craned her neck to reach the grass inches beyond her nose. Birds lined one of the branches above her head, chirping encouragement. If she moved to the left just a foot, the line would relax and her wish would be granted.

Trucks rumbled down the road, their brakes screeching as they yielded for the ambulance. A bicyclist nearly put himself in the ditch as he strained for an extra look at the squad cars' flashing lights. Making the sign of the cross, he regained control of the bike and pedaled swiftly away. Was he thanking God that he hadn't ridden into the gully or that he didn't need the ambulance?

Cars with multiple antennas rolled into the parking lot behind the ambulance, gravel crunching under the tires. The occupants called to one another as they exited their vehicles and extracted equipment from their trunks.

"Kyle!"

I concentrated on Page the way a bad swimmer focuses on the beach when they've gone out too far.

"Sunny." That was all I could get out.

He sprinted past me into the arena. I was by myself again, but not alone. An officer lifted a giant roll of yellow plastic tape from his trunk. Another took the loose end and the two men tied it to fence posts and shrubs, cordoning off Bright Hope.

Closing my eyes, I thought of the medicine wheel. Round and round we go. Jake had cautioned me to be careful, that my next move could have consequences. How could I have caused this? I had been home, convalescing. Why did I feel like this was my fault?

"Go inside." Page stood next to me. "Get out of the sun. I'll be in soon to talk to you."

Nodding in assent, I trudged through the arena and went to the office. Dixie and Izzy were still huddled together, their arms around one another, Izzy as gray as an old sheet. Dixie looked up at me when I entered the lounge.

"What did she see?" She stroked her daughter's head. "She keeps mumbling about Ed. I don't understand."

"He's dead, Dixie. I'm sorry." I looked pointedly at Izzy. "I think that's all I should say right now."

Beyond the window pane, Chuck stood under the oak tree talking to a man taking pictures of his pants legs. Bright Hope was a crime scene again.

Time to make a fresh pot of coffee.

Lately it seemed that whenever there was a crisis, I made coffee. As I measured out the grounds, the medicine wheel came to mind again and I remembered Jake saying each choice we make triggers a decision in someone else. What action had caused this violent reaction?

Ed buying Foggy? Ed giving charge of the new place to Chuck instead of Henry? How did they feel about that? Was it a promotion or a demotion? The bidding against Sal? And what about Mrs. Sims' revelation? Had Ed really thought about marrying Dixie? Had he been that serious about Equestrian Escapades? About her? I looked at Dixie and Izzy. How did they feel about it all?

Page came through the screen door and squatted before Dixie and Izzy. "I am very sorry for your loss. Do you know where we can find Brisa?"

Dixie shook her head. "You tried her cell phone?"

"I left a message asking her to call me." He looked at me. "In there."

I followed him into the office and pointed at the open pass-through as he closed the door behind us.

He nodded and whispered, "No pun intended but this is horse shit! Please tell me you don't think it was an accident. It's too frickin' neat!"

I kept my voice down. "There's something you should know that I kept forgetting to tell you." I explained how Sunny had charged me and told him about the leather strap Izzy found in his stall. "This was no accident. Poor Sunny was set up."

"That's some serious premeditation."

Preparation…forethought…planning.

I grabbed the desk calendar. "The thing with Sunny happened

before Frank was found. Two weeks ago. Whoever killed Ed was already planning it."

"God, what a mess!" said Page, writing furiously, "Should be an interesting autopsy. Who was here this morning?"

"Dixie and Izzy, of course. Chuck was banging around in the back of the barn, feeding or mucking stalls."

"Are you sure it was Chuck? Exactly what did you hear?"

I gripped the edge of the desk to steady myself. "You think the noises I heard could have been Ed getting beat to death?"

"Relax. Unless that horse made no noise while someone beat him and Ed, this happened before everyone got here." Page caught my eyes. "Are you up to recapping your morning for me? I'd like your version before I talk to the others." When I nodded, he said, "Give me as much detail as you can remember."

I did, although relaying what happened when Izzy found Ed Duran took awhile. Dealing with the police and making more coffee had kept memory of that frightful scene at bay. Recounting it meant reliving it. Suppressing the choke that gripped my throat, I did my best to explain what I saw.

When I finished, Page sighed, "You came early because Jake dropped you off? Then you weren't expected to be here so soon."

"No."

"Dixie and Izzy are usually here by then, aren't they?"

"They always start at seven. They arrived right on schedule."

"But why kill Duran on this morning? Why not tomorrow or last week?"

"Ed doesn't go by the horses, not even Brisa's. Occasionally, he cut through the arena but I never saw him near the stalls. Someone gave him a reason to be there."

Page flipped his notebook to a clean sheet. "I'd better start talking to the others."

"I called Doc Lemmer, our vet. Sunny might be injured."

"I'll alert the officer out front to let him in. We've got to move that horse eventually anyway. We need to get Duran's body out."

"Can that wait until Doc Lemmer gets here?"

"It'll have to. I've asked the spatter experts from the lab to come. We're not moving anything until they take a look. Might be good to have the vet here though. We need pictures and the flash might set off that horse."

"When you move Sunny, Dixie or Izzy should help, too."

"I'll send for them when we're ready."

He went out to the lounge and asked Izzy to recount her morning activities. At first Izzy spoke like a misfiring engine, her words halting and without cadence as she struggled to control her shock.

"I got here. Kyle was here. Surprised."

"Why?" asked Page.

"Ankle."

"Go on. What did you see? How did things look?"

"Normal."

"What did you see that was normal?"

"Henry with the tractor. Jorge mucking Raider's stall."

"OK. What next?"

"Kyle was in the office. Coffee ready. And she had messages in her hand. Mom was outside with a horse."

"Do you always work Sunny first?"

"No. Thought we'd get harness work out of the way. He and Foggy only ones driving right now."

"So you broke your routine?"

"No routine. If you work the same horse at the same time in the same way, they anticipate. I always vary the work order."

"So your doing Sunny first was happenstance?"

"Yes."

"Now tell me what happened after you told Chuck to get Sunny ready."

"I went into the arena and Chuck went to get Sunny. Then I

heard him shouting so I went to see and…then…" She drifted to silence.

"You're doing fine," said Page, stroking her with his words. "I know this is hard. Take a deep breath. Good. You went to the stall. Was the door open?"

I didn't hear her answer so she must have nodded.

"OK. You went in."

"No," she said, barely above a whisper. "I couldn't."

"So you stayed outside in the barn aisle. Is that correct?"

A pause.

"And you saw Ed Duran lying on the stall floor? Face down?"

"Up. His eyes…"

"And Sunny was in the stall. Moving around? Tied up?"

"In the corner. So terrified."

"Was he tied?"

"I don't think so."

"Then you sent Chuck for help?"

"Must have."

The screen door banged and then Doc Lemmer entered the office, ducking his head to miss the door jam. Short, curly hair and wire-rimmed glasses gave him a boyish appearance that was overshadowed by a look of deep concern. I briefly explained what had happened and then introduced him to Page. He escorted the vet out and the two men huddled near the tack room before hurrying down the aisle.

Ten minutes later, two evidence techs told us to leave so they could look at the lounge and the office. Izzy tried to go into the barn but she was turned away. Taking her hand, I led her outside to the shade of the oak tree where Chuck leaned against the fence. That's where Page found us when he asked Dixie to help move Sunny to an empty stall. Izzy begged to go along but her mother was adamant. She was to stay outside with us. The mare nickered then and Izzy went to her.

"You all right?" I asked Chuck.

He didn't focus on me. His jaw was set but he nodded in the affirmative. "I tend to horse. No one takes care of her."

An eon passed before Dixie came through the arena doors, rubbing her hands on her jeans. As Izzy hurried over to meet her, I followed, looking over my shoulder at Chuck. He didn't raise his head to watch us.

The three of us stood in the middle of the parking lot, unsure where to go. It was ninety degrees but Dixie was shivering. Other than a haunted look on her face, goose bumps were the only sign that the scene in the stall had unnerved her.

"How's Sunny?" asked Izzy, rage spicing her words like red curry. "Was he hurt?"

"I think so. I don't know how badly."

Izzy stiffened, clenching her fists. Red spots flared in her cheeks.

"How could someone…? Whoever did this…" Her right hand moved over the knife hilt. Then, almost in a whisper, "I'm gonna kill him!"

Dixie grabbed her daughter's shoulders and shook her. "I think we've had enough killing."

I sided with Izzy. There was no way to explain to Sunny that he had been abused so he would become a murder weapon. Would Sunny revert to the frightened beast I'd seen two weeks before, attacking anything that came near him or could Izzy's love heal him again? I hoped so because the alternative, a trip to the glue factory, was unthinkable. If that happened, whoever killed Ed Duran would also be responsible for killing Sunny. And if Sunny was put down because of this, Izzy would have to stand in line behind me.

Anger helped. It gave me something to hang on to when nothing around me made any sense.

Giving her daughter a final squeeze, Dixie turned completely around, her eyes taking in the groups of police roaming the property. "I need to walk this off. Lots to think about."

She started around the south side of the barn. Izzy followed, more slowly. I was a good five paces behind, moving slowly to ease the strain on my ankle, when Izzy stopped suddenly and came back toward me.

"What about Brisa? This is gonna kill her." Izzy flinched. "Jeez, I'm sorry. What a lousy choice of words."

"I know what you meant. How about you? How are you doing?"

"Nothing like a good cry. I keep wanting to puke and I did that already. You did, too. Didn't you?"

I nodded.

"Sunny was beat again. That's why he attacked Uncle Ed."

We went around the corner to the rear of the barn. With the exception of the new crime scene tape across the back door, everything looked ordinary. The tractor rolled by, turning the soil in the field behind the house. Two guys were painting the farmhouse and another was bent over a piece of equipment, oil can in his hand.

Izzy touched my arm. "Remember when you were hanging up the signs and Sunny was all upset? I didn't have to unlatch his stall door that day either. It was open a few inches."

There were two possible explanations for that. The first was that the latch was too noisy. The second, and more likely, was that once Sunny went berserk, the culprit made a hasty exit in order to avoid discovery or injury. It was a minor detail but I knew Page would be interested.

"Wait," said Izzy, coming to a sudden stop again. "Isn't that Brisa's car by the house?"

It sure was. What surprised me even more was that Sal's Corvette and Nolan's car were parked right next to it. Where were they? Why were they here on a Tuesday? And how the heck could they ignore all the sirens?

CHAPTER 15

I wasn't the only person asking those questions. Followed by two uniformed officers, Page strode out the back door of the barn, shoulders square and eyes locked on the cars. Their holsters were unbuckled. The two uniforms walked around the house and then followed Page up the steps to the front door. Seconds later, they went inside.

Dixie and Izzy exchanged looks.

"What?" I asked.

"Those three together," said Dixie. "That's one heck of a coincidence."

"And one hell of an alibi," said Izzy.

An hour passed before we were allowed into the lounge again. I made sure Izzy was in the office with me when the deputy coroner took Ed Duran's body out. That may have been a bad decision. A black body bag had to be better than the picture of pulverized Uncle Ed that was now her last memory of him.

When Doc Lemmer reappeared, he was soaked with sweat and his entire body drooped like a plant that hadn't been watered in a week. He set his black bag next to the door and poured himself a mug of coffee.

As he stirred in three envelopes of sugar, he said, "The evidence people are finished with Sunny. I sewed up his shoulder and put a couple of stitches in the flank as a precaution. That sedative will last a few hours. When I come back, I'll give him another if he needs it. Right now, I'd advise cleaning him up, getting some Corona on those scrapes and giving him a good rubdown."

Izzy was out of her chair and through the door before the vet had finished his sentence.

"Keep an eye on her, Dixie," Doc Lemmer said. "She's probably in shock. If she's not, she should be. You, too, for that matter. Ghastly scene. I'm going home to clean up. I'll be back about four to check on things."

With his departure, stillness settled over the lounge like an evening fog filling the low points in a meadow. As hard as I listened, the only thing I heard was the usual traffic noises drifting in from the road. Dixie and I sat quietly. I don't know what she was thinking. I was consumed by the brick pattern in the fireplace and the cobwebs in the corner. When Dixie stood up suddenly, I gasped.

"Sorry," she said. She walked to the fireplace where she rested her hand on the mantle. "Since we came inside, I've been trying to figure out what's going on in that farmhouse. What are those three up to?" She turned toward me. "The cops are going to have fun sorting this out. Practically everyone I know was mad at Ed these days."

"Including you?"

"I ignore most of what he says…said. Ultimately, he always did the right thing. It just took him awhile to get there sometimes."

"You think he would have given up the Foggy thing?"

"I didn't like the way he was handling Nolan or Brisa and he should have behaved better with Sal but yes, he would have dropped it. Brisa doesn't want Foggy and he always did whatever she asked."

"Brisa told me Ed had some sort of contract with all his farm employees. Were they mad about that?"

"Absolutely. Henry was furious. Poor Jorge begged me to keep him on my payroll and not turn him over to Ed."

"Were you going to?"

"Ed said if Jorge was paid by the farm, I wouldn't have to deal with payroll and work hours and tax forms. Less for me to worry about with Frank gone."

"If you transferred Jorge to the farm payroll, he'd have to sign an employment contact like the others?"

"No. He doesn't live on the property so he couldn't trade room and board for work. It didn't matter. Bright Hope has payroll no matter what because of Izzy and me so Ed's offer was pointless."

"This contract thing was put into place before Frank disappeared?"

"Oh yes." Her eyes glazed over. She was in the past. "Not long after Ramon left. Ed told us he got the idea from some golfing buddy." She straightened. "No matter how many times he tried to explain it, it sounded completely screwy to me. It just seems, I don't know, sneaky? Frank didn't think much of it either. He warned Ed that it would come back to bite him. Maybe it did."

I bit my lip, then forged ahead with my next question. "Dixie, did you know Ed had a big insurance policy on Frank?"

"Yes, I knew. He came to me about six months ago and asked if Frank and I had any life insurance. Health and liability is all we can afford because liability for this kind of business is so expensive."

"So he took out a policy on Frank's life? Why not yours?"

"He probably did. I don't know. Ed might have had a similar conversation with Frank about it."

"Or Izzy?"

"Lord, I hope not. She doesn't need to be thinking about her parents dying."

I merely looked at her.

"Yes, I guess she does."

"Izzy called Ed uncle. They were close?"

"I used to ride over to Penzler's so early I'd be the first one there. The second person was usually Ed. Naturally, we got to talking. One day, he brought Brisa out to Bright Hope. Back when it was on Stable Road. Typical pre-teen girl, she was totally nuts about horses. Ed went directly to Frank and offered to pay the equivalent of board and training if we would give Brisa private riding lessons. Frank said yes immediately."

"And that started your relationship with the Durans."

"Ed was always around because of Brisa. Izzy bonded with him immediately. He insisted Mr. Duran was his father and suggested the uncle part since Frank wouldn't allow her to address him as Ed."

"And then you moved up here."

"When we needed more room, Ed suggested we bring Bright Hope here. It was perfect. Secluded but near the highway." She let out a sorrow-infused sigh. "Nothing lasts forever. Change is part of life, I guess."

"What happened?"

"Frank started talking about moving right after that developer's billboard went up on the corner at Kelly Road."

"When did that happen?"

"During the winter. Maybe February. He said we'd be forced out by developers soon and he wanted to move while we had a chance to find a place with reasonable rent. At first, it was just talk but right before he disappeared, he was looking at properties in Wisconsin."

"I got the impression Ed would have protected you guys. He didn't seem interested in developers. Didn't he buy the new place to keep them away?"

"What are you getting at?"

"I'm trying to understand the relationship. Izzy called him uncle; Mary Penzler told me about Ed's plans to partner with you in

Equestrian Escapades; a huge life insurance policy with Ed paying the premium..."

Dixie stared at me like I had three heads and then all the color left her face. Her eyes filled with tears. She turned back to the mantle.

"I couldn't understand why Frank was suddenly so anxious to leave here. We had a couple of fights about it. I swear, I swear it never occurred to me that Ed was the reason."

She dashed out, the screen door banging behind her. Judging by the stricken look on her face, Dixie had just realized how strongly Ed Duran felt about her. I was glad I hadn't mentioned the marriage rumor.

When Page returned to the lounge, he looked like he'd been through a car wash without the car. I pulled a Coke from the vending machine and passed it to him.

"How about some nice cold caffeine?"

"Thanks." He popped the tab. "Nolan, Sal and Brisa were inside that house, sitting at the kitchen table, coffee cups in front of them like it was perfectly natural for them to be there. They claimed it was a strategy session for how both men could keep their horses. Brisa was about to buy insurance from Nolan to cover the new place and sign a construction contract with Sal for some work she wants done here."

"How could she do that unless she already knew her father was dead and she had control of his company?"

"My thought exactly but they alibi each other."

"Any chance they were in on it together? They were all mad at Ed."

"Togetherness doesn't rule them out as individual suspects. I'll tell them it does hoping one of them might slip up eventually. The coffee was cold, Kyle. The fake creamer had congealed in the cups."

"Brisa knows the morning routine. She'd know when to sneak

into the barn." I came to a mental dead end. "I can't see her killing her father."

"Me neither. Sal or Nolan but not her. Maybe they set this up to provide themselves with an alibi and she's clueless."

"How did she take the news?"

"I didn't tell her. Not in front of the others. I have the three separated now and they're being questioned. I left Brisa in the kitchen but they all know something's up. Hard to ignore all the activity." He scrunched the empty can. "What's been happening with you?"

I told him about my conversation with Dixie.

"Regular Peyton Place around here." He turned to go. "I've got to break the bad news to Brisa. You know, you should see a counselor. Whether you feel it now or not, you were traumatized. Remind me and I'll give you a name."

With Page gone again, I was alone in the office. The sudden lack of activity was not a good thing. Page's words stirred my hodge-podge emotional soup. Anger and horror, seasoned liberally with pain and frustration, threatened to boil into a complete meltdown. My ankle hurt like crazy. Cast or not, multiple trips through the sand arena had strained it. I found the aspirin and took three, remembering too late that I had an empty stomach.

When a muffled, agonized shriek reached me, I knew Page had told Brisa about her father. Could anyone sound that distressed and be guilty of murder? There was little time to ponder it as he guided a stricken Brisa to the sofa where she sat rigidly straight, arms wrapped around herself, eyes locked on the fireplace.

"I'll be back in a few minutes to talk to you," he said. "Kyle will stay with you."

I glared at him but he was already out the door. Good, ole dependable Kyle. We can count on her to make coffee, hold everyone's hand, and take charge in a crisis. What if I didn't want to stay with Brisa? What if I just quit, went home, and crawled into bed? To hell with this! Ed Duran haunted me, my ankle was sore, and three aspirin were burning the lining off my stomach. Why didn't he assign someone to stay with me? Where was my extra support?

My private pity party didn't last long. One look at Brisa reminded me that my father wasn't a mushy mess inside a body bag or a pile of bones in the morgue and my mother hadn't died nor was she a widow.

I approached her. "Would you prefer to be left alone?"

"No. Please stay." Brisa gripped herself more tightly. "Do you like it here? The work I mean?"

"Yes. I do."

"I can tell." She gulped. "I have to take over the businesses now. I...I'm not a math whiz. I'll screw it up. And the guys won't work for a woman. Look how they ignore Dixie here. How much worse will it be on the construction sites?"

People talk about the strangest things when confronted with devastating news. My grandmother told me the bereaved usually voice regrets about unresolved issues with the deceased. She ought to know. She'd been to as many funerals as weddings in her sixty-odd years. Brisa wasn't troubled by things she hadn't said or didn't do. She worried about her father's businesses. I sat next to her and put my arm around her shoulder.

"I'm sure your attorney and Greg Lacey will be happy to help."

"How can they? When Daddy took the books to the new guy, he met with a different attorney, too. I don't think he was very happy with the old one."

"Did he tell you why?"

"No."

"When did he make the change?"

She popped up and whirled toward me, hands on her hips. "Why are you asking me these questions? You think you're the police?"

I held up both palms. "Sorry. You seemed to want to talk about your father's business and what you said made me curious. Going to a new accountant, switching attorneys. Those are serious moves."

Her shoulders dropped as she pulled tissue from the box and blew her nose. Then she looked at me.

"They are, aren't they?"

She sat down at the table and stayed there until Page collected her. Before they went out, she turned to me and said, "About four months ago."

They left me with a ringing telephone and no desire to answer it. It occurred to me I should call the clients but by now the media had the story and there was nothing more I could tell them anyway. There, however, was one call I felt I had to make. Lori Boc had saved my life and she deserved to hear about Ed Duran's death from me.

"How did he die?" she asked after I explained that he had been found in Sunny's stall.

"The police aren't sure."

"Any remote chance it was an accident?"

I fudged. "It could have been, I suppose. Sunny charged me one day."

"Really?" She paused. "Still, they can't think Sunny killed him. Are they that stupid?"

I assured Lori that the police aren't stupid.

"They'd be better off looking at Brisa. She called me last night. She was still hoppin' mad about the Foggy thing."

"Lori, people don't kill each other over a horse."

"Sure they do. But it wasn't just that. The day after the garage fire, Henry and Chuck told Brisa they were going to quit."

"Did they say why?"

"Ed promised Henry for a year that he would run the new farm. Chuck was furious because he didn't want to go to the new place and raise vegetables. He wanted to stay by the horses. They told her everyone's fed up with that goofy work-for-rent contract and she'd better convince Ed to get rid of it or find new workers."

"I remember what you said about Bright Hope being a haven. Would Brisa kill her own father to protect it?"

"Who knows? Maybe. Does anyone know how anyone else truly feels about something?"

For the rest of the day, I stayed in the office, avoiding outside contact as much as possible. I was exhausted and my usual polite banter was becoming vitriolic disrespect. All I could think about was a bloodied Ed Duran lying in Sunny's stall, who had put him there and why.

Dixie was off the hook. Not only was I with her when Ed was discovered, she would never harm an animal. Izzy was capable of killing someone but her anguish in front of Sunny's stall had been real. Remorse? Had she murdered Ed Duran because he had killed her father? No. Like her mother, she would never injure an animal to accomplish her goal. If she had wanted Ed Duran dead, she would have slit his throat with her big knife and been done with it.

Lori's revelation about Henry and Chuck was a surprise until I thought about it. The farmhouse at the new place would be perfect for Henry's family. It had taken Ed a year to put the deal together. Had Ed been promising Henry the new place but always intending it for Chuck? And how had that crazy work contract affected Henry's ability to earn enough to bring his family over?

The contract would have impacted Chuck's earning power as well. Until Lori's comments, I hadn't given much thought to Chuck as a killer. However, if Chuck was running the equipment racket, he'd be mad at having to reorganize everything. Perhaps the reason Chuck was being moved to the new place was to stop the trafficking in stolen equipment. If Chuck suspected that Ed knew about it, would he have killed him? What would Chuck do with the money he made selling stolen equipment? How much did a race horse operation cost?

Lori made a good point. It appeared to me that Brisa was close to her father but I didn't know them at all. Behind closed doors, they might have hated one another. Was confiscating Foggy the last straw, forcing her hand? Or was Equestrian Escapades the final blow?

What about Sal? Most of Brisa's motives applied to him. I couldn't overlook Nolan either. He had plenty of motive. What was it Mary had said? Nolan would find a way. Did that include murder?

Looking at all the customers and all the farm employees, I couldn't figure out who killed Ed Duran. It got worse when I tried to connect his death with Frank Villano's.

Did that mean there was no connection? Not a chance. It was there; I just wasn't smart enough to see it. Perhaps if Page figured out who killed Ed, he'd have back door access to a motive for Frank's killing.

And that's what I said to him the next evening after Jake and I laid waste to one of Liz Page's spinach lasagnas. After dinner, she and Jake went into the kitchen, leaving Page and me to mull over the case.

"If you can figure out who killed Ed," I said, "that will help you with Frank's killing, won't it?"

"That's my approach, yes. Why?"

"Ed moved the farm accounting to Greg Lacey. There may have been a reason that would help explain what's been going on."

"I looked into that. Lacey told me that when Frank disappeared, Ed was convinced something was wrong but didn't know what. In an effort to find out, he took his books to a new accountant. The books were clean. Lacey didn't find anything wrong."

"But that action might have alerted the bad guy that Ed was concerned."

"I asked everyone about that. Ed passed it off as a simple case of prudent business practices plus a whole lot of convenience. He told Dixie he wanted someone who wasn't affiliated with Duran Building and Grading to do the farm work. His accountant is down in Bannockburn. Greg Lacey is in Libertyville. That's at least ninety minutes of saved drive time when he was out at the farm. The shorter drive meant less spent on gas, too."

"A dead end."

"Yeah. I'd hoped for more from that lead, too."

"How about Brisa, Sal or Nolan? That meeting was pretty convenient."

"Brisa insists she was buying insurance from Nolan and he swears he has the paperwork to prove it. We're following up on that."

"What about Sal?"

Page snorted. "He claims he and Brisa were discussing rehabbing the farmhouse. Instead of Equestrian Escapades, she wants to develop a therapeutic riding camp and use the house as a bunk house for the kids."

"And you don't buy that?"

"No, I don't. Not yet anyway."

"Something is bothering me. When I told you about someone beating Sunny, we both thought keeping Sunny riled up showed premeditation for killing Ed. What if it was premeditation for killing Sal? After all, Sunny is Sal's horse."

Page scowled. "Are you saying that Ed wasn't the one who was supposed to die? Could you be wrong about that horse?"

"Someone chased Sunny around the stall, forcing him to step on Ed. I promise you Sunny did not kill Ed. Sunny was just part of the weapon."

"OK, but my point is that the killer knew exactly who he was killing. It was no mistake."

"Oh I agree, but what if that person was planning to kill Sal for some reason and then got mad at Ed and took advantage of the set up designed for Sal?"

He thought about that for a moment. "I see what you're getting at."

"Sal's been making a lot of noise about the stolen equipment. He filed police reports. He talks about it constantly."

"And he accused Ed of being behind it so that brought focus on Ed and the farm. Your theory is that Sal was going to be killed to shut him up."

"It would look like an accident because the crazy horse did it."

"So when Ed became a problem..."

"A convenient murder method was already in place."

"Look, if we stay with the heavy equipment angle, we have all kinds of possibilities."

"The farm is a great place to hide stuff until it can be shipped somewhere else."

"The ETs found yellow paint traces in the shed."

"They did? What kind?"

"We didn't test it."

"If you knew what it was, wouldn't that help the case?"

"I may order that test to prove a fact for court but if the task force can solve this thing without it, all the better. Paint analysis is incredibly expensive."

I'd never thought about what crime lab tests might cost although I had a heart-stoppingly good idea about the cost of lab tests for medical treatment. The first hospital bill had arrived. I almost had to resuscitate myself after reading the amount. It was easy to understand why Page wanted to put off any tests he could.

"They bring the stolen equipment to the farm," I said, picturing shovels, dozers and loaders all rolling through the farm in the dead of night. "They alter its appearance and then ship it out. Wait a minute. Why would they need to alter the appearance? It's all yellow, isn't it?"

"I asked myself that same question so I got on the Web a

couple of nights ago to look it up. Ford farm tractors are blue. John Deere is green and yellow, but primarily green. As for construction equipment, Cat, Volvo and Komatsu are all yellow. So were most of the other brands I checked out. I assume it has something to do with visibility."

"Then the paint is used to obliterate special markings like company logos?"

"Probably."

I pushed at my bangs. "Oh my."

"What?"

"I think I saw them moving equipment last week. Before Frank was discovered." I ticked off the days on my fingers. "Last Thursday morning, a big piece of yellow something was at the far end of the northeast hay field."

"And you think it might have been stolen equipment because?"

"The farm tractor is a John Deere. John Deere is green. The manure spreader is green, too."

Page perked up. "Any other equipment you've seen regularly?"

I pondered that. "Some weird looking thing they tow behind the tractor that makes the round bales of hay and some other gizmo they use to cut the hay. Both are green."

"But you saw something yellow. How big was it?"

"Big enough to notice."

"What happened next?"

I didn't answer. My mind had hold of something. Page didn't pester me.

"I spotted the yellow thing on Thursday morning," I said when it came together. "Frank's skeleton was discovered Friday afternoon. What if the farm was used as a stop-over point? What if someone knew that Frank was in the manure pile and what if they knew that he was about to be found? They'd move everything off the farm so they wouldn't be discovered."

"And they might set fire to an outbuilding to destroy any

evidence of their activities." Page leaned back. "I think we just found the motive for the fire. We've always assumed someone at the farm set that fire. No one else had access or familiarity. How about Henry?"

"He had smoke inhalation. Dixie saw the paramedics working on him and they wouldn't treat a person unless there was a real injury."

"Maybe Sal is right and Duran was running equipment through and started the fire to cover it up."

His words pried a memory loose.

"Remember I told you about standing at the rear barn door, looking out toward the fields, and seeing that yellow equipment?"

Page nodded.

"Well, what I'd forgotten until this moment was that Ed saw it too. Ed was next to me that morning." I looked at Page, barely able to speak I was so horrified by the next revelation. "Did he know or suspect enough to understand the significance? If he understood the implications, he wanted to be sure I didn't. When he sent me home after Chuck found Frank's skeleton, he was protecting me, trying to keep me out of it. If I wasn't around to answer questions, I might not be tempted ask any."

Another thought surfaced with equal force, confronting me so directly that I squeaked.

Page stared at me. "What?"

"The loader. I'll bet I saw the loader. Dixie saw it too. The day before, Dixie yelled at Chuck and asked him why he wasn't using the new loader she'd seen."

"I'll be…An IDOT loader was stolen two weeks ago." It was Page's turn to be stunned. "State equipment has giant black letters painted on it."

"A loader with Illinois Department of Transportation painted on the side would get noticed immediately if it was anywhere but at an IDOT project."

"Assuming we're right about this, sounds like Dixie could have ended up in the manure too. She's probably lucky to be alive."

Jake came in and set a plate of cookies on the table. "Maybe, but Dixie'd be dead if someone wanted her to be. Same with Kyle. Rather than kill people, your bad guy removed the evidence."

"Good point," said Page, "but then how do we explain Villano and Duran? Somebody murdered them."

"Stealing equipment requires more than one person," I said. "Could there be an accomplice? Maybe an outsider?"

"There's got to be a whole network of people moving stuff from place to place until they get it out of state. Bright Hope is probably the last stop for stuff headed north."

"The outsider is the killer?"

"Even if that's true," said Page, "the insider knows about the killings. Was probably there when they happened. At the very least, the insider would be an accessory."

"Perhaps," said Jake, "your insider views those killings as unavoidable? A means to an end? Regrettable, but part of the cost of doing business?"

"What an awful thought," said Liz, passing her husband a coffee carafe. "Death, a cost of doing business."

Page snorted. "Nolan would say that's why there's insurance."

"Speaking of which," I said, "did I tell you Ed paid for the life insurance policy on Frank? Dixie told me Ed talked to her about life insurance about six months ago." I helped myself to a cookie. "You know, all kinds of things happened within the last six months. Frank told Dixie he wanted to move Bright Hope. He started looking at other properties up in Wisconsin right before he disappeared."

"Frank must have suspected something," said Jake, "and he wanted to get away from it."

Page looked at me. "You don't think Ed being hot for Dixie was the motivation?"

CHAPTER 16

"No, I don't. Even if he was, Dixie was all Frank all the time and I'm sure he knew that. It isn't always about sex, you know. And thanks to me opening my big mouth, now Dixie thinks it is." I shook my head. "I'm positive Ed being hot for Dixie wasn't what had Frank worried."

"Maybe Ed talking about life insurance set him off."

"Especially so much. That would sure get me to thinking."

Page pulled his notebook out and flipped through the pages. "Let's see…six months ago Ramon disappeared."

"Four months ago," I said, "Ed got a new attorney and a new accountant."

"Six months ago Frank told Sal to stay away from Brisa. Too bad we can't establish an exact time line. It might help to know which came first, Ramon's disappearance or the conversation about life insurance."

Liz said, "You two think whoever killed Frank Villano also killed Ed Duran, right?"

Page nodded. "It sure looks that way."

"If you're assuming it had to be someone connected with Bright Hope, then why not stay with the motives of the people at the stable?"

"Motive?" I asked, reaching for another cookie. "There are so many. Can we assume Frank died because he stumbled onto the equipment thing and that was the motive no matter who shot him?"

Page nodded. "That's as good a place to start as any. How about Sal killed Duran to protect his business?"

"We know Ed was interfering with Sal's love life. Sal still has a thing for Brisa. With Ed gone, he can pick up where he left off. If he marries her, he certainly won't have to worry about competing with Duran Building. He'll practically own it."

"Duran asked you to spy on Sal. If Sal knew, it might have motivated the attack on the bridle path."

"If Sal was stealing his own equipment and using the insurance money to buoy up his company, he can stop doing that now that Ed Duran is dead."

"No more failing business if the competition is dead. And no more chance of getting caught stealing."

"The insurance company investigation of him would end."

"Does he have an alibi?" asked Jake.

"Not one that counts."

Page put his coffee cup down. "How about Duran killed Frank Villano and then Dixie or Izzy killed him because they found out about what he'd done?"

"Weak for Dixie, plausible for Izzy. Dixie told me that Izzy's grief has become hatred. She worries that Izzy could kill whoever murdered Frank. You must have noticed that machete she wears. That's no pocket knife and she doesn't use it for cutting baling twine."

"You exaggerate but I get your point. I wonder if she's always worn it." Page frowned. "Still, if someone died every time they were wished dead, we wouldn't have a population problem on this planet." He went silent for a moment and then snapped his fingers. "Brisa kills her father to get her hands on her inheritance and on Sal. Maybe she was opposed to Equestrian Escapades and all that meant. Remember the marriage rumor and she *claimed* she wanted to open that riding camp for kids with problems.

"Lori told me you can't know what goes on inside a family.

Maybe Brisa wanted to get her hands on her inheritance but I can't see her beating Sunny. Sal's reluctance to buy him could be explained by plans to use Sunny to kill Ed but Brisa wouldn't hurt the horses."

Liz chuckled. "You two could be at this all night. It sounds to me like you don't have the piece you need to pull it all together."

She was absolutely right so we didn't work on our puzzle any more that evening. The Pages shared pictures of their June vacation to Utah's Bryce Canyon and although I thoroughly enjoyed the slide show, my mind returned to Bright Hope several times.

Dixie had seen a loader. That thought bothered me well after I returned home. When I slept, it wasn't my cast that woke me up every hour all through the night. It was Tuesday morning again and I was back in front of a blood-stained stall. Had Izzy seen the loader too?

Chuck was in the office when I arrived the next morning. He shifted his weight from one foot to another while I turned on the computer and placed my tote under the desk.

"When Miss Dixie comes, I want to talk to her. Very important that Brisa not fire us. Not our fault work not done."

"I don't understand."

"When he sees manure so high, Ed thinks we don't do our work." Chuck gave me his one-shoulder shrug. "Henry had me fix fence. That took up time. Said that was most priority."

"And you were so busy fixing the fence that you didn't have time for other chores, like spreading manure."

"Henry had long list for me. When I ask him about the manure, he told me it can wait." He looked into my eyes. "Was he wrong?"

"Keeping the horses safe is the most important thing so if the fences were bad, that had to come first."

Chuck seemed relieved. "I told Ed I had no time when he asked about the manure being so much."

"You told Ed that Henry kept you busy doing other things?"

Chuck nodded. "He should know I'm no lazy oaf. Henry wanted me to do other things."

As he walked away, a shiver scampered down my spine like two squirrels chasing each other on a tree. Had Henry kept Chuck busy purposely to keep him away from the manure and Frank's body? How bad had the fencing been? The maintenance took place weeks before I started at Bright Hope so I had not seen the fences in disrepair. I made a mental note to ask Dixie or Izzy about it. About an hour later, I had my chance when Izzy came into the office.

I handed her a message from Nolan. "And Brisa called. She's staying at the house for a couple of days to work on farm stuff. She wondered if she could ride Chicken later."

"Says here she'll be late? Let her know I'll have Jorge leave him saddled in the stall." Izzy sank into the stool, her hand over her mouth. "Will I ever stop seeing Uncle Ed's dead body? Every time I think about him, that's what I remember."

"From what I understand, those types of images stay with us our whole lives. The edges fade and maybe someday, you'll be able to examine the scene more clinically."

"Detective Page wants me to see a counselor."

"He told me the same thing."

"Will you?"

"Probably. I hope talking about it will take the nightmares away."

She stared at me. "You're having nightmares? Me, too."

"Yeah, well..." I stood up, not wanting to dwell on the macabre scene we'd both witnessed. Whenever that memory surfaced, my stomach turned. "I had a chat with Chuck this morning. He's concerned about his job."

"All the guys are spooked. No one knows what Brisa will do about that contract."

"I don't think Brisa will make any sudden changes. Besides, there's always work to be done on a farm, isn't there? Chuck told me he spent a lot of time repairing fences this spring."

"Mom didn't think they were bad until Henry explained he had already talked to Dad about it. Then he showed her a board that had ants all over it. Picture horses trotting down the road and playing tag with the cars."

"That actually happened?"

"A couple of years ago, we had Maida, Raider and two others out in the front ring while Jorge did some repairs in their stalls. Next thing I know, cars are honking like crazy. I ran out to the front just in time to see Maida trot up to a stopped car and poke her head in the driver's window."

"Hokey smokes. How did you get them back into the barn?"

"We ignored them."

I must have looked unconvinced because Izzy chuckled. It was good to hear her let down a bit.

"I'm serious," she said. "Maida's tail was waving like a flag as she bounced from one car to the next just like that Looney Tunes skunk bounces after girl cats. Every time I got close to her, she took off. Trust me; there is no way a person on foot is going to catch a horse that doesn't want to get caught. I was so mad. There I was, standing in the middle of the road screaming at a horse that was laughing at me."

"She could have been killed!"

"I was frantic. Mom came out eventually and pulled me back inside the barn. She made me work a horse. I don't remember which one. About twenty minutes later, Maida appeared in the arena. She stood there, watched for a bit and then put herself into her stall. It was just amazing."

"What about the others?"

"They followed her right in. Raider put himself away too. Jorge and Mom grabbed the others."

"And no one got hurt?"

"If it hadn't been a holiday, we might not have been so lucky. There would have been truck traffic and trucks can't stop fast enough to avoid a stupid horse that wants to play in the street. Anyway, when Henry said Chuck needed to replace the fence, all he had to do was talk about Memorial Day and he got no argument. Converting to vinyl was a big project. It took Chuck weeks."

That answered that but I had another problem. "I need to ask you a straightforward question."

She cocked her head.

"What's with the knife?"

Her hand edged toward it but she stopped herself. "What do you mean?"

"You know what I mean. That's not for normal barn work. You carry a pocket knife for that. What are you afraid of, Izzy?"

She looked at her boots, then slowly rose from the stool. "Better get back to work."

"Why did you ask me to check out security at other barns?"

"I don't know what you're getting at."

"Look me in the eye and say that."

She whirled toward me, right hand on the knife sheath, eyes blazing and lips snarling. "Jeez, you're a pest! No wonder you can't hold a real job."

That hurt but I ignored it. "You're spooked. Why?"

"Leave me alone!"

"Izzy, what?"

She dropped her head as an emotional dam broke and wracking sobs forced her onto the stool again.

"I'll call your mother."

"No!" She stretched out and grabbed my hand, her fingers locking so tightly around mine that my knuckles cracked. "She can't know!"

I waited. Seconds ticked by as Izzy struggled for control.

"I saw stuff," she said, barely more than whisper. "Construction equipment. Sat by the shed late at night. Gone the next day."

I felt my jaw drop. "How did you find out about it?"

"One night, I couldn't sleep. Wanted to jump out of my skin. I came back to the barn. To make sure everything was all right. With Maida when I heard an engine rumble."

"So you went to investigate."

She gulped back a sob. "Engine noise from the shed. Stayed on the north side of the garage, in the shadows. Saw this idling Bobcat get loaded onto a flatbed."

"Did you recognize anyone?"

"No headlights. Most of the time, faces were toward the truck." She shook her head slowly. "I tried. Jeez, I tried, but I couldn't make them out. Not without giving myself away."

"And you told someone about this."

"Dad." She squeezed my hand again. "Do you get it now, dammit? Dad's dead because I told him what I saw!"

Her words broke a mental dam; remembered conversations and observations flooded my mind. What had Page said about a timeline?

"How soon after you talked to him did he disappear?"

Izzy shuddered. "A week."

"Did you talk to anyone else?"

"Right after Dad went missing, I told Uncle Ed. He told me to keep quiet; he would check it out."

"So you kept quiet."

"Until last week. I kept watching though. Something got my dad killed. I had to know what it was."

"And you saw a loader by the shed."

"I told Uncle Ed about it."

"Was he alone when you told him?'

"The first time. Friday morning. Right before they found Dad's skeleton." She shook off her rising emotion. "The second time, Sal was with him. Chuck and Henry, too. Sal was yappin' at Uncle Ed again about stealing equipment. I told him to lay off. His damn loader had been behind the shed and I wouldn't let him get away with blaming Uncle Ed. Not for something he was doing himself."

"When was that?"

"Sunday, after his stupid macho display in the lounge."

I pushed at my bangs. Before the garage fire; a fire set to get rid of evidence. But the paint evidence was by the shed. Had someone burned down the wrong outbuilding? Did Sal know we called the first building the garage and the second the shed? Would he have made that mistake? Maybe. There was one other person to consider. The person on the outside would know to burn down a building but might easily have mistaken which one.

Izzy had been watching me. "You agree with me. Dad and Uncle Ed are dead because I opened my big, fat trap."

"No, I don't. Wasn't Ramon already missing when you spoke to your father about what you saw? Your talking only confirmed suspicions he already had. Same with Ed, I'm sure." Something else clicked into place. "This is the real reason you wanted me to ask other stables about security, isn't it? You wondered if others had unexplained nighttime activities."

"I hoped it wasn't just us."

"One of us needs to tell the police about this."

"You do it. I…I can't tell it again."

I telephoned Page as soon as Izzy was recovered enough to go back to training.

"Boy, do I have news for you," I said and relayed what Izzy had told me.

"It's coming together. That fills in a lot of blanks." He paused, then said, "Can you come into the station this afternoon? I have something I want to show you."

"I really shouldn't leave until five. Taking off early might require explanations."

"Gotcha. See you after work."

Jake and I had dinner plans that included two thick ahi tuna steaks and some summer squash on the grill. I let him know I'd be delayed Of course the afternoon dragged as I waited for the clock to give me permission to leave and drive to the Vernon Hills police station. When the time arrived, I yelled goodbye to Dixie and hurried off.

The problem with traffic at five o'clock is that one can't go anywhere in a hurry. Cutting in and out, honking and swearing only gets a person to the next red light a few seconds before anyone else. It took me every bit of forty-five minutes to make the trip. My nerves were raw by the time I pulled into a visitor's slot in the VHPD parking lot but it wasn't driving stress that had me jumpy. I couldn't let go of Izzy's revelations. I called Page from outside and found him waiting for me when I entered the building. He led me to an interview room that was bare except for a table and two chairs in the center. A shallow box lay in the middle of the table.

"This is Detective Beekly," said Page.

The bald detective leaned against the wall, his round tummy pressing against his belt. He nodded a hello, squinting at me through wire-rimmed glasses that sat on a face so bland it looked like a mask. I'd seen him before but neither of us mentioned it.

Page pointed at the box. "Take a look. Does any of this stuff do anything for you?"

I peered inside. "This is what you got sifting the manure? It doesn't seem like much for what? …four days of work in the hot sun?"

The top layer held safety pins, some stones, bits of paper, a belt buckle, a curry comb, several hoof picks, and a decayed leather strap, all tidy in their plastic evidence bags. I pushed a few of the bags aside to get a look at what lay underneath. More of the same. I moved the bags around again. One of the dung-encrusted pebbles caught my eye.

I picked up the packet, held it up to the light and carefully examined its contents. Nature does not make perfect ovals.

Tiger-eye? Perhaps Baltic tiger-eye?

I stared at it. There was an obvious answer as to why it was there. It had come out of a ring Henry stopped wearing, a ring that once adorned his right hand index finger. The only finger on either hand that had not had a ring on it. I looked up at Page. Suddenly it all made sense. I didn't have all the facts so he would have to connect the dots, but now I understood the look on Henry's face when Ed Duran announced that Chuck would be in charge of the new farm. And now I knew that Henry, not Sal, had been moving the equipment through the farm. I even knew why.

Page watched me closely. "You've got it, don't you?"

"I think so," I said, "but you'll have to pull it all together."

"I can do that."

"There's something else," I said after reminding him of Henry's naked ring finger. "Chuck told me Henry kept him so busy with chores this summer that he couldn't spread the manure like he normally would."

"Henry didn't work on the manure because he was too busy in the fields. Bumper crop of hay this year. At least that's what he told me." Page rubbed his chin. "And he said Chuck was repairing fences and that took priority."

"If they truly needed to be fixed, they would." I pushed at my bangs. "Put a little syrup on the wood and it would be covered with ants in no time. How long does a body have to cook before the flesh decomposes entirely?"

"Depends," said Beekly, "but if we're talking about summer, not long. Three weeks, four tops."

"So if Henry kept everyone away, Frank would literally disappear."

"The bones would remain and even though the DNA was

destroyed by the compost heat, the teeth were there so the coroner could always ID the body from dental records. I don't think dissolving Frank was the idea."

"Maybe Henry just wanted to hide the body until he could move somewhere else. A rush burial."

"That makes more sense. Dixie told you that dung heap is never completely gone. Henry buried Frank deep and counted on months' worth of manure on top of the body to prevent it from being found, even after they started spreading again."

"As foreman, Henry could control how much time was spent on that versus other chores."

"He didn't plan on Ed Duran getting ornery about it."

"Or on Chuck complaining."

"Or on Ed deciding to put Chuck in charge of the new place." Page hit the intercom. "Zucker, get in here. I think we've nailed it." He looked at Beekly. "Get a warrant, take Zucker and get ready for a little visit to Bright Hope. I'll be along in a minute."

He turned to me. "I assume you're headed home. I'll call you when it's wrapped up."

All the way home, uneasiness plagued me. It was like being back in the bog with mosquitoes crawling over my arms. I'd overlooked something terribly important. After just a few blocks, I couldn't stand it anymore. Turning the car around, I drove toward Bright Hope as fast as I dared, trusting my instincts that I was doing the right thing and that I would get there in time.

There was no sign of police activity at Bright Hope. Brisa's car was under the tree but Dixie and Izzy were gone. I hurried through the arena and looked out the back door. The tractor was parked nearby. Where was Henry?

Hooves battered a stall wall. Sunny. I gimped to his stall as quickly as the cast would allow. He was circling, plainly agitated but I didn't see any signs of injury. The stall door was latched.

"Easy, boy," I said, watching him closely.

Sliding the latch back, I began the same type of patter I'd heard Izzy use with him. He stopped his frantic dance, dropped his head and came to me. After hugging him, I checked his flanks. No welts. Why was he so upset?

Next door, even Divot was awake. Clearly something had happened but what?

Chicken nickered. I patted Sunny and left him. The door latch on Chicken's stall was already back. I looked over my shoulder, listening intently but hearing nothing except for normal horse sounds and chipping sparrows overhead.

Inside Chicken's stall, Brisa was on her knees, moaning softly, left hand on the crown of her head. Blood oozed between her fingers, running down her arm and off her elbow, droplets soaking into the shavings.

"Brisa! What happened?"

"Don't know. Someone just whacked me on the head."

Voices. Coming closer.

I searched frantically for some type of weapon. The seconds I wasted on that useless reflex nearly cost us any chance of escape. I stopped thinking and hoisted a confused Brisa to her feet and half-dragged her out of Chicken's stall. There was no time to get to my car. We needed to hide somewhere long enough for Page to arrive with the cavalry. But where?

The feed room? With Foggy?

The voices went quiet.

With Brisa's arm draped across my shoulder, I limped down the aisle. Then, propping her against Divot's stall, I reached in to Sunny, patting and reassuring him before pushing Brisa inside. Whispering that she wasn't to make a sound, I guided her into the corner under the water bucket against the wall. From the aisle, we couldn't be seen. But if anyone came into the stall and Sunny went nuts, we were toast. I held my breath and waited.

Seconds later, heavy boots clomped down the aisle. A stall

door moved. Henry swore. Things were quiet for a minute. Henry walked away and stopped. At the feed room. Then the boots came closer. Sunny screamed in anger. If I'd ever needed proof of Henry's treachery, that squeal was it.

Sunny blasted the rear of his stall with both hooves; the thunderous connection rang in my ears. Teeth bared, he charged the door, whirled and charged again. Then, legs planted apart and chest heaving, Sunny stared at his stall door.

There was a moment of silence but it was long enough for me to hear sirens in the distance. Then boots hurried away.

I let out a sigh of relief, rose slowly and left the stall, looking right and then left. No sign of anyone. Something lay on the floor in front of Chicken's stall. I knew what it was before I went over to examine it. A leather strop.

Returning to Sunny's stall, I slowly approached the chestnut gelding. Sunny hated Henry Slavin and that hatred had protected Brisa and me. I had gambled on that and it paid off. All very logical.

However, when I wrapped my arms around Sunny's neck, sobbed into his mane and thanked the most wonderful horse in the whole world for saving our lives, I wasn't being the least bit rational.

CHAPTER 17

The cavalry did arrive, spurred on by Jake, who called Page when I wasn't home by seven o'clock. After Brisa was sent off in an ambulance, I told my story and went home to Jake's arms. The ahi tuna waited until the next day. The task force began a search for Henry Slavin. I found out later that Page called Lori first.

Bright Hope shut down the next day. I worked in the office but Dixie and Izzy stayed with Brisa at the house. Squad cars collected all the farm workers, leaving the place deserted except for me. When Jorge returned, I went home; feeling disconnected from the action and with no clear understanding of what was happening.

That evening, Jake grilled the tuna and summer squash while I made a salad and fussed about being left out. As we cleaned up the kitchen after our meal, I glanced periodically at the medicine wheel.

Izzy saw a Bobcat. If she had ignored it, if she hadn't told Frank, how different everything would have been. Five whole minutes passed before I peeked at the wall clock again. Jake shot me a look. Watched pots never boil. I heard my grandmother's voice in my head. Her admonition was written on his face. I plopped myself down on the ottoman blocking his view of the television.

"They should have Henry by now."

Jake shifted slightly to the right. "Didn't Ian Page tell you he would call when it was over?"

"What if someone got hurt?"

"Page knows what he's doing."

"But -."

" - Kyle, let go of it. The police have it now and there's nothing you can do." A look of resignation crept into his eyes. "You're not going to settle down, are you?"

I got up again and walked to the sliding door that overlooked the patio. The evening sun painted the sky with flamboyant pinks and purples. Shadows stretched across the flagstones. Swarms of gnats hovered near the lilac bush. Soon the temperature would drop and the bugs would go away but for now, it was their dinner time and I was glad to be indoors.

Finally, after another agonizingly long ten minutes, the telephone rang. I dove for the receiver.

"Hello?"

"We got him. It's over."

"Thank goodness! Was anyone hurt?"

"There was no showdown. As soon as we found him, Henry gave up. He was hiding out in a motel near the state line. He's confessing to a video camera as we speak."

"Shouldn't you be there?"

"Zucker and Beekly are taking care of it. I thought I'd better call you. Knew you'd be jumping out of your skin by now."

"Jake is sick of my pacing."

Page chuckled. "I knew that."

"Can you tell me anything?"

"Not much to tell that we hadn't already figured out. I'm leaving in about an hour. I'll stop by on my way home and fill you in, if that's OK with your boyfriend."

"It's OK with me."

Jake and I killed time debating which television reruns to watch. Law and Order won simply because it was already on and both of us liked the episode. When Page finally rang the doorbell ninety minutes later, we were in the kitchen discussing the merits of fruit versus chocolate topping for our vanilla ice cream dessert.

"We were right about the motive for killing Frank Villano," Page said as he entered the living room.

The short walk from his car to my front door in the ninety-percent humidity coated his skin with perspiration although it had not melted the satisfaction and barely suppressed excitement shining in his eyes. He and Jake politely shook hands and then I pushed both men into the kitchen where the ice cream was already turning soft. I scooped a dish for Page.

"Henry ran the stolen equipment through the farm," said Page, reaching for the chocolate topping. "Frank, following up on what Izzy told him, caught them and they killed him like we thought. Henry said Frank didn't say a word. Just looked at them and then at the front end loader. When he turned to walk back into the barn, he got a bullet in the head."

"Henry shot him?" My spoon stopped halfway to my mouth. "Just like that?"

"He insists he didn't pull the trigger and he's givin' up the guy that did. The same guy, by the way, who set the garage on fire. Our theory about an outsider was correct."

"But Henry hid the body." Jake made it a statement, not a question. "Bet he meant to move it but never got around to it."

"I asked him about that," said Page. "Every time he tried to dig Frank up, Chuck or one of the others thought he was going to spread manure and offered to help."

"So he had to put off spreading," I said. "He must have been happy with his hiding place, though. The more manure that piled up, the more buried Frank was. When Dixie finally made an issue of it and he actually had to start spreading again, there was still plenty of stuff covering Frank."

"Henry tried to arrange it so Frank'd stay buried forever by keeping Chuck busy with other chores. When I interviewed Chuck, he said he figured they'd get to the manure eventually and if Henry wasn't worried about it, there was no reason he should be. After all, Henry was the foreman."

"Except Henry forgot one thing," said Jake, "Life is beyond our control. Frank's bones showed up after, what, just one day of digging?"

"I don't know much about farm work," Page said, "but it seems to me that the flaw in Henry's plan was that he couldn't dictate where fresh manure would be dumped without calling attention to the situation. Instinctively, Chuck and Jorge dumped their wheelbarrows as far away from the barn as possible for as long as possible. The near end, where Frank was buried, didn't get as much piled on."

"Henry tried to solve that," I said. "Ed said something about the guys heaping up the manure instead of spreading it. Henry must have used the tractor's bucket to dump more manure on top of Frank, only he couldn't remember exactly where Frank was. Ed noticed the mound was getting higher instead of lower."

"How did Henry get Ed into Sunny's stall?" asked Jake. "And did he bang Ed on the head or did Sunny do all the work?"

"Henry told Dixie he thought Sunny was a better horse for Brisa than Foggy," I said. "Was he laying groundwork to tell Ed the same thing?"

"Looks that way. As for the how, the autopsy confirmed a severe blow to the head but Sunny did a lot of damage. Duran bled to death, although the pathologist said the head wound would have killed him eventually."

Again Duran's beaten body haunted me, reminding me of how my forgetfulness might have cost him his life. Logically, I knew that Henry and Ed Duran had been headed for a violent confrontation but that didn't remove my culpability. I gripped the edge of the counter. My trembling wasn't caused by the ice cream's chill.

Jake watched me closely for a minute and then said, "So it was Henry stealing Sal's equipment."

"Sal made himself an easy target," said Page. "Every time he bought something, he bragged about it. When he started moving equipment himself, he beefed about it. Henry always knew where Sal's equipment would be because Sal advertised it. Henry told his partners and they would steal it."

"Even I knew where he had a new backhoe parked," I said. "He screamed it at Ed the day they had the fight. Henry must have heard." As I took another bite of ice cream, brain freeze reminded me of something. "Hokey smokes. Sal told Dixie that backhoe was stolen the very next day. No wonder he was convinced Ed was the culprit."

"Do you know exactly why Henry killed Ed?" asked Jake.

Page nodded. "He was mad as hell that Ed put Chuck in charge of the new farm. From the day Duran announced he was going to buy the farm across the road, Henry planned to live there. The big house at the new farm was perfect. He stepped up the pace on the stolen equipment so he'd have enough money to bring his family over from Europe by the time Duran closed the deal. Then Duran passed him over in favor of Chuck. He lost it."

"And used poor Sunny to trample Ed to death. Much as I feel for Henry, what he did to Sunny is unforgivable! Did Henry spook Maida? Did he put me in the bushes?"

"I'm afraid so. He confessed to that, too."

"To scare her off?" asked Jake.

"To get his hands on that shell casing. He said he never meant for Kyle to get hurt—"

"That's a load of BS and you know it! He pushed her off the trail so no one would find her."

"He claims he knew Lori would eventually. If it makes you feel any better, the state's attorney will probably add assault and attempted murder to the list of charges because of it."

"Those will get dropped eventually." Jake glowered. "She's still in a cast, for Pete's sake."

"I see the doctor tomorrow." I asked, "I'll be fine."

"You can barely walk. Bet he puts you in plaster."

I decided against a retort. Page looked like he wanted to get going and I still had some questions to ask. "Do we know the real reason Ed gave Chuck the job?"

"No," said Page, "but personally, I think Duran suspected something was going on with Henry. He put that contract into place, had the books checked by a new accountant and then he popped out to the farm for that surprise inspection."

"But he never found anything," said Jake.

"In a weird way, he did," I said. "He told me his nitrogen levels were down and we were watching Chuck on the manure pile when he said it."

"Duran had certain levels of nitrogen in his hay cutting calculations," said Page. "Told me all about it the first time we talked. When the measurements weren't what they should have been; he knew something was going on. Especially when his numbers were off kilter for the entire season."

"Is that what he told the sheriff on Monday?"

"You know about that?" Page snorted. "Why am I not surprised? Yeah, he explained about the hay. Guess he had that part figured out the minute Frank's skeleton was found. Henry didn't take Ed's detail-mindedness into consideration. Duran's been around the block a few times so he smelled something and I don't mean shit. Duran didn't have it all figured out but he was getting close."

"But he didn't know who did it."

"Right up to the end, Duran thought the reason for Frank's murder was that workers were moving drugs through the place. At least that's what he told the sheriff's deputy. He tried to tie Ramon into it."

"Was he right? Did they kill Ramon Gutierrez, too?"

"Henry doesn't know. Until Frank was shot, he thought

Gutierrez went back to Mexico. Now he's not so sure. The only concrete fact we have about Gutierrez' whereabouts is that he wasn't in the manure with Frank."

"Drugs or equipment, you can't tell me that the other workers didn't know what Henry was up to," said Jake. "They live right there."

"Chuck may not have actively participated but he didn't report it either. None of them did."

"I wonder if that's what Ed was thinking about when Chuck was working on the manure pile." I remembered Duran standing next to me in the barn door, the two of us watching Chuck labor with the pitchfork. There had been a look in Duran's eyes. Now I tried to analyze that look without success. Only he knew what he thought that day and now it didn't matter.

"Looks like Brisa's going to be without workers, whether or not she gets rid of that contract."

"What about that meeting in the kitchen?" I asked. "What was that all about?"

"Brisa told the truth. She met with Sal and Nolan to figure out a way to solve their financial problems so they could keep their horses. Nolan finally produced a copy of the insurance he wrote on the new farm. No contracts were signed but Brisa showed me the canceled deposit check to Sal. She planned to move all the workers over to the bigger house at the new place and rehab the house behind Bright Hope."

"I remembered what you said about the therapy camp. That's what made me think Brisa was in danger. That's why Henry went after her. Another Duran messing up his plans for the new place."

Page nodded. "Yup."

"One last questions. Did you tell Henry about the tiger-eye?"

"When the sifting ended and we still hadn't asked him about it, he thought he lost it somewhere else."

"How close were you to the answer before you saw the tiger-eye?"

Page smiled. "Pretty close. It was your conversation with Izzy that did it. That and you kept asking what we'd found in the manure. I began to wonder what we might have missed. When you picked that one bag, out of all those other little bags, and held it up to the light, I realized it was more than just a stone. The lab would have identified it eventually but it might have taken us awhile to connect it with Henry. Funny. We thought we'd get Frank's killer by identifying Duran's killer. It was just the opposite." He set his empty bowl in the sink. "I gotta get home. Liz will want the rundown too."

We walked him to the door. After the men shook hands, I gave Page a firm hug.

"Thanks," I said. "For everything."

"Same here."

Page went out to his car, waving as he slid into place behind the steering wheel.

"Nice of him to fill us in," said Jake. He watched through the screen door as Page pulled away.

"He answered a lot of questions."

"He didn't mention how soon you two would be working together again."

"What's that supposed to mean?"

"Nothing. It was a snide remark and I shouldn't have said it."

He went outside and sat on the top step of the cement stoop, propped his elbows on his knees and stared out into space. There was something about the way his black hair hung down his back, the way his shoulders hunched forward. I wasn't sure what I felt at the moment. It was a jumble.

What had he said to me that night in the Italian restaurant? If we couldn't talk about the little things, how would we handle the big ones? I thought about his comment for a minute and then went outside to join him, lowering myself to the bottom step. Leaning back between his legs, my head rested on his chest. He dropped his arms and wrapped them around me, his chin on the top of my head.

"You sounded jealous," I said.

"I am...maybe...sort of. Hell, I don't know."

"I'll take that as a yes."

"I know you two don't have a thing going. It's more..."

"We're friends. There's no chemistry between us."

"Was there?"

"No."

I thought back to the first time I'd seen Ian Page, sitting on a patio with plates of fried chicken in our laps and talking about the state of modern primary education. Page was stag that night. Liz had been ill.

"Always a connection, but nothing sexual."

"I've known you less than a year and twice you've been caught up in some murder investigation with him. Is that how it's going to be with you?"

"I don't plan to get involved, you know. If I had known Frank Villano was buried in that manure, I would not have taken the job."

"Baloney. You would have jumped at it." He drew his arms together and gave me a quick squeeze. "You couldn't pass up the chance to poke your nose in."

"That's not fair. The task force works lots of cases I never hear about and solves them without any input from me. But if something happens to the people close to me, I have to help. There's no choice."

"Sure there is."

I thought about that for a moment, remembering the medicine wheel. "You're right. There is always choice, but I couldn't live with myself if I could help and I didn't. It's part of me."

Jake squeezed my shoulders again. "I know."

I whipped around. "Then why are you giving me such a hard

time?"

"Because you feel responsible for Ed Duran's murder. You believe that if you hadn't gotten involved, he would still be alive."

I shrugged. "Maybe."

He was right, of course, but I didn't want to admit it. I turned back toward the street without saying more.

My soul hurt. There was nothing about this that could be called a happy ending. The bad guys would be prosecuted and sent to jail but Henry was now separated forever from his beloved family, Dixie was a widow and Izzy had lost her father. Who knew if Sal's business would recover? And, because of me, Brisa was an orphan.

"Henry decided to kill," Jake went on. "Maybe it was supposed to be Sal and Ed got it instead. Either way, Henry made the choice to become a killer and nothing you did could have changed that."

"It's what I didn't do that haunts me. I kept forgetting to tell Ian about Sunny's beatings. Had he known, he might have kept Ed alive."

"I doubt it. You're looking at this with hindsight. At the time, neither of you knew enough to put it all together. But let's say you did remember to tell him. What would have happened?"

"I don't know. Dixie might have moved Sunny out for awhile?"

"And Henry would have stabbed Ed...or shot him...or poisoned him. Ed's actions, not yours, are what got him killed."

Jake waited quite awhile before he said, "You never saw a counselor about any of this."

"I think I just did."

"There's a line in a Chippewa prayer. It goes 'I ask for wisdom and strength; not to be superior to my brothers, but to be able to fight my greatest enemy, myself.' Call the counselor." Jake pushed me upright. "We'd better go inside. I need to get going soon."

After Jake went home, I went out to the patio, lit the citronella candles and settled on the chaise. Jake did not mention the prayer again and yet the last line had troubled me continually since his departure. There is an adage that expresses the same sentiment: we are our own worst enemy.

Guilt can wipe out a person, destroying emotional well-being, expelling hope and happiness as surely as salmonella dehydrates us. Untreated, both can destroy us from within.

I stared up at the sky. Although I couldn't see the stars, I knew they were there. The night was conducive to lofty thoughts about humankind but all that came to mind was Ed Duran's beaten body and the medicine wheel. I was a long way from hopelessness but just a few steps from constant sadness. I went inside and left a message with the counselor's answering service.

The following day's routine at the barn was as it had always been; Dixie in the outside ring, Izzy in the arena while Chuck and Jorge did chores. The only noticeable change was that the John Deere was parked in front of the shed instead chugging out in the fields.

My doctor had given me a good scolding but he had removed the air cast. Now I sat quietly in the office, my ankle wrapped in a new Ace bandage and propped on an open drawer. A pair of crutches leaned against the wall within easy reach.

I nursed a mug of coffee, unable to work. The mail gave me something mindless to do that didn't require a lot of focus. I'd just finished opening the last envelope when Brisa came in. She sat on the stool, her hands wrapped around a bottle of water.

She let a long sigh. "I'm numb. My doc says I'll be angry eventually but right now, I'm just numb." She straightened her shoulders. "What are your plans? For working here, I mean."

"That depends on you, I guess. Duran Building is my employer. That's you now."

"Daddy wanted you to get the office straightened up. Are you finished?"

I pointed at a short stack of manila folders. "Nearly. Once

those records are into the computer, things'll be in good order."

"How long will that take you?"

"If I push, I can have it done by the end of next week."

Her eyes widen. "So soon?"

I shrugged.

Brisa knotted her eyebrows. It was something I'd seen her father do when things weren't quite as he wanted them. I pushed away the twinge of remorse.

"I think," she said, "you're being optimistic. I'd estimate that will take you at least three months."

I stared at her. "Oh-kay."

Then, in her dark eyes, I saw a woman who would survive and be successful running the businesses that she had inherited so tragically. The fear she had exhibited the day her father was killed had been replaced by confidence, a bit shaky perhaps but it was there. She was, after all, her father's daughter.

"I'd say you'll finish up right about the time a new part time person is fully trained and ready to take over. Even if Dixie hires someone tomorrow, it will be months before they have everything nailed down."

"That's true," I said. "Shall we say my contract is up at the end of the year?"

Brisa nodded. "And, for any extra time you have available, perhaps you can spend it at Duran Building and help me sort through that mess?" She didn't wait for a response. She pointed at my foot. "That's a new bandage. How's the ankle? How are the hospital bills? Is your insurance covering them?"

"The ankle is fine. I'll be on crutches for a week and then I'm supposed to walk on it. Pretty much everything is covered because my injury was an emergency. The follow-up visits may not be."

"Duran Building will cover those and anything else your insurance doesn't pick up."

I pushed at my bangs. "That's not necessary."

"Yes, it is." Her voice was firm. "You were hurt because of Henry. Henry was our employee. I insist." She rose from the stool, her eyes misty. "Daddy would want it that way so don't argue."

She fled the office then, leaving me with the impression that adapting to the business world would be a lot easier for her than adjusting to the loss of her father.

"It's going to take a long time for her to get over losing Ed," said Dixie, resignation in her voice. She came in and sat on the stool. "I heard what she said about your bills. If she hadn't taken care of it, we would have."

I bobbed my head but when I didn't answer, Dixie didn't say anything more. She sorted through the mail I hadn't yet opened.

"Looking for something specific?" I asked.

"A check from Nolan."

I had suspected that. "Any luck?"

She held up an envelope. "I think so."

Dixie grabbed the letter opener, slit the envelope and pulled out a single slip of paper.

"Saints be praised." The first real smile I'd seen in a long time spread across her face. "It's not the whole thing but it's a serious start. I wonder where he got the money."

Nolan had said the finder's fee for writing my insurance wouldn't be much, but he must have made a bundle in commission for the policies he wrote for the new farm. Brisa had meant what she said about Nolan keeping his horse. I put the check in the bank envelope.

The telephone rang. Dixie waved and left me to the deal with the call.

"My goodness, Kyle." It was Margaret, my Office Right Staffing Service supervisor. "Every time I read something in the paper about that stable, I think about how that assignment almost came through us. The very thought makes me sick. Imagine the liability."

I laughed. "Yes, you were right."

"So you took the job as an independent?"

"I did. By the way, thanks for the referral to Greg Lacey. Great guy."

"Ed Duran hired you right? Will his daughter let you go now?"

"Not for another couple of months." I briefly explained Brisa's plans for my future. "I'm available after the holidays so I'll need an assignment."

"You're not going to stay independent?"

"If something comes along where I have to be, I'll certainly consider it but I'd rather be a temp. It's a lot easier."

"Hmmm."

"What does that mean?"

"I just had an idea. I have to have some surgery and I've been putting it off because we didn't have anyone we thought could work in our office. My doctor said I can't wait much longer. Would you consider working for Office Right? As a time card supervisor?"

"Sure."

"Good. We'll talk about it in a month or two."

When I met Jake for dinner that evening, I relayed Margaret's offer.

"That's great," he said. "It must be a relief to know you already have a job lined up."

"It is, but I'm not crazy about doing payroll."

"Is that what Margaret wants you to do?"

"She said I'd be a time card supervisor. Processing time cards sounds like payroll to me."

Jake nodded. "And boring to me."

"I could do with something really boring for change."

He laughed. "OK. How about a long boring weekend up north? Together."

The End

Contact the Author

Please visit:

www.lindamickey.com
and
www.dollarsandsense4writers.com

Be sure to read:
- Greased Wheels: A Kyle Shannon Mystery
- Defective Goods: A Kyle Shannon Mystery
- Chicago Dawn
- Dollars and Sense for Writers: A Guide to Managing Your Writing Business

CPSIA information can be obtained
at www.ICGtesting.com
Printed in the USA
FFOW04n1727100715
14865FF